The Unlikely Genius of
Doctor Cuthbert Kambazuma

Donal,

May da Choist be
with ya,
All the best,
Chris

This story is for us, and for them,
but mainly for us …
remind me again, which are you?

The Unlikely Genius of Doctor Cuthbert Kambazuma

Chris Wadman

JONATHAN BALL PUBLISHERS
Johannesburg & Cape Town

Author's Note
This story is set in Zimbabwe. Until 2009, the local currency was Zimbabwe dollars.
Rampant hyperinflation, with hundred-trillion-dollar notes being the highest denomination
finally in print, forced the government to legalise the use of foreign currencies
for transactions, and since then US dollars have become widely used.

Published in trade paperback in 2012 by
JONATHAN BALL PUBLISHERS (PTY) LTD
PO Box 33977
Jeppestown
2043

ISBN 978 1 86842 460 3

Twitter: http://www.twitter.com/JonathanBallPub
Facebook: http://www.facebook.com/pages/Jonathan-Ball-Publishers/298034457992
Blog: http://jonathanball.bookslive.co.za/

Edited by Lynda Gilfillan
Text design by Triple M Design, Johannesburg
Cover design by Michiel Botha, Cape Town
Printed and bound by Paarl Media, Paarl
Set in 11/16pt Latin 725 BT

Contents

The truth changes colour depending on the light and tomorrow can be clearer than yesterday.

Eve's Bayou – Kasi Lemmons

1

Teddington Chiwafambira's Million-Dollar Mango

It takes a special calibre of man to slice, peel and consume an over-ripe mango while manoeuvring, with only one knee, the antiquated oversized steering wheel of a battered ZUPCO omnibus hurtling along at breakneck speed. Teddington Chiwafambira was, indeed, just such a man. Untroubled by his motley cargo of seventy or so lunatics, three distracted Mental Health Superintendents and two terrified orphans, he wiggled his portly posterior into position, wedging his lukewarm Coca-Cola between his sweaty thighs. Squinting at the road ahead, he rested his knee against the base of the worn steering wheel. Guided by habit, his hand reached quickly into a tatty plastic packet swinging to and fro like a frenetic pendulum from the window winder. He snatched up the nearest fruit, noting with irritation its small size and a nasty rash of brown speckles. But he had other matters on his mind, far more pressing. His

1

bothered expression contrasted with the image of smiling revellers painted in bright colours on the sides of his omnibus, under the words from a much-loved jingle, 'Chibu-Chibu-Chibuku … the beer of good cheer.'

Grabbing his knife from its resting place in the speedometer socket, Teddington sliced off the bottom of his mango. The knife clattered to the floor as he lifted the fruit to his mouth, using his teeth to clasp the skin and peel it back from the fruit. It was a well-practised drill. He took a large bite, grinding his teeth from side to side to break the fruity fibres, sucking furiously to stem the flow of juice that pooled on the grubby red driver's seat before disappearing through a slit into the foam cushion below. In less than a minute, nothing remained but the white pip which he gnawed at pensively for some time, before tossing it from his open window.

Teddington was an angry man. A flurry of calculations consumed his thoughts, and his mind churned like a giant adding machine. How could this bag of mangoes cost him twenty thousand dollars today, when last year it had been only two hundred dollars, and the year before that, a mere two dollars? Who could say what next year's price would be? A million dollars, perhaps – maybe a million just for one!

'Bloody ridiculous! *Zvinoshamisa!*' he muttered. 'Whatever next – a billion-dollar banana?'

Had his ZUPCO omnibus driver's salary escalated by a thousand times? Well, had it? Of course not! He had only ten thousand dollars left in his Post Office savings account and, with bread now costing almost four thousand dollars a loaf, it was clear that he would not make it through the remaining two weeks of the month.

'What sort of life is this?' he grumbled, '*Hazvikwane kana kudyiwa nembwa!* Not even fit for a dog!'

It was a discussion he had had a thousand times with himself, drifting, as always, to an escape – a fantasy where, without warning, he packed it all in and headed south, down to the border town of Beitbridge. Ignoring the relatively minor inconvenience of having neither a passport nor an entry visa for South Africa, he pictured himself paying a guide to lead him across the crocodile-infested waters of the 'great, grey-green, greasy Limpopo River'. If undetected by the authorities – statistically, extremely likely, given the hundreds of thousands who had gone before him – he would shortly find himself, bum in the butter, in the bustling metropolis of Johannesburg. They say that if you throw a stone high up into the air on a busy Johannesburg street, when it falls it will almost certainly hit a Zimbabwean square on the head – so plentiful are his people in Egoli, a city built on the abundance of gold, a place of boundless opportunity and jobs aplenty. As a driver, he pictured himself manning an airport shuttle, raking in fistfuls of tips – not in these worthless Zimbabwean dollars but in rands, real money that could buy you real things in proper shops. Colour TVs, branded footwear, Camel Lights – you could have it all. All he needed was a million dollars, the probable price of a paltry freckled mango twelve miserable months hence, to get him across the border, with just a little to tide him over until he could find employment. And that, he realised, grinding the omnibus's recalcitrant gears, was precisely his problem. How could he possibly raise such an amount? A million dollars! That was several months' wages for a ZUPCO driver of his standing, including his Christmas Box – a thirteenth cheque which, that year, was no certainty.

Once again, Teddington Chiwafambira felt thoroughly trapped. His fantasy deflated like a punctured tyre and his mind returned reluctantly to the more mundane journey at hand. His was a charter to Harare's Parirenyatwa Hospital, where the newly appointed Matron Matambanadzo awaited her new Ward G20 patients. He had fetched them earlier that day from Ingutsheni, Bulawayo's primary facility for Adult Mental Health. As for the two orphans, someone from Child Welfare had managed to persuade his Ingutsheni counterpart to let them onto the bus for free – funds were tight, if not non-existent. Assurances that the children would at all times be under the watchful eye of the three Mental Health Superintendents addressed any concerns about their safety. It was a straightforward arrangement, nothing could go wrong. Upon arrival, Matron Matambanadzo would arrange their transport to the nearby William Westward Children's Home.

Wiping beads of sweat from his furrowed brow, Teddington glanced in his rear-view mirror. In the first row, two of the super-intendents had fallen asleep on each others' shoulders, their duet of shameless snores clearly audible above the noise of the engine. The third superintendent stared blankly ahead – apparently oblivious of the dignified, well-dressed gentleman seated next to him who end-lessly repeated the words 'Go on, then!' followed five seconds later by 'Come on, then!'

Exemplary was the behaviour of the occupants of the second row, mesmerised as they were by the twirling of a partially straightened paper clip between the fingers of the man in the middle. Behind them, an elderly zealot stood on his seat, his neck bent against the roof of the omnibus. Laying claim to the prophetic title, Elijah, and with a voice as hoarse as the hiss of an Eyptian goose, he was all hellfire and brimstone, with little reprieve. Teddington knew the old man well from previous trips. This one had been in the system for life. Holding the attention of nearly all the passengers with his fa-natical rhetoric and sweeping gestures, to the superintendents, doz-ing or vacant alike, the prophet was truly a Godsend. In the murk of his greasy rear-view mirror, Teddington could just make out, at the very back of the bus, the two orphans peeping anxiously over the seat backs. He sighed heavily. Surely this was not the life he was destined for, driving around in the baking heat with this lot. Clearly, it was all a mistake. One way or another, it had to be rectified.

His mind plunged into another Olympiad of fiscal calculations, rounding off sums to the nearest hundred thousand dollars. A sud-den, sharp tap on his shoulder caused him to swerve precariously.

One of the superintendents stood behind him, doubling over theatrically, with his hands clasped over his crotch and a pained expression on his face. Teddington nodded, scanning the road before him for a suitable place to stop. Up ahead, a cluster of buildings lined the roadside. The aging omnibus lurched dangerously as Teddington veered off the tar onto the gravel shoulder without slowing. Pedestrians, chickens, goats and dogs scattered in all directions as the bus skidded to a halt next to a lone petrol pump, a plume of orange dust rising in its wake.

2

The Unfortunate Truth about Learnmore Chitsanga

There was nothing elaborate about the layout of the William Westward Children's Home. Its box-like administration building was flanked by two double-storey wings, each with a dormitory upstairs and classrooms below. Paget on the left for boys, and Fairbridge on the right for girls. Their whitewashed walls were stained with dust and rust-coloured streaks that trickled down from faded red corrugated-iron roofs now buckled and lifting.

. Established in 1947 by Sir William Westward, a prominent Southern Rhodesian parliamentarian, just one month before his failed attempt at landing the country's highest office, the home had initially been a farm school under the Fairbridge Scheme. It was one of several such schools in Rhodesia, Canada and Australia, taking in neglected children from the crowded cities of post-war Britain. Here they were provided with – in order of importance – discipline, shelter and schooling, and usually a solid grounding in agriculture.

Following the colonial scramble away from Africa in the 1960s, and the consequent dismantling of the Fairbridge Scheme, the home's almost eighty hectares of prime farmland had not been tilled in decades. The orphanage had been taken over by a group of charities under the guidance of the Anglican Church, and become a refuge for local orphans at a time when 'local' meant 'white Rhodesian'. After many heated rows and much door-slamming in the nearby St Luke's Church Hall, such exclusions eventually came to an end. Twenty years later, there was not a white face in sight on the twisted frame of the jungle gym, as the 'local' population dwindled.

Over the years, the ravages of Africa's three-letter plague had swelled the ranks of the William Westward beyond capacity. In the struggle to accommodate an ever-increasing number of children, the games room below Paget dormitory – once home to a treasured ping-pong table and dartboard – had been cleared to provide space for more children. A few were lucky enough to have one of the old heavy iron beds, but the rest had to make do with a flattened coir or foam mattress on the floor, lined up in rows and covered by threadbare blankets.

From here, the children left for school each morning, walking in a neat line; the little ones – twelve years old and under – to Msasa Primary, and the seniors to Msasa Secondary. Few now wore the regulation khaki shirts and shorts for boys, or the navy-checked school dresses for girls. Only one child possessed a blazer, with the Msasa Technical School emblem embroidered on the pocket – a simple, stark silhouette of a spreading msasa tree under a crescent moon, above the spirited motto 'Reaching for the Stars'. The rest of the children wore whatever bits of clothing had, over time, been donated to the William Westward, hand-me-downs passed from generation to generation – usually in the form of oversized T-shirts and boxer shorts. Some wore takkies without laces, or plastic yellow-and-red Bata flip-flops, but mostly they went barefoot.

Inscribed in thick black permanent marker on the back wall of Paget, partially concealed by an aging mulberry bush, were the words, 'Learnmore Chitsanga has only got one ball! *ANE CHENDE RIMWECHETE!*'

3

A Single Moment that would Ultimately Influence the Tide of this Nation's History

When the dust cloud had settled, Teddington noticed a crowd of surprisingly well-dressed individuals standing next to an omnibus up ahead that bore the red, green, gold and black colours of 'Chiyangwa & Sons Charters', the once-premier, privately owned transport service. Lying on his back on a length of oily tarpaulin, with his legs poking out from underneath the vehicle, the driver was tinkering with the undercarriage. Joyful cries rose from the stranded group at the sight of the sky-blue ZUPCO omnibus. Gathering up their bags, they trundled towards Teddington's omnibus just as the three Ingutsheni superintendents hopped off and went behind the store to relieve themselves.

From the advancing group, a man – clearly a figure of some authority – stepped forward. He was greying slightly at the temples, and wore a fashionable tweed coat reinforced at the elbows with corduroy patches. Clearing his throat, he climbed aboard.

'Excuse me, and good afternoon to you, sir. As you can see, our journey home has been hampered by mechanical difficulties. Would you be so kind as to allow us to squeeze onto this bus for a ride through to Harare? We are only thirty in number.'

Teddington was in no mood for this malarkey.

'Can't you see? This is a privately chartered vehicle – and anyway, look around, it's full.'

'Indeed, it does look quite full, but –'

Teddington knew he must nip this line of questioning in the bud.

'Hey, old man, do you need an earbud? *Hausi kundinzwa here*? As I said, this is a charter liner, not a charity liner. Now run along back over there to help your driver with the repairs.'

The gentleman's face dropped.

'Please sir,' he began to plead, 'we've been standing out here in the blazing heat all afternoon, and this morning we were also standing out in the open sun, addressing a gathering in Masvingo. We are tired now.'

'That's enough!' cried Teddington sternly. 'Off my bus, old man! *Buda mubhazi mudhara!*'

'We will, of course, reward you handsomely.'

'Off, I said!'

Mister Lennard Chavundukwe, MP, retreated hastily from the omnibus to break the bad news to his colleagues. An animated bunch, they took it badly.

'Jesus Christ!' bellowed one fashionable young man with a goatee beard and prominent sideburns, throwing his hands up in frustration, 'Can you jolly-well believe it!'

Lennard Chavundukwe covered his ears in a gesture of pained frustration.

'Now, now, Cromwell,' he admonished, 'don't you start again. Please. We'll get there eventually.'

Shaking their heads in disbelief, the group turned to Teddington. He ignored them, and not without some measure of satisfaction. This was his omnibus, and only he would decide who could climb aboard. From behind the restless crowd, the three superintendents emerged from their toilet break, eager expressions on their faces. Teddington turned the ignition key and the omnibus burst into life with a shudder, but the three men ambled right past, crossing the road towards the beer hall. With their own superintendent now on the other side of the country, there was no one for them to answer to.

'What the hell ...!' Teddington muttered impatiently, sounding his horn in a series of angry blasts.

Without looking back, the superintendents wagged their fingers dismissively in Teddington's direction. The one who had been desperate for a toilet stop minutes before made a tippling motion towards his mouth, followed by a back-in-five gesture with spread fingers. Before Teddington could protest, the three men had disappeared into the din and darkness of the beer hall. Teddington scowled, his mind defaulting instantly to his desperate calculations. The spectre of a billion-dollar banana rose before him.

In that instant, he finally snapped. This was a rare instance, the ramifications of which would reach far beyond his wildest imagination, a single moment that would ultimately influence the tide of this nation's history.

4

Colonel Reginald Threscothic and his Wife Marie Discover the Infant Thomas in a Guava Tree

Thomas Threscothic did not stir as the telephone began to ring on Mai Rutivi's desk. It was late, twilight was falling, and Mai Rutivi, secretary to the headmaster at the William Westward Home, had already left. From his office, which was arguably less of an office and more of a converted broom cupboard, Thomas seldom heard the phone ringing, even when his hearing aids were in place.

The contents of Thomas's office were scant. Beneath the small window, through which he kept an eye on the playground and followed the movement of the woodpeckers in the msasa trees outside, stood an old wooden one-piece school desk with an empty inkwell sunk into the top right corner. It was small, built for a schoolchild; even so, at twenty-four, Thomas sat in it quite comfortably. He kept his books and stationery in the desk, as well as a clipboard of obsolete duty rosters, a list of children's names, a

Shona Language Exercise Book (Intermediate Level), and his reading book, *Nicholas Nickleby*, which he had treasured since childhood and was now attempting to reread for the third or fourth time. As a reader he was painfully slow, struggling to maintain his concentration, but he did love stories, particularly those that ended well. Also inside his desk was his Bible: hard-covered, with a faded blue cloth exterior, its language formal and archaic. It did have some pictures, though – stark black-and-white sketches of the prophets, the creatures of Noah's Ark, ancient temples and the like, a brochure of an age long past.

Thomas's childhood memories of the William Westward Home, where he now spent his days as a general helper, were not something he could recall at will, like a sequence of coloured frames from *Tintin* or *Asterix* in his mind's eye. They came to him rather as a feeling, striking in its intensity – a sense of being completely alone and unspeakably afraid. Like an ache in an old man's shoulder before the rain, he could neither tell nor control when they might grasp at him. It was at the William Westward that Colonel Reginald Threscothic and his wife Marie had found him, all those years ago, as he sat wedged between the overhanging branches of a guava tree on the farthest fringes of the playground, hiding. With just his sad green eyes blinking in the dappled light, even a small flock of bronze mannikins, the most timid of finches, felt safe enough to flit about in the branches around him, pecking at wisps of his ginger hair with which to line their nests. As members of the St Luke's Anglican congregation in Greendale, the colonel and Marie had been regular Sunday visitors to the William Westward for over two decades. With no offspring of their own, they derived much joy and fulfilment from their interaction with the children, particularly the little ones. Never once had they thought of adopting; they were, after all, far too old by then – the colonel almost seventy, and Marie already in her late fifties. Watching the mannikins at their delicate task, Marie had known at once that her prayers had been answered. She waited for the last of the finches to disappear before gently scooping the frightened child into her arms.

'This,' she had whispered to her husband, 'is the child that we ourselves could never have.'

The colonel, a man of deep but hidden emotions, knew that silence was the only correct response to these things he did not understand. The boy's arms were badly scarred, and as Marie lifted him down she noticed his narrow torso was similarly marked. Was this, she wondered, an explanation for what seemed to be a constant look of surprise on his face? Enquiring at the home as to the child's origin, they were told only that little Thomas had been brought there, tucked into a broken wicker cradle, by a concerned person. As for the scars, they could only assume that he had fallen, and from quite some height, too. His age was estimated at between two and three years.

The couple visited the boy as frequently as was permitted. He loved to be held as much as they loved to hold him, but he did not speak, and showed no response at all to sound. A visit to the ear specialist revealed that both eardrums were badly perforated – the three tiny bones of the middle ear disrupted. The doctor reassured them, however, that with hearing aids the boy should be able to develop and function almost normally. In order to receive the constant care and attention needed for his speech to germinate, it was agreed that the boy would move in and live with the aging Threscothic couple, if only for a while. They lived less than a mile from the home, and both being retired, had sufficient time for the difficult task at hand. Six months later, the boy – although still painfully shy – had acquired a babble that, over time, increasingly resembled words. Marie could not even think about returning their precious Thomas to the home and felt quite beside herself at the merest suggestion. After an intervention by the Anglican archbishop, the difficult process of Thomas's adoption was concluded, and the child formerly known simply as Thomas became Master Thomas Threscothic. Given the colonel's considerable age and Victorian upbringing, he considered it appropriate that the child call him Father, and his wife, Mother, instead of Daddy and Mummy, terms that would remain in use well after the good colonel's passing.

Outside, night fell gradually as Thomas rearranged his duty rosters, daydreaming intermittently. Gathering up his plastic juice bottle and an empty yellow Dairy Board ice-cream container that now served as his lunch box, he closed the door of his tiny office behind him. The headmaster's office door was ajar and the light still on. Mister Joseph Chiswa, known affectionately to children and staff alike as Baba, meaning 'father' in Shona, often worked well into the night, catching up on the paperwork that piled up as he kept a watchful eye on the children throughout the day.

Thomas knocked softly on his door.

'Another late night for you, Baba?'

The headmaster sighed heavily. 'It's the monthly report for the Board of Trustees. Due tomorrow.'

'Well, good luck with that, and good night. I'm leaving now.'

'See you in the morning, Thomas. Bright and early!'

Pausing behind the wheel of his mother's worn-out yellow Datsun 120Y before setting off home, Thomas glanced up at the Fairbridge dormitory. The dim flickering of a candle could be seen passing from one window to the next. It must be the Home Matron, Betty Mukadota, so he thought, doing her final rounds, checking on the little ones settling down after lights out.

Thomas couldn't help wondering where they would find space for the two new children arriving from Bulawayo the next day. He glanced at his watch. It was six twenty-five, almost dinner time. Thursday evenings were special for Thomas and his mother, a social occasion of sorts, courtesy of their neighbour, Mister Mucheche, and his satellite dish. Thanks to a bit of creative wiring, their friends, the newsreaders from CNN, were transported across the world and into their living room.

Eagerly, he set off home.

5

Mister Lennard Chavundukwe, MP, and his Stranded Group are Rescued

Teddington glanced at the beer hall across the road. Dancing to the soulful singing of a voice blaring from a roadside speaker was an enthusiastic albeit elderly man wearing a tattered coat. No sign of the thirsty superintendents, though, as the old man's elbows and knees gyrated in fits and starts, punctuated with the odd pelvic thrust.

Unable to wait a second longer, Teddington leapt from his driver's seat onto the dusty roadside and marched across to Lennard Chavundukwe's restless group.

'Right, then,' he roared, 'I'll take you. I'll take the lot of you to Harare. But let me warn you … it will cost you.'

A ripple of surprise passed through the crowd.

'How much?' Mister Lennard Chavundukwe, MP, asked cautiously.

'One million,' Teddington announced, pursing his lips – a million would get him there, to Egoli.

'What? A million dollars!' exclaimed Cromwell Shimwa, tugging at his goatee beard in horror. 'That's extortion … it's more than twice the going rate!'

'Whatever!' Teddington replied nonchalantly. 'Take it or leave it!'

'Okay, okay, okay!' Mister Lennard Chavundukwe, MP, hastily intervened as Teddington walked back to his bus. 'But is there enough space for all of us?'

'Hand over the money, and there'll be more than enough space – I can assure you.'

Teddington held out his palm and rubbed his thumb and index finger together. 'Come on, show me the money!'

An excited chatter erupted as each person searched his or her wallet for the fare.

Teddington's heart was racing. In all his twenty-nine years, he had never done anything like this. The money was quickly collected and handed over to Cromwell Shimwa, who counted it with remarkable speed and aptitude. Reminding himself that these were desperate times, and that desperate times called for enterprising solutions, Teddington grabbed the huge wad of notes and stuffed it into all his available pockets.

'Right!' he shouted, ignoring one or two notes that had floated to the ground as he pushed his way determinedly through the crowd, 'Wait here until I call you!'

Teddington boarded his ZUPCO omnibus, shoving aside Elijah as he entered.

'Toilet break! Toilet break!' he yelled, at the top of his lungs. 'All off, come on, we don't have much time. All off!'

There was a stunned silence – save for Elijah's husky monologue.

'All off, toilet stop!' Teddington called out again, this time using sweeping arm gestures to guide the passengers towards the open door.

'One-two, one-two! Let's go! Let's go!' he shouted, clapping his hands.

To get them moving in the right direction, Teddington grabbed the man with the twirling paper clip from the second row. Marching him briskly to the door, he shoved him down the stairs before starting on the next passenger, continuing in this way till the bus was cleared. Blinking in surprise at the bright sunlight, the erstwhile passengers huddled in a large group, uncertain what to do with their unexpected freedom. Flicking his wrists impatiently like a traffic policeman, Teddington ushered them towards the trees behind the General Store. Mister Lennard Chavundukwe's group stared open-mouthed in amazement, fumbling nervously with their suitcases.

A slight movement at the rear of the bus caught Teddington's eye. The heads of the two orphans popped up one after the other, like a pair of of meerkats. He felt a pang of regret. As an uncle to twenty-three nieces and nephews, ordinarily he was fond of children. The girl could not be more than nine, and the boy eleven or twelve at the most. But his resolve was firm. His escape to Egoli, the Eldorado down south, could not be compromised.

'Now, children, you too! Toilet break,' he purred, with a salesman's instant smile. 'We'll be off again in five minutes.'

The boy and girl emerged cautiously from their hiding place, each clutching a small plastic packet, the entirety of their worldly possessions. As soon as they were out, Teddington called down to Mister Chavundukwe's bewildered group.

'Well, do you want to go or not? Quickly! On the bus, then! All of you! It will soon be dark!'

Loading the bus quickly was imperative – given the unpredictable temperament of the Ingutsheni lot, it was only a matter of time before suspicions were aroused.

Before the last of the passengers had taken their seats, Teddington set off at breakneck speed. People tumbled down the aisle, howling their objections, but for neither man nor beast would he stop, not until he had reached his final destination.

In this heightened state of excitement, Teddington finalised the remainder of his plan. The temporary absence of seventy mental patients would hardly raise an eyebrow, he knew, but the disappearance of a ZUPCO omnibus – that was sure to set the police on his trail. The bus must be delivered to its designated destination, Ward G20 at the Parirenyatwa Hospital. Once there, he would abandon both it and its new occupants and flee with his million-dollar wad to his room in the high-density suburb of Hatcliffe, to pack and say hurried goodbyes to his brothers. Then, in the early morning, he would set out by long-distance mini-bus taxi for the Beitbridge border post – hopefully before ZUPCO's top brass got wind of his nefarious deeds.

Craning forward over the steering wheel, he shifted the knobbled gearstick into fifth, his wretched omnibus reaching speeds hitherto believed mechanically impossible.

6

Becky Anderson's Secret Admirer

The whitewashed pebbles lining the driveway, recently painted by Marie's gardener, Leviticus, reflected the dim light of the Datsun's headlamps as Thomas drove slowly up to the house and parked under the tattered shade-cloth garage next to the kitchen. Against the night sky, Thomas could make out the silhouette of Father's now rusty ham-radio tower with its lattice of iron beams, a monument perhaps to Father's lifelong attempt to reach out beyond the confines of his own small world, broadcasting his protest at the status quo. The shell of a derelict aviary lay behind the house, built by Father two decades previously to house the collection of injured birds rescued by his wife – a space that had doubled as the home of Thomas's grey rabbits. Legions of offspring had been spawned in the oversized brick hutch roofed with an asbestos sheet that could be lifted to view the furry occupants, once a source of daily delight.

In the fast-fading light, a thicket of msasa trees concealed the clearing that had become central to the lives of both Marie and Thomas over the years. Through the flyscreen flap of the back door, Thomas could see his mother standing in the kitchen, mashing potatoes in a saucepan. Glancing up over the rim of her bifocals, she waved at him with a smile.

Somehow, despite the scarcity of all but the most basic of foods, and her late husband's ever-shrinking Rhodesian Railways pension, Marie always managed to find two pieces of frozen hake for their Thursday meal, to be baked in white sauce, and served with peas and mash on trays by the television – a welcome break from the formality of the dimly lit dining room. For the neighbours, Tadius and Evlyn Mucheche, a romantic couple in the old-fashioned sense, Thursday night was date night – chicken korma and a bottle of Mukuyu wine at the Sitar restaurant in Newlands, setting the satellite decoder onto CNN before they left just after seven.

Thomas had never had many friends. He found if difficult to say the right things in company, or, for that matter, anything at all. Who would be interested? He preferred to listen. Beamed into his home from somewhere far away, to appear in black and white on Father's ten-inch Telefunken, CNN provided just the solution. He loved nothing more than to sit back in Father's old Parker-Knoll wingback, next to his mother, with his hake, mash and peas on his lap, eyes glued to the box. It was not so much the content of the news that fascinated Thomas, but rather those who delivered it.

'Look, Ma! It's Richard!' he cried as the familiar face of Richard Quest flashed across the screen.

Marie tilted her head and peered over her bifocals, 'Yes indeed, it is Richard, isn't it?'

'So who's your favourite, Ma?'

Giving it some thought, Marie replied, 'Well, it's difficult to say, Thomas. They are all quite special, aren't they … each in their own different way. But I do like that Jonathan Mann.'

Aware that his query was not so much seeking an answer as calling for a question, she waited a while before continuing.

'And who's your favourite, Thomas? Is it still that Monita Rajpal?'

Thomas's brow furrowed. 'Hmm,' he eventually conceded, 'yes, I do like Monita, of course, but sometimes I also like Hala Gorani. And I must say that Colleen McEdwards was excellent last week.'

Thomas's answer to this most significant of questions took the same form each Thursday – only the names rotated. Typically, each presenter remained the favourite for a week, although Femi Oke, the animated weather-woman, had once featured two weeks in a row.

It was a game mother and son liked to play. Although he would never tell his mother outright – it was his secret, touching on that awkward subject of the fairer sex – his all-time favourite was Becky Anderson. Deep down, he believed himself to be uniquely in touch with the emotional state of each of his treasured news presenters, in particular, Becky. For instance, he could tell, just by listening to her voice or looking into her eyes, whether or not she was having a bad day. Pondering endlessly the possible reasons for her unhappiness, he knew with certainty that should she, or any of them for that matter, call on him for assistance, or even just for someone to talk to, he would always be there for them, no matter how great or small the problem.

That particular night, dominating the news was Scotland Yard's recent decision to release, for the first time ever, a list of Britain's Top Ten Most Wanted. From behind square-framed spectacles – perched on an enormous hooked nose – one Inspector Rajiv Gupta rejected concerns that the notoriety that accompanied appearing on the Most Wanted list might in fact encourage criminal behaviour. To be on the list, he asserted, was 'not actually cool', adding that any information provided by the public concerning the Top Ten would be invaluable.

At half past eight, Marie took the trays through to the kitchen. She would be off to bed shortly. Thomas remained a while longer, but in truth it was not much fun watching on his own. Ten minutes later he turned the set off. On his way to bed, he noticed Marie's light was still on and put his head around the corner to say goodnight.

Marie was lying in bed, reading her Bible. In her left hand she held the misshapen crocheted cross that Thomas had made for her from red string at Koodoo Range Preparatory School. A bookmark in her Bible ever since, its edges by now were soft and frayed.

'Everything all right, Ma?' Thomas asked, noticing a wince of pain as she shifted position.

'Yes, Thomas, fine … just a bit tired, perhaps.'

He hesitated, concerned, but didn't press her. 'Good night, Mother. God bless you.'

'Good night, Thomas, my boy. God bless you too.'

Spiderman, in various action poses, decorated the duvet cover on Thomas's pine-based bed. Next to it was a side table, and against the wall, the cupboard that contained his few clothes. Nothing had changed since his childhood – even the faded blue teddybear-patterned curtains remained.

A brass-framed photograph of Mother and Father stood on the side table, the two of them sitting on a wicker settee in the shade of the verandah. The colonel sat bolt upright, as was his habit even while watching the cricket on television. One hand was balanced on the handle of his walking stick, while the other rested gently on his wife's knee. He faced forward with a resolute look, while Mother had turned to him with a contented smile that spoke of the forty precious years of marriage they had enjoyed together.

Basking in front of the picture frame was Edwin Swales VC, a toy crocodile. Shortly before the colonel's death, the family had visited a crocodile farm while on a motoring holiday along the KwaZulu-Natal south coast. Having spotted the stuffed animal on a shelf in the curio shop, Thomas had stared with unusual fascination and longing, anxiously refusing to leave until the colonel, usually famously frugal, finally relented and made the purchase.

Made of olive-coloured velvet and stuffed with cotton wool and lucky beans, three jagged ridges were sewn along Edwin's back and one along his tail, just like a real crocodile. His mouth was a line of neat black stitching. Most impressive, however, were his eyes. A pair of olive-green plastic marbles with black centres were firmly secured in raised velvet sockets, affording the creature an uncanny, almost lifelike appearance. Once back on the motorway, a sign came into view. Edwin Swales VC Drive, it said. 'Hoorah!' whooped the colonel, recalling an evening of single-malt with the legendary Durban bomber pilot in early 1945 at an airman's pub in Cambridge, just weeks before his heroic death in the night skies over Germany – and that is how the crocodile got his name. Edwin Swales VC was the last gift Thomas had received from Father, and it remained his most prized possession.

The walls of Thomas's room were bare but for an odd-sized series of portraits cut from magazines and newspapers – Winston Churchill, Mother Teresa, Robert Mugabe, Desmond Tutu, Mahatma Gandhi and Nelson Mandela – all bordered with rudimentary wooden frames, hung by the colonel with a great sense of purpose. It was his intention that the lives and philosophies of each should act as beacons to guide Thomas through life's journey. In truth, the hanging of the 'Great Ones', as he called them, was the colonel's final act of rebellion against the values of his own father, which he despised openly and with great passion.

Major Albert Threscothic MC OBE, at one time the commanding officer of the King's Own Camel Corps, had been a living embodiment of shameless brutality, colonial fervour and ill-conceived ideas of racial supremacy, all of which prompted his son to embrace an ideology far removed from that of the average white Rhodesian of his generation. The colonel could never forget the fateful Christmas of 1920. After three helpings of turkey and gammon, and twenty-three double gin-and-tonics, the Major got it into his head that he had been 'lied to' concerning the contents of the liquor cabinet. Or was it the pantry? The riding crop came out, and no one was spared. His servants, his children, even his wife bore the brunt of his fury; the beatings were merciless, the name-calling and slurs unrepeatable – all, he claimed, in the name of the Empire and the attendant morality and progress it had brought. Late that night, as the colonel – all of seven years old at the time – lay under his sheets nursing the welts on his back and buttocks, a compulsion came over him. He sat up, lit a candle, and reached for his notebook.

'That man,' he wrote, 'is a piece of shit. I shall live my life to be everything he is not.'

7

Two Cheers
for Democracy!

It was twilight as Teddington's omnibus burst into the city of Harare, passing the smokeless smokestacks of the industrial sites, hurtling under the railway bridge and up Charter Street, where third-generation Indian traders now jostled for shop space with the recent wave of Chinese retailers – Zhing-Zhongs, the locals called them. Teddington weaved skilfully through the downtown streets and on to Second Street Extension. From here, it was an easy finish to the Parirenyatwa Hospital.

Cries of dismay rose from the passengers as he passed the city's central omnibus terminus without slowing. With a concerned frown, Lennard Chavundukwe walked briskly up the aisle and tapped Teddington on the shoulder.

'Excuse me, driver. Are we not stopping at the Ruzende Street terminus?'

Instinctively, Teddington went on the attack.

'What's wrong with you people? I've done nothing but accommodate you at every turn, and all you do is complain. *Munenge Chembere!* I told you back at the Growth Point that I needed to make a quick stop at the hospital before the terminus. Now, if you'd kindly take your seat instead of distracting me, we'll get there quicker!'

Mister Chavundukwe, uneasily mindful that there may have been some irregularities concerning the swift disembarkation of the omnibus's former occupants, decided to accept Teddington's explanation. He shrugged his shoulders and returned to his seat, pacifying his companions along the way.

As Teddington turned into the main gates of the Parirenyatwa Hospital, he fought hard to control his nerves, his knee bouncing up and down like a jackhammer. The guard at the entrance recognised him, and, assuming that this was the monthly transfer of patients from Ingutsheni, he raised the boom and waved the bus on.

Teddington brought the tired, hissing machine to rest right beside the main entrance of the G20 Ward Block. Snatching up his bag of mangoes – the root cause of all this tomfoolery – he leapt from the driver's cab and down the stairs, locking the door to secure the passengers until after his escape.

'Oi, what do you think you're up to, driver!' Cromwell called out, banging violently on the window.

Teddington did not pause to answer, but dashed through the swing doors into the G20 Reception. To his horror, the unmistakable figure of the Ward's recently appointed new matron, Miss Beatrice Matambanadzo, stood by the front desk, ready to commence her evening rounds. Rumours about her abounded – her vicious temper, her merciless disposition, the secret meals that fed her gargantuan size.

Acutely aware of the matron's fearsome reputation, Teddington realised he must act quickly and decisively, or his game would be up.

'Mai Matambanadzo, good evening. *Manheru, makadini,*' his voice quavered. 'You'll find the Ingutsheni patients in my ZUPCO bus at the back door. A lively lot this time … far livelier than usual … *Iboka revanorwara nepfungwa!* … So I've locked them in until your attendants can take custody of them.'

He fumbled in his pockets.

'Here's the key. In the meantime, may I, er, use your bathroom?'

Matron Matambanadzo regarded the young man with silent suspicion. Narrowing her close-set eyes, she watched him as he walked awkwardly towards the toilet.

Relieving himself at the urinal, Teddington drew in a few deep breaths as he scanned the room for windows through which he might escape. There were two tiny ones right above the urinal, but this being the country's chief psychiatric facility, it was hardly surprising that they were barred.

Not usually a religious man, Teddington prayed silently that the matron had moved on. He eased the door open a chink and peeked out, eyes wide, expecting the worst – but the corridor was empty. Breathing a sigh of relief, he walked as calmly as he could to the reception entrance before sprinting across the darkened hospital parking lot to Second Street Extension, his entire body tingling with anticipation.

Minutes later he was on his way home in a minibus taxi, all according to plan. He had pulled off an unimaginable heist. He had a million dollars in his pockets, and he was free – free to start a new life down south, far away from this basket case of a country, he told himself.

The orderlies of Ward G20 could only gasp at the sight of thirty highly agitated passengers banging on the windows of the omnibus. Their protestations filled the cool evening air.

'Let us out, for God's sake! *Uri kuda kuita sei?*'

'*Chii chirikuitika pano apa!* What the hell is going on here?'

'Do you know who we are!'

Faced with the impossible task of herding this mob into the reception hall, the three orderlies retreated inside. Without question, they could not possibly do this alone. The senior orderly reached for the mouthpiece of the two-way radio to summon security from the hospital's main gate.

Through the windows of G20 Reception, the anxious orderlies watched as the security guards exited the guard house across the deserted parking lot. There were three of them, rubber batons swinging from their waists as they eagerly mounted their bicycles – big, shiny Chinese ones, with carry-baskets in front.

At the sight of the guards, the imprisoned passengers renewed their protests, whistling and calling out, 'Let us out! For goodness' sake! Let us out!'

The guards propped their bikes up against the wall and quickly ran towards reception. Grinning with amusement under their shiny Fawcett Security Company peaks, they entered. A visit to G20 was always a welcome distraction.

'Okay, okay guys. We can see what the problem is!' one of the guards called out to the orderlies, gesturing with his thumb towards the omnibus.

'Can you get them all into the examination room through that door there?' the senior orderly enquired tentatively.

'Sure, where's the key?' asked the youngest and most enthusiastic of the guards. Snatching it from the orderly, he withdrew his baton from the loop on his belt. He had absolutely no intention of using it, but its removal was an essential part of his training. He was now what his instructor would have termed 'at the ready'.

Marching purposefully towards the omnibus, he unlocked the door and stepped into a noisy near-riot, the wind momentarily stripped from his youthful sails. Panic-stricken, he banged the baton against the metal frame of the front seats.

'EVERYONE OFF! INSIDE THE BUILDING! NO TROUBLE, YOU HEAR!'

A storm of objection followed, which he silenced with a few meaty thumps on the nearest seat. Sensing he meant business, the mob fell silent and began to gather their belongings and file down the aisle.

Much to the alarm of Lennard Chavundukwe, the first to enter, the walls of the examination room were padded. It was not long before all thirty of G20's newest admissions were pressed up against one another, shielding their eyes from the sharp overhead lighting.

The senior orderly stepped forward.

'Good evening, ladies and gentlemen. We trust you had a good journey from Ingutsheni? Welcome to your new home here at G20, in this, the sunshine city of Harare! You should be very happy here. Now please empty the contents of your pockets into those empty cake tins over there, and leave your suitcases and handbags by the door. You won't be needing them here.'

A fragile, fretful woman at the front of the group covered her eyes. 'Oh, my God! Ingutsheni!' she exclaimed in a high-pitched wail. 'Whatever next? It's another one of their plots, you know! I told you we should never have gone to that rally!'

Cromwell Shimwa stepped forward, clearing his throat with an officious 'Ahem'.

'Listen here, mate. This is obviously some kind of mistake. We are perfectly normal citizens with absolutely no connection to Ingutsheni whatsoever.'

This kind of denial is, of course, extremely common in a mental institution. The senior orderly had encountered it often before, countless times, in fact, but never en masse, so to speak. He felt distinctly uncomfortable.

'Right, then bring out the straitjackets!' he barked at the junior orderlies.

The stunned silence that followed was punctuated by a subdued clunk as the fretful woman fainted, collapsing in a pitiful heap. The senior orderly was clearly unsettled. His eyeballs quivered behind his immense spectacles, the lenses of which were as thick as the base of a Coke bottle, and equally frosty. He must report this to Matron Matambanadzo, he must make it more of her problem and less of his, or there would be trouble – big trouble – that much was certain. Leaving the examination room, he walked quickly to the Matron's office, wiping his glistening brow with his handkerchief.

He paused at the door before knocking gingerly, for Matron Matambanadzo was temperamental at the best of times. Inside her office, the matron was finishing a snack. It was her habit to conceal a loaf of brown bread in her top drawer, next to her paper punch and a box of paper clips. A tin of apricot jam and some margarine wrapped in greaseproof paper were in the second drawer, along with a bread knife. Whenever she felt peckish – a near-constant sensation – she would treat herself to a sandwich, using one of the patient's case files as a plate. Once devoured, she would dust the crumbs into the wastepaper basket, and then, using her fingers, she would scoop up any remaining dollops of jam and margarine before licking them clean again, as a matter of general hygiene. After putting everything back in their designated places, it was back to business for a contented Beatrice Matambanadzo. Her sandwich fetish was an open secret among the staff; they all knew that when knocking on her door they should allow at least a minute for her to complete the ritual. Premature entry would be suicidal.

The senior orderly waited uneasily for what seemed an age before knocking again.

'Dammit! Who is it?'

His reply was timid. 'Er, it is Boniface Mazingi, Matron.'

From behind the door, he heard a deep sigh of annoyance followed by a shameless belch. Drawers slammed shut, followed by the sound of two spurts, presumably from an aerosol can.

'Okay, come in.'

Mazingi entered the office and stood to attention in front of Matron Matambanadzo's desk. The air was thick with conflicting aromas. He immediately recognised the overpowering sweetness of toilet freshener, a commodity hard to come by these days. A hint of apricot jam, as expected. And something else, which irked him in particular. Garlic, perhaps?

'What is it now?' she said, glaring at him.

'The new patients, Matron – a very restless lot. They all claim to have been delivered here by accident and do not look as if they want to be settled in.'

'Well, why bother me? Get the, er, what's he called … psychotherapist, to, er, examine them!'

Mazingi remained silent.

'Can't these people just do their job?' she muttered to herself.

'Ordinarily we would, Matron, but, as you might remember, the psychiatrist left last week, following the doctors' wage dispute. There are no doctors left in this ward, Matron,' Mazingi reminded her, referring to the unresolved national strike, where doctors had thrown down their stethoscopes and syringes, demanding a salary increase of 8 000%.

'Well, then you'll have to sedate them! Sedate them all. Every last one!'

'With what, Matron? We ran out of sedatives some months ago due to the hospital drug shortage.'

'What do you mean, no sedatives! So what have you done in the past when there were no sedatives?'

Mazingi shifted his weight uneasily from one foot to the other. This was a tricky question to answer.

'We have found, on occasion, Matron, that some of them calm down a little if you let them have a cigarette or two.'

'A cigarette or two. Very good. Get them each a box from the cafeteria,' she ordered. 'Tell them they can go home once they have smoked their box. That should provide some distraction.'

A smile came to her lips; the problem had been solved. If truth be told, she possessed no relevant medical health qualifications whatsoever for the position of Matron of Parirenyatwa's Mental Health Ward. Moreover, her propensity for violent outbursts rendered her far less stable than the majority of patients under her care. It was only through the influence of her uncle, a permanent secretary in one of the government ministries, that she had landed this job. Even then, he had only arranged it to obtain some relief from the constant badgering and relentless belligerence that disturbed the otherwise calm waters in which the extended family boat had sailed. To her credit, though, she had a flair for spotting opportunities, and could be suprisingly shrewd in securing them.

Boniface Mazingi sent one of his staff off to the canteen to buy three cartons of Madison Reds, the strongest toasted cigarettes in the land. One whole hardpack of twenty for each patient. On the man's return, Mazingi instructed him to open the cartons and place the individual boxes on the medicine dispensing trolley, which he personally wheeled through to the examination room. A heated argument had in the meantime erupted between the patients and the orderlies. Cromwell Shimwa, now restrained in a straitjacket, hurled insults at the orderlies.

'Silence!' bellowed Mazingi. 'Silence!' But his cries were completely ignored until one of the security guards gave an ear-piercing whistle.

'Thank you,' the senior orderly calmly continued. 'Now, we are aware that you've had a long day on the bus, and so we have organised some cigarettes to calm you down. Due to budget constraints, there is only one box each. Once you've finished your box, you'll be free to go home.'

A disbelieving silence ensued, followed by a cacophony of protest.

Cromwell Shimwa shouldered his way through the crowd.

'I,' he declared in a loud and authoritative voice, 'am Cromwell Shimwa, president of the Youth League of the Movement for Democratic Change, the official opposition party of this country. I no doubt

speak for all my colleagues in the Youth League, and also other es-
teemed senior party members here tonight – including the honourable Member of Parliament, Mister Lennard Chavundukwe, MDC
Shadow Minister of Law and Order – when I state that we wish to
register our extreme dissatisfaction with the treatment meted out
to us here today. Through some bizarre misunderstanding, we have
been imprisoned in what is clearly an institution for the mentally
infirm – and a poor one at that, might I add. To add insult to injury,
we are now called upon to smoke a box of cigarettes each, against
our will. We absolutely refuse to do this!'

'Hear, hear, Cromwell, hear hear!' came the chorus of agreement.

'Good show, Cromwell, let them have it!'

An unforeseen complication threatened, however, to fracture
their unanimity. Some of them were smokers. Heavy smokers, in
fact. It had been a long day at the MDC Youth Rally in Masvingo,
and a hot, frustrating journey back to Harare, with the added stress
of this latest imposition. Quite simply, a number of them could have
done with a smoke right then. One such person, a Mister Jonathan
Katsande, stepped forward.

'Yes, no one here should *have* to smoke any cigarettes! Not unless
they want to, that is!'

Already anxious at the prospect of administering such unconven-
tional medication, Mazingi shook his head. There was a ripple of
consternation. Mister Katsande again stepped forward, driven by
an uneasy craving for nicotine.

'Okay, okay, okay! We are a democratic organisation, a fact upon
which we pride ourselves, particularly in view of the autocratic cli-
mate in which we currently find ourselves in this country. Now, let's
put this issue to the vote.'

'This is absolutely ridiculous!' retorted Mister Chavundukwe.

'But sir,' Mister Katsande responded timidly, 'a selective use of
democracy would be a betrayal of the very principles we as the MDC
hold dear.'

Mister Chavundukwe threw up his hands. 'What can one say? Okay, have your election. But I for one shall abstain.'

A chorus of non-smokers followed suit.

'Me too, I also abstain.'

'Let's boycott the election.'

Sensing his opportunity, Jonathan Katsande did not hesitate. 'Okay, those who wish to abstain from participating in the election, raise your hands.'

'Right, we have fifteen absentions.'

'Okay, those who have not exercised their right to abstain, and wish to vote against the distribution of the cigarettes, please raise your hands.'

'Nine against,' called Mister Katsande, counting the raised hands.

'Those who wish to vote in favour of the distribution of the cigarettes, please raise your hands.'

Eleven eager hands shot up.

'Eleven for, and nine against. Right, then, Orderly, let's have those cigarettes.'

A torrent of complaint ensued. All but the smokers were bewildered.

'Well, there you bloody well have it! Two cheers for democracy!' uttered Cromwell Shimwa in disgust. 'Preposterous! We are thirty in number, yet we have a total of thirty-five votes and absentions – either some people voted twice, or the electorate included those who should correctly have been excluded. The result should be struck down immediately!'

In truth, it was the orderlies and the security guards, eager to exercise, for once, their democratic right to vote, who had pushed through the motion. An ad hoc form of gerrymandering had clinched the result.

Mindful of his tyrannical superior, and of the clear instructions given to him with respect to the distribution of a box of cigarettes per patient, Mister Boniface Mazingi resolved to stamp out any further debate. From his point of view, the outcome had been ideal.

He moved quickly around the room, dispensing the Madison Reds.

'Right, you've had your election. A democratic process has been followed and a legitimate result achieved. If you didn't want the cigarettes, you should have voted against them, which you failed to do. So here they are! Smoke away, or it's the straitjacket for the lot of you!'

Jonathan Katsande took a deep drag of his Madison, savouring the smoke in his lungs for quite some time. Yet, surrounded by the gasps and splutters of his colleagues, he did not feel entirely comfortable with the results of the election.

8

Matron Matambanadzo's Big Fish

Knocking tentatively on the matron's door, Boniface Mazingi tensed his thigh muscles and closed his eyes in fearful anticipation. Two minutes passed before a gruff voice sounded from within.

'Who is it?'

'Boniface Mazingi, Matron.'

'I can't hear. Speak up, dammit!'

'Boniface Mazingi,' he loudly repeated.

'Wait.'

He waited patiently for the sound of aerosol spurts and drawers opening and shutting to die down.

'Come in – if you must!'

Mazingi entered the office and assumed his position at attention in front of the matron.

'What is it this time, Mazingi?' enquired the matron. 'Can't you see I'm busy?'

'Yes of course, Matron, very busy. But I thought you would want to know that the new arrivals have been subdued, in accordance with your instructions.'

Matron Matambanadzo stared at him for several seconds. 'Is that all you came here to tell me, Mazingi?'

'Er, there is something else, Matron, but perhaps it is not worth mentioning.'

'This better be good, Mazingi.'

'Er, Matron, the new patients from Ingutsheni. They claim to be from the MDC Youth League. One's calling himself Cromwell Shimwa. He claims to be President of the MDC Youth League.'

'Yes, Mazingi, and I am the Queen of Sheba! Have you forgotten that this is a mental institution?'

Boniface Mazingi shifted his weight uneasily from one foot to the other.

'Another claims to be a member of parliament, also for the MDC. Lennard Chavundukwe, he says. I think I recognise his face from ZBC. He was on the news a few weeks ago, if I'm not mistaken.'

The matron's eyes lit up with interest. An MP in her custody; this could do wonders for her party credentials. And Lennard Chavundukwe – one of the country's best-known political figures. A senior lawyer for many years, he was highly respected both locally and abroad for his intellect and integrity, even by those whose political loyalties lay with the government, although none would be heard saying as much in public.

The matron's mind immediately began plotting – she must maximise her kudos from this remarkable stroke of fortune.

'Bring him to me immediately.'

'Yes, Matron.' Mazingi was off like a shot to the examination room, jumping at the chance to clock up some eager-beaver points with his despotic superior. The air was so thick with smoke it took some moments to locate Lennard Chavundukwe, who was leaning against the back wall. Mazingi grabbed him by the arm and pulled him out into the corridor. The MP's face looked ashen as he stumbled behind Mazingi, gingerly holding a half-smoked Madison between thumb and forefinger.

'Where are we going?' he coughed, his eyes watering.

'To the matron,' Mazingi said, 'and you'd better be who you say you are, or there'll be trouble for both of us.'

Lennard Chavundukwe did not reply. By now he had begun to suspect that this whole exercise had been orchestrated by the CIO, the dreaded Central Investigation Organisation, which frequently interrupted MDC gatherings and detained its members.

Boniface Mazingi could hear the matron chattering excitedly over the telephone as he stepped forward and knocked on her door yet again. This time he did not have to wait long; the matron cut short her call mid-sentence. 'Mazingi, is that you?'

'Yes, Matron. I have Mister Lennard Chavundukwe with me.'

'Well, don't just stand there, Mazingi, bring him in!'

Mazingi entered the matron's office, pulling the confused patient along by the arm. The matron immediately recognised Lennard Chavundukwe. Her heart leapt with joy.

She stared at him with narrowed eyes. 'Mister Chavundukwe – I take it you are *the* Lennard Chavundukwe, Member of Parliament?'

'That I cannot deny. I am indeed Lennard Chavundukwe, Member of Parliament.'

'And that makes you think you can smoke in my office? For goodness' sake, throw that thing out of the window!'

The matron only needed to give the command once for Lennard to scramble to the window to rid himself of the appalling sedative.

'Now, Mister Chavundukwe, what is your illness, are you a ...' Drawing a blank, she turned to her subordinate. 'Mazingi, what's it called again? You know, like most of them?' she enquired, pointing in the general direction of the G20 wards.

'Schizophrenic?' suggested Mazingi cautiously.

'Yes, that's it. Are you a schizophrenic, Mister Chavundukwe?'

'Good heavens! No, definitely not. We came from a political meeting in Masvingo this afternoon and our bus driver seems to have dropped us off here by accident this evening. I am definitely not a schizophrenic.'

Matron Matambanadzo stared hard at him for a couple of seconds and smiled. She couldn't believe her luck. 'Well, Mister Chavundukwe, if you weren't a schizophrenic before, I can assure you, you certainly are one now! Take him back to the examination room and post extra guards at all the exits, Mazingi. These are dangerous people, they must not be allowed to escape! And get me a list of all their names.'

Beatrice Matambanadzo wasted no time in calling back her uncle, George Maramba. This was indeed *the* Lennard Chavundukwe, she confirmed. She could hear the excitement in his voice. This was a stellar event for him too, in these topsy-turvy days of ZANU-PF snakes and ladders, with various factions of the ruling party jostling for pole position in the remote hope that His Excellency, Robert Gabriel Mugabe, might one day step down from the presidential podium.

'Oh, my God! Oh, my God! Oh, boy! This is big, Beatrice! This is very, very big!' her uncle squealed with exhilaration. 'Do you have any idea how big this is? I'm going to phone Party headquarters; the president must be informed. We've got a whole bunch of them this time! Thirty, you say? And an MP! A big fish! Oh, my God! Marvellous! You've done well, Beatrice. *Iwe ndiwe wepamoyo pangu*. You know you've always been my favourite niece. There's a promotion in this for you, my dear. Matron of the Mbuya Nehanda Maternity Home. The whole darn thing! I'll see to it. Just sit tight. See you in ten minutes.'

9

Two Orphans Lost at Zama Zama Growth Point

It was almost midnight, and still the Trustees' monthly report was not finished. Joseph Chiswa's eyes felt tired and heavy. The shrill ringing of his secretary's phone outside his office startled him. Who on earth could be calling at this hour? With a sigh, the headmaster slid his chair back, taking care not to bump his desk for beneath his desk lamp on a large dinner plate, he had neatly placed the minute inner workings of a pocket calculator. He had taken it apart that morning, using a tiny screwdriver, one of a series he kept in the top drawer of his desk. Striding purposefully out of his office and into the hall of the administration block, he snatched up the receiver.

'Hello, Joseph Chiswa speaking … Ah, yes, is everything all right? … Those two little ones who were supposed to have arrived this evening, you mean? … Yes, I was wondering where they'd got to … Lost? Oh, dear … any idea where? … With a group of … what?

Lunatics, you say? You must be joking ... Okay, so where exactly is this Zama Zama spot? Sorry, the line isn't good, did you say thirty kilometres past Chivu ... Okay, I'll try to make a plan in the morning. Let's stay in touch.'

The news of the children's disappearance troubled Joseph. Even though they had not yet arrived in his care, they had already become his responsibility, he felt. Despite the best intentions of the staff at the Department of Welfare, for whom he had developed much respect and affection over the years, he knew it was highly unlikely that they would have the means to do anything at all to find the children. Perplexed and uncertain as to his next move, Baba Chiswa returned to his office, donned his spectacles, and took out his miniature screwdriver. Tinkering with mechanical objects had always helped him think. He examined the buttons of the disassembled calculator with a large magnifying glass, holding them up to his desk lamp with a set of tweezers and then carefully scraping bits of grime from their edges with the tip of a pin. As he worked, he pondered the plight of the two orphans. Did they have food to eat? Where would they sleep? Were these lunatics dangerous?

Contemplating his options and obligations, he came to the inevitable conclusion – he must go out and look for them himself. Thomas should come as well, he decided; two pairs of eyes would be better than one.

10

The State's Obligation
to Protect Citizens from Themselves

Mental Illness Ravages MDC Leadership
Harare – *Herald* Reporter

*Health administrators at the Parirenyatwa Hospital's G20
Psychiatric Ward were startled on Sunday evening when thirty
MDC activists required urgent admission, suffering from mental
illnesses ranging from schizophrenia to chronic depression. The
patients admitted included the MDC's Lennard Chavundukwe,
MP for Marondera West, and Cromwell Shimwa, president of the
MDC Youth League, an organisation that has gained nationwide
notoriety in recent months for unprovoked attacks on peaceful
ZANU-PF gatherings.*

*The group attended an illegal political gathering in Masvingo
yesterday morning before boarding a privately chartered Chiyangwa*

44

& Sons luxury coach bound for Harare, which broke down near the town of Chivu. It was there that the group persuaded the driver of an empty ZUPCO bus en route to Harare to transport them to their final destination at the central Harare Bus Terminus on Ruzende Street. The ZUPCO bus driver, whose identity was not known to The Herald *at the time of going to print, was fortunately diligent enough to take notice of the peculiar behaviour exhibited by the passengers, including facial distortion and violent outbursts. Based on his correct analysis of his passengers' mental condition, the ZUPCO driver had the good sense to deliver the group directly to Parirenyatwa Hospital's G20 Psychiatric Ward. The group is believed to have been highly agitated, and may have engaged in conflict among themselves. The extent of any injuries inflicted during such conflict is not yet known.*

The ward was visited by the Minister of Safety and Security and the Minister of Information and Communications, to personally ensure that all necessary steps had been taken to provide adequate treatment to the afflicted persons. The Minister of Safety and Security praised the courage and diligence displayed by the bus driver. He said that if our hard-won democracy is to withstand the assault of Western imperialism and its agents – the root cause of economic decline in recent years – all Zimbabweans should follow this example.

Parirenyatwa Hospital psychiatrists have not yet ruled out the possibility of mass hypnosis, a controversial method popular with Western Intelligence Agencies such as Britain's MI5, and America's CIA.

In response to this, the Minister of Information and Communications stated that the admissions might yet provide further evidence that the MDC are mere puppets of Britain's Tony Blair and his merry band of gay gangsters described by the President as lower than dogs and pigs, hell-bent on preserving and promoting their own imperialist interests in retaliation for the government's successful land redistribution exercise, which has seen settlers of British descent being forced to surrender land stolen by Britain during its colonial occupation of Zimbabwe, and redistributed to landless black Zimbabweans.

The Minister of Information and Communications told The Herald *that, for the sake of their own wellbeing, the patients will be held indefinitely for observation and treatment.*

The Herald's editor and layout technician shot uncertain glances at each other.

'Is there a problem?' asked ZANU-PF's Minister of Information and Communication, otherwise known simply as 'The Spin Doctor'.

'Is it, er, how does one put it? Er … true?' ventured the editor cautiously.

'Of course it is, you buffoon! I wrote it myself, didn't I! How do you think we got the picture? Now stop asking stupid questions and let's get going with the printing!'

Moments later, a photographer emerged from the darkroom with a photo. It had come out beautifully. The unfortunate replacement passengers of Teddington's omnibus were lined up outside Ward G20 in three rows, like a high-school sports team, with the shortest ones kneeling in front, the middle row sitting, and those at the back, including Lennard Chavundukwe MP and Cromwell Shimwa, standing. All were tightly bound in white straitjackets, and from the mouth of each dangled a lit cigarette. Various facial expressions of indignation, outrage and confusion conferred upon the group a sense of abject lunacy. On either side of the hapless group stood a collection of beaming security guards and other hospital personnel, most prominent being Matron Matambanadzo, holder of an O-level pass certificate for domestic science, wearing a white doctor's coat, with a stethoscope dangling from her ears.

The Spin Doctor positively glowed with pride. With the article completed, the alterations to the front page layout took less than five minutes.

'Get the machines rolling,' he cried as he grabbed his jacket from the back of the editor's chair and made his way to the car park. It was well past midnight – late, but certainly worth the delay in printing.

As he slumped into the back seat of his ministerial Mercedes, the sound of the printing press was music to his ears – a symphony of words.

All his! Simply glorious!

11

The Theft of *The Herald* from Mister R Utsichingoka's General Store

It is therefore my obligation, Joseph Chiswa hastily scribbled, *to inform you, the Board of Trustees, that payment of the children's school fees in these hyper-inflationary times will be the William Westward's greatest challenge.* With that, his report was finally complete. Having worked well past midnight the night before, the headmaster felt weary as he dropped the bundle of pages onto Mai Rutivi's desk for typing. He glanced at his old Seiko wristwatch. Despite countless sessions of complex microsurgery under his magnifying glass and screwdriver, its sturdy hands consistently lost time. Ten to ten, it said, which meant it was actually closer to ten past. It was already mid-morning. He and Thomas must set off at once.

Mile after mile of farmlands flashed by, most of it fallow. Tall grass and msasa saplings covered fields once green with maize and tobacco. Thomas knew little of the various arguments concerning the land resettlement process. In *The Herald* he had read that the land had been given back to those from whom it had been unlawfully taken many decades before. Fair enough, he thought. But he had also heard that, lacking even the basics – seed and fertiliser – the new farmers did not stand a chance. With no pesticides, tractor fumes, farmers or farm labourers, the birds, it seemed to Thomas, had flourished – and that pleased him. Leaning back in his seat, he scanned the wooded fringes of the road ahead. Lilac-breasted Rollers and Fork-tailed Drongos swooped from the sagging telegraph wires. Flocks of Quelea rolled across the empty fields in swirling waves that baffled the eye. He knew all the birds, even those he could not name.

Stark naked but for a pair of dirty white Bata takkies without laces, an elderly man waved frantically at them from the roadside, startling them. They might have driven straight past otherwise. Zama Zama Growth Point – General Store appeared, its name hand-painted on the building's wall, and underneath it, in smaller, italic script, the name of its proprietor: Mister R. Utsichingoka.

'This is it, Baba Chiswa! This is the place!'

Music blared from bulky speakers outside the beer hall across the road as they drew to a halt. Joseph Chiswa eyed the hall with a sense of foreboding.

'Let's try the store first, Thomas.'

Inside the General Store, a contest was in progress. The shopkeeper – presumably Mister R Utsichingoka – and a would-be reader were jostling for possession of a rolled-up copy of *The Herald* across the store's concrete counter. With a loud grunt, the would-be reader yanked the newspaper clean out of the shopkeeper's hands, falling heavily onto a pile of empty crates.

Mister Utsichingoka leaned over the counter and wagged his finger, 'I've told you ten times today already – no money, no newspaper. Now give that back and get the hell out of here!'

The man glanced at the shopkeeper, and then at the newspaper in his hand. Without a word, he jumped to his feet and fled across the road to the beer hall. Mister Utsichingoka swore blue murder, but it was too late.

'It's madness in here today. Here – and in there!' he exclaimed, pointing across at the beer hall. 'It's been going on non-stop since yesterday evening!'

With a jerk of his head in the direction of a pile of newspapers, he muttered, 'And if the headline in today's *Herald* is anything to go by, there's madness going on in Harare too! It's spreading around the country like VD!'

'Have you by any chance seen two children?' Joseph enquired, 'We understand they were accidentally left here by a bus driver yesterday ...'

'A lot of people arrived yesterday, and a lot of people were left here – and it wasn't by accident, either. I saw it all, with my very own eyes. The driver kicked all his passengers off his bus, and loaded on a whole new bunch from that broken-down bus up the road. It's been chaos here ever since.'

'So you haven't seen the children?'

'Children? No. But you could try the beer hall across the way. A lot of passengers from the bus headed straight there. But I warn you, many went in, and so far almost none have come out. If the kids aren't in there, try the village. It's behind this store.'

12

Teddington Fails to Change Direction in Mid-Air

The sun streamed through the window of Teddington's room, waking him with a start. Just as well – he had intended to flee Hatcliffe well before dawn in order to catch a bus from the city centre to Beitbridge by seven. With a panicked jerk he sat upright and glanced at his watch. Ten past twelve! He gasped with horror. If he wanted to get to Beitbridge by nightfall, he had to move fast. His burning thirst and pounding headache induced a wave of regret. What he had intended as a quiet evening of heartfelt farewells at his brother's house had escalated into quite a soirée, funded largely, and most unfortunately, he now realised, with his ill-gotten gains. His brother's youngsters had been sent to the shebeen several times during the evening to replenish the scuds – two-litre plastic barrels of Chibuku beer that resembled Scud missiles – which had attracted a small but surprisingly thirsty crowd. At three that morning,

Teddington, awash with bonhomie, had sponsored a couple of crates of Black Label quarts, considerably more expensive, which disappeared within minutes of their arrival – just as well, considering that their hasty distribution had barely preceded the third visit of the evening from his brother's irate neighbour, Mai Hungwe. Clad in a scarlet towelling dressing gown and matching slippers, she arrived brandishing a long bamboo cane. Her two children, by then weeping with frustration, were due to write their A- and O-level examinations the following day. Her hidings – indiscriminate, if not sadistic – scattered the revellers into the night, Teddington included.

Frantically squeezing his spare set of clothing and shoes into an old Zimbank sports bag, he was startled by a sharp rap on the door. Teddington froze with dread. A second later, a more decisive knock followed.

'Open up, Chiwafambira! *Tivhurireyi!* It's the police!'

Teddington's eyes widened. Instantly resolving to make a run for it, he hastily zipped up his bag. In a single, improbably smooth movement, he leapt onto his bed and out of the window. At the zenith of his trajectory, he spotted a hefty constable lying in wait for him below. Hoping to change his direction, he peddled his legs frantically in the air, like a long jumper, but to no avail. Within seconds he had been handcuffed and frogmarched to the waiting ZRP Land Rover. On their way back from their exams, Mai Hungwe's two children, wearing their regulation straw boaters, observed the scene with apprehension bordering on embarrassment – could their mother be responsible for this? Sure, it had been noisy, but getting the cops involved, well, that was over the top.

Teddington bumped his head on the frame of the canopy as the constables pushed him into the Land Rover and slammed the door shut, locking it with a rusty Yale padlock before setting off. Both relieved and delighted, they had now fulfilled the Spin Doctor's orders, issued outside Ward G20 just before midnight the night before. It had been a long night, tracking down the elusive Chiwafambira.

Recognition and reward lay ahead, no doubt.

'Hey, Chiwafambira! *Uzvichenjerere!* Big trouble in store for you, my friend. The minister, Mister Spin Doctor himself, he wants to see you!'

Teddington gasped with horror. If ministers were involved, particularly the Spin Doctor, a jail sentence was inevitable; years of hard labour at Chikurubi Prison lay ahead.

To impress the nation's propaganda chief, the constables had procured some ancient leg irons. Clamping these onto Teddington in the car park outside the minister's office, they shuffled him along, his chains clanking.

13

Adulterers Repent in the Crocodile-Infested Waters of the Munyati

A volley of festive shrieks and cheers rang out from inside the beer hall as Joseph and Thomas crossed the road, apprehensive but undoubtedly curious. Strings of bottle tops hung from the tavern's doorframe down to the floor. Poker-faced, Joseph cautiously parted the strings. Inside it was dark and hot, the air thick with the stink of sweat and stale beer, the din deafening. A long table dominated the room around which most of the revellers sat on benches. Others stood unsteadily behind them, or were slumped over the unattended bar counter. A few had collapsed where they stood, and had been rolled to the fringes of the room, sweating and snoring. Empty scuds were strewn across every surface. The till lay open, its cash drawer looted.

In front of each person seated at the table was a tin mug or a jam jar. A man – under these, and only these circumstances, a figure of authority – walked along the one side of the table. Using his right hand, he filled each container with Chibuku from a scud. With his left he poured a generous dash of paraffin from a bottle. His task complete, the revellers at once began to shout. 'Shuddup! Shuddup!'

One or two placed a finger in front of their lips. 'Sssshhhhhhh.'

A man stood up on a chair and banged two pots together. Silence fell as he yelled, 'Okay! Ready! Steady … wait for it!'

For a moment, nothing happened. Then, from the darkness, a bold, crystal-clear voice called out. 'Come on, then!'

The cue, it seemed, for a game by now well established. The reveller at the top of the table snatched up his mug, swallowing his drink in several trembling gulps. Exactly five seconds later, the voice exclaimed 'Go on, then!'

As if by clockwork, the contender across the table from the first knocked back his drink. Appalled, Joseph and Thomas watched as the contestants responded, one by one, each to his team's specific directive – the game proceeding smoothly until it reached the end of the table. The last man up ignored his call, completely mesmerised, so it appeared, by the twirling of a partially straightened paper clip between his fingers. A thunderous cry went up from the winning side – yet another in a seemingly endless series of pointless victories.

'Let's go,' Joseph Chiswa said, 'it's clear that the children aren't in here.'

Blinking at the bright sunlight, the two men crossed the road to the village, where circular thatched huts and small brick dwellings ran down towards a river behind Mister R Utsichingoka's General Store. From the water's edge came the sound of agitated voices.

'Let's try down there,' Joseph suggested.

Just as they began their descent, a middle-aged man appeared suddenly from behind a tree. He was wearing a dark suit, fashionably cut but heavily creased, and a thin navy-blue tie, on which the scales of justice were embroidered. Trapped in his hair were bits of msasa bark and a small orange feather from the breast of a rooster.

'Gentlemen! Good day!' he called out in clear hot-potato English.

'Good day,' Joseph replied cautiously.

'Benedict Toriro Tsoko QC. Formerly of Gray's Inn, Chancery Lane. And now village headman. How may I be of assistance?'

A hint of alcohol reached Joseph as they shook hands.

'We are, er, looking for two children. We understand they were left here accidentally yesterday by the driver of a bus.'

'Children. Hmm. I've seen some children, but whether they are the two you are seeking, or merely someone else's, I cannot say. Follow me, gentlemen, a search party is in order!"

A group of teenage boys came into sight, playing barefooted in a dusty clearing with a ball made from old fertiliser bags tightly bound with twine.

'Lads! Over here, lads, I've got a task for you. Hurry, now!' Benedict Tsoko QC called out loudly.

The boys stopped their play and stared at him blankly. One set off at a run.

Turning to Joseph, Benedict Tsoko clicked his tongue in annoyance.

'Kids.' he said. 'No jolly respect these days!'

The boy quickly returned with an older man dressed in brown trousers and a faded Manchester United shirt. He addressed Benedict Tsoko in Shona, but the latter responded in English, 'As headman of this village, I've called these boys to assist my guests in searching for two missing children.'

The man interrupted him. 'Did you say you are the headman?'

'Indeed.'

'Impossible! I am the headman! *Uri kunyeba*! Who the hell are you?'

Frantic shrieking and wailing rose from the direction of the river, the leadership wrangle was temporarily placed on hold while everyone moved hastily to investigate.

A tall, fearsome man, standing high up on a tree stump near the water's edge, pocket Bible in hand, towered over a large crowd. Villagers from all around, it seemed, had abandoned their daily chores to witness for themselves the arrival of Elijah – a preacher, it was rumoured, of continental fame.

'Repent! Confess! Beseech the Lord for his forgiveness!'

He recited harrowing extracts from the Book of Revelations in English, and an equally enthusiastic translator stepped forward to assist – whose translations, Joseph Chiswa noted, betrayed flamboyant artistic licence, if not a disturbing taste for the macabre. Several women had fallen to their knees, wailing in anguish.

'In these waters be baptised! Let your sins be washed away!'

Fear rippled through the unsettled throng. There were crocodiles in the river, everyone knew that. A terrible choice must be made – to brave the perilous waters of the Munyati River, or to suffer eternal damnation. Several chose to flee, swiftly making their way back to their own villages and the relative safety of their own churches. Others remained where they were, paralysed by the weight of such a troubling decision.

A group of men, fearing the wrath of God above all crocodiles, waded cautiously into the murky flow until only their heads and shoulders could be seen above the surface.

'Repent!' cried Elijah feverishly. 'Repent and save your souls!'

The near-submerged men launched simultaneously into a startling anthology of adultery, each confession tainted with the same woman's name. Shrieks of indignation emanated from the womenfolk waiting on the banks, who turned and pointed at the shamed woman in rage. Under a hail of stones, the men sought cover in deeper waters until a cry of '*Garwe! Garwe*! Crocodile! Crocodile!' sent them scrambling up the slippery banks, where the women lashed at them with sticks. Within minutes the crowd had dissipated, leaving only a few tree-bound spectators, some of whom began to topple from the branches as they howled with laughter.

Alone on the river bank, Joseph and Thomas could not suppress their smiles. A boy, one of the footballers, approached them. Clearly, he had overheard their discussion earlier about the missing children.

'Come, I will take you to them.'

Up near the road, a woman had taken the two children in the day before. She opened her door to Joseph and Thomas, and there they were, crouching behind a small table. It took some coaxing to get them to come out – in their short lives they had been given little reason to trust anyone, and the events of the past two days had done little to dispel that sentiment. The girl, Ruth, was small enough to be carried, but would not allow Thomas to lift her up. There were no white people, and certainly none with flaming red hair, in the remote corner of Matabeleland where she came from. Joseph, with his gentle voice and patient manner, finally gathered her up in his arms. She clung onto him, nestling her head into the nape of his neck, with tears rolling down her cheeks as they went to the car.

Thomas tried talking to the boy, who was slightly older. Sullen and defiant, he refused to look up, and neither would he move. When Joseph returned from the car and asked the boy for his name, he simply shook his head and stared silently at the floor. Joseph asked again. This time the boy responded in a voice unusually deep for his size and age – unsettling perhaps, thought Joseph – two-toned at times, like a mouth organ, with a warbling higher octave. Regus was his name, he said. And his father would be coming to fetch him. No amount of persuasion could convince him otherwise. Finally, they had little option but to gently grab him under the arms and propel him in the direction of the car, his legs and feet dragging behind him. Mindful that he might try to escape in mid-journey, Thomas sat in the back seat with the children. He tried to speak to them on the journey home, first in English then a few words in Shona, a language which he generally understood, though, despite his daily exercises, and much to his embarrassment, he still struggled to speak. But the children were from the south-west – they knew Ndebele only.

In the end, the four sat in silence, intensely aware of one another, but each alone with his or her own thoughts.

14

The Spin Doctor's Distaste for Colcom Pork Pies

So outlandish was the Spin Doctor's front-page picture and article combination that most members and supporters of the MDC – and, more importantly, the public – believed it to be true. Government spies infiltrated into the ranks of the MDC soon reported mayhem in the organisation. No one knew what to do next. Nothing like this had ever happened before. The MDC president, puzzled in the extreme, called one of his trusted advisors to ask, 'Is it true we've been working with the British?' and was greatly relieved to be told it was not. A consultation with a private psychiatrist was hastily arranged to extract an opinion on the veracity of the newspaper report. Once it was established that there could be no truth in it at all, and that it was just another wicked ZANU-PF ploy to destroy its opposition, the party's lawyers were instructed to be on standby to prepare an urgent application to the High Court for the members' release.

In response to all the intelligence filtering through to the ruling party, the Minister of Safety and Security called an urgent Politburo meeting. There was only one item on the agenda: how to maximise the damage that this fortuitous event would cause the MDC. The President himself was summoned. Wailing sirens from two dozen motorcades could soon be heard making their way across Harare to ZANU-PF headquarters.

The Spin Doctor's proposal that the MDC psychiatrist should be encouraged to see the error of her ways was snapped up unanimously. Two plainclothes Central Intelligence Organisation units were dispatched at once – one to collect her, another to collect her two children from Highland Schools. The children were to be given granadilla ice lollies and placed behind reflective glass in an interrogation room at Harare Central, so that their mother could see them while a polite CIO officer offered her tea and handed her a dossier containing photographs of terrible car accidents, all of which, he suggested, could have been so easily avoided.

The plan was executed faultlessly. The psychiatrist promptly produced a report concluding mass hypnosis by agents of a Western government to be highly probable under the circumstances. This she submitted to the MDC before catching the first available flight to South Africa with her children and alarmed husband – much to the delight of the CIO officers who drew lots for her electrical appliances, and carted away the remainder of the family's furniture using a fleet of recently privatised police vehicles.

The Politburo knew that the exercise with the psychiatrist would buy them only a few days before the inevitable court process began, but that was all they required. Thereafter, court applications could be opposed, legally at first, and then through a myriad of 'judicial delays' and 'postponements'. Finally, a friendly judge, lured by the promise of a lovely spread of land in the Mazoe Hills, with a citrus orchard and a nice little herd of Aberdeen Angus, could be relied upon to refuse the application on spurious grounds. Doubt-less, an appeal would follow – appeals were wonderful, they could take could take several months, if not years, by which time the captive MDC members would hopefully have succumbed to a genuine range of mental illnesses.

The Spin Doctor was detained in further important meetings until after two that afternoon, leaving Teddington waiting in leg irons and handcuffs, stiff with fright, in the reception area. It came almost as a relief when Teddington heard the sirens of the motorcade dying down in the car park below, and the footsteps of the energetic minister striding up the stairs three at a time. The dozing ZRP constables leapt to their feet in a hotchpotch of salutes and apologies.

'Not now, not now! I'm busy!' the Spin Doctor barked at them, not even noticing Teddington. 'Wait until I call you!'

With that he disappeared into his office, where he could be heard on the telephone either barking orders at *The Herald's* editor, curry-ing favour with Eastern and Middle-Eastern diplomats, or speaking in hushed tones, using codenames on his secret mobile phone, to members of his particular faction of ZANU-PF, pontificating as to how the latest events might improve their position in the presiden-tial succession struggle. Such was the demanding life of the Spin Doctor.

At two-twenty, the Spin Doctor ordered a Colcom's pork pie and a Coke, which his secretary promptly brought through on a tray. Hungrily, he tore the pie out of its little blue box and helped himself to a large mouthful. As he chewed, he lifted the crust with the tip of his Mont Blanc pen to inspect the pie's contents – a solid ball of processed pink meat, not dissimilar, he thought, to the Colcom's polony roll which he so detested. The idea that the same product could be packaged as two different dishes irritated him enormously. He screwed up his nose at the thought, and reluctantly swallowed a mouthful before getting to his feet and briskly flinging open the door of his office.

'Get this thing out of here!' he ordered his secretary. 'From now on, I want steak and kidney!'

As he turned back to his office, he noticed the two constables and their captive waiting on the couch. With the same obsequious flurry of salutes as before, they leapt at once to their feet.

'So, this is the bus driver?' said The Spin Doctor, a wry smile appearing on his face.

'Yes, sir, we caught him at his house trying to escape through the window,' the older of the constables replied.

Teddington felt a hot flush of panic.

'Sir,' he stammered, as he tried to stand, the leg irons jangling. 'It was only a million, sir. I'll give it back, all of it. Sir, I promise.'

The Spin Doctor was perplexed.

'Ha! A paltry million dollars! That's chicken feed compared to what you've done for us. More like five hundred million, is what you deserve.'

Teddington gulped with disbelief. The smile broadened on the minister's face; an idea had come to him,

'That's it!' he exclaimed, 'An agricultural sort of fellow, are you?'

Wide-eyed, Teddington shook his head. This was all too much for him – evidently, years of hard labour lay ahead in the cabbage patch at Chikurubi Prison.

'Not to worry. We can make a plan about that! Come into my office. Please.'

Teddington shuffled forward.

'Good heavens, constables!' the Spin Doctor exclaimed in shock at the leg irons. 'Is this how you treat a national hero? Release the man immediately, and get your ugly faces out of here!'

Dumbfounded, the constables hurriedly liberated Teddington and departed.

The Spin Doctor shook Teddington's hand. 'I'm so sorry about that, Mister … er?'

'Chiwafambira. Teddington Chiwafambira.'

'Come into my office, Mister Chiwafambira. I'll need to make a couple of calls to get you on your way. Would you like some tea and a steak-and-kidney pie?'

Teddington nodded suspiciously. What if the pie were poisoned?

'Tea and a pie for the gentleman,' the Spin Doctor instructed his secretary.

Inside his office, the Spin Doctor made a call to *The Herald's* photographer.

'I've got the bus driver. Be here in five minutes with your camera.'

Teddington shifted uneasily in the plush leather chair opposite the Spin Doctor's desk. What might they want with a photograph? A mug shot was all that came to mind.

The Spin Doctor made another call. This time his tone was genial.

'David, how are you, Comrade? … Good, good, good. Where are you? … Can you be here in ten minutes? I need your assistance with something.' He tossed a copy of *The Herald* to Teddington.

'Seen this, have you?'

Teddington's eyes bulged at the sight of his omnibus and its unfortunate erstwhile passengers, all strapped in straitjackets. He scanned the article. Despite the minister's praise, he still felt perplexed and uneasy.

'Excuse me, sir, it says here that the driver noticed strange behaviour among the passengers. Sir, I must be honest, I never saw any strange behaviour.'

The Spin Doctor sighed heavily, rolling his eyes.

'Chiwafambira! You may know that, and I certainly know that, but *they* do not!' he said, his hand waving in the general direction of the window. 'And I'd advise you strongly to keep it that way, or really, there will be trouble! All you need to know about your actions is written in the article. Are we absolutely clear?'

'Yes, sir,' Teddington meekly replied.

'Now, read it again so that you know exactly what it is that you did.'

Teddington re-read the article slowly, then skimmed through the other news items on the front page: 'Bumper Harvest for Manicaland' and 'Chinese Tourists Expected in Droves'.

The photographer arrived and was ordered to take several shots of the minister shaking Teddington's hand as both of them smiled at the camera. Ideas for the accompanying article whirled through the Spin Doctor's head: 'Minister Congratulates Diligent Bus Driver' – nice and simple as a title, he decided.

Slow, purposeful footsteps could be heard entering the reception. A brisk knock soon followed. The Spin Doctor leapt up and opened the door.

'Comrade Shuranyama! Come in.'

Comrade David Shuranyama's enormous frame seemed to fill the whole room. Though only in his mid-thirties, he had already developed the corpulence of one who has enjoyed a lengthy ride in the first-class dining carriage of the Party gravy train, acquiring in the process that ultimate symbol of political triumph, the much-coveted triple chin. The first chin appears at the bottom of the face, then the second arrives and nestles below the first. The third 'chin', however, is that sizable sea-cucumber-like bulge which appears at the base of the skull, just above the neck, where it is most likely to draw attention to itself as it proudly inflates and deflates depending on the angle of the bearer's head.

'This is Teddington Chiwafambira. The ZUPCO driver responsible for bringing those MDC lunatics to the Pari last night,' the Spin Doctor said, motioning his comrade to sit down on a gigantic couch.

Comrade Shuranyama responded with a chortle that came from deep within his belly.

'I saw your signature all over that one! How on earth did you manage to do it?'

'Well, to be honest, Comrade, it was one of those scripts that could just as well have written itself!'

The couch vibrated as the comrade doubled up with laughter, tears streaming from his eyes as the Spin Doctor recounted the previous night's events. With a wheeze, he turned his frame towards Teddington.

'Looks like we can take a trick or two out of your book, eh, Teddy-Boy!'

Teddington responded with a nervous giggle.

By now, the late afternoon sun was streaming through the windows of the minister's office.

'We need to reward Mister Chiwafambira here for a job well done,' the Spin Doctor said. 'Let's step outside for a second to discuss what I have in mind.'

The two men sauntered out into the ministerial foyer, leaving the door slightly ajar. Teddington shifted uncomfortably as he strained to hear their voices.

The voices in the foyer got louder. 'But what we really need is a nice big one, with all the amenities. Not one of those useless little ones on the A2 list. And no delays!'

Comrade Shuranyama again responded with a chortle, and the Spin Doctor continued, 'He doesn't have much of a background in that field – after all, he's a bus driver. So we need to find someone to run it. That's where you come into it, Comrade.'

Comrade Shuranyama clapped his hands together with glee. The sound startled Teddington.

'I've got just the place for him,' he said. 'Charming spot. Not too far from town either, out in Goromonzi. It's got everything you're looking for, and more. I can take him out there tomorrow morning, if you like.'

'Perfect!' came the minister's response.

As the two men appeared at the door, it suddenly dawned on Teddington who this David Shuranyama actually was. He recognised him from photos he had seen in the newspapers – Comrade Hitler Jesus, they called him, a ZANU-PF strongman, seldom referred to by his real name. Many opposition supporters had felt the punishing end of his steel-capped boot. Initially in charge of the less formal aspects of the government's land-reform process east of Harare, it was said that he could raise a band of supporters and clear a whole district of commercial farmers and their families in less than a week. He had become an almost mythical figure in the War Veterans Association, even though he could not have been much older than nine or ten at the end of the war against Ian Smith's Rhodesian army in 1980.

'Chiwafambira, it seems that Comrade Shuranyama here is to be your knight in shining armour.' The Spin Doctor beamed.

'I've got a busy day tomorrow, Chiwafambira. Be outside this building at six-thirty in the morning,' Shuranyama instructed. His smile had gone.

Teddington nodded frantically. He tried to speak, but could not.

All three men shook hands. Comrade Hitler Jesus disappeared into the car park and sped off in a shiny black BMW X5, careening through the rush-hour traffic.

Overcome by an unsettling mixture of relief, suspicion and anxiety, Teddington made his way back home. In the dim light of his room, he turned on his splattered hotplate and made himself a small pot of sadza, which he ate plain, and without pleasure. Playing the events of the day over and over in his mind, trying to make some sense of it all, he spent the evening alone. After the embarrassment of his arrest, he resolved to remain out of sight of family and neighbours until the next day at least, when he might have some clarity regarding his situation.

15

A Man of Infinite Mystery with Rustling Plastic Shopping Packets

On the outskirts of Harare, Joseph Chiswa spotted a hitchhiker up ahead – a curious dreadlocked being clouded in a haze of smoke with a khaki canvas bag slung over his shoulder and a multitude of plastic shopping packets in his hands. Remembering all too clearly his years as a pedestrian, Joseph could seldom pass a hitchhiker without the heavy hand of guilt tapping him on the shoulder. Since the passenger seat was vacant, he slowed and pulled over. Expecting the man to scramble towards the car, he was surprised to see him saunter up slowly.

'Where you fellas off to, then?' the man asked, leaning his wrist on the Peugeot's roof, holding a hand-rolled cigarette, and smirking slightly as he stuck his face through the window on the driver's side. Though bloodshot, his eyes had a puckish glint.

'Not far,' Joseph said, 'just up the road … to the William Westward, in fact. Do you know it?'

''Course I do. That's perfect. Mind if I catch a ride?'

'Not at all. Hop in.'

The rustle of plastic shopping packets filled the car as the man slumped into the passenger seat with his canvas bag on his lap. At the back, Thomas noticed the orphans tense. As for the new passenger, he pulled the door shut and at once closed his eyes, appearing to be sound asleep, the very picture of relaxation. Only his lips moved – almost imperceptibly – as he drew breath.

Joseph stole glances at the man.

'So, been on a long journey?' he asked after a while.

The man remained still and quiet. Perhaps he was asleep, after all. Then his eyes opened slowly.

'Been here and there, I suppose,' he said with a look of amusement. 'You know how it goes.'

'Yes – I suppose I do,' Joseph replied, for lack of anything better to say.

Slowly and inconspicuously, Thomas leant forward and squinted over the man's shoulder, curious as to what might be in the shopping packets at his feet. One contained roots that seemed to be caked in clumps of red soil. A sprig of herbs bound with twine stuck out of another. Nothing unusual. Protruding from the third, however, was the furry tail of some poor creature – wagging, it seemed, with the motion of the car.

The faded signpost indicating the entrance of the William Westward came into view.

'So, what line of work might you be in?' Joseph asked. Evidently, he too had noticed the mysterious packets.

The slumbering passenger raised his eyebrows and swivelled his eyes towards the driver.

'Oh, you know, a bit of this, a bit of that,' he said, flicking a stray dreadlock from his face. After a pause, he added, 'I'll hop out here, before the gate.'

Taking up his packets and canvas bag, he climbed out as the car came to a halt. He closed the door and leant through the window. 'I suppose you could say I solve problems for people … you could say I fix things.'

'What sort of things?' the headmaster pressed.

'I thought you'd ask that.' The man stared intently at Joseph. 'This, for example,' he exclaimed, holding up a Seiko wristwatch.

'Eh, that's mine!' Joseph cried, snatching back the watch.

'So it is!' the man replied with a grin.

Joseph checked his watch against the time on the Peugeot's dashboard clock. To his surprise, they were synchronised. For the first time in years, his Seiko was accurate, miraculously fixed. As he looked up, he saw the man strolling off down the verge of the road. Equally amazed, Thomas quickly rolled down his window and called out, 'What's your name?'

'Cuthbert,' the man replied over his shoulder as he wandered off towards the msasa woodlands lining the road, 'Doctor Cuthbert Kambazuma. If you haven't yet heard of me, you soon will!'

In seconds, he was out of sight.

* * *

The matron, Betty Mukadota, cooed with delight as the Peugeot pulled up outside the home. Loved by children and staff alike, with the countenance of an angel – or a princess – Betty's ample girth matched the extent of her generosity and joviality.

'Hurrah for the rescue party!' she called out, clapping her hands together, doing a little dance.

Thomas's face lit up with pride. He seldom found himself at the centre of a drama.

'Do you think there are two more mattresses in the storeroom for these two, Betty?' he asked.

'Luckily there are, my dear Mister Thomas. We checked this

afternoon and laid them out in Paget and Fairbridge. I'll take the children up and show them where they'll be sleeping.'

'Betty, thank you. I'll come and say goodnight before I leave this evening.'

Returning to his office, and with an hour or two left before dinner time, Thomas passed the time paging once again through his dog-eared copy of *Nicholas Nickleby*, itself a tale of journeys and rescues – not too dissimilar to their own, he thought with a measure of satisfaction. At ten past seven, conscious that his mother would shortly be serving dinner, Thomas locked his office and made his way up to Fairbridge dormitory. He found little Ruth on a thin foam mattress, squeezed into the far corner of the large room. With a threadbare blanket pulled over her face, he could not tell if she was asleep or merely hiding.

'Good night, little Ruthie, sleep well,' he whispered, gently patting the top of her head.

As he made his way up the Paget stairs, the shrieks of dozens of excited voices and the sound of beds scraping across a parquet floor reached him. A tiny bat had flown in through the dormitory window, sparking a commotion. Standing on their beds or mattresses, some armed with old wooden tennis racquets, the boys leapt up and down in an impromptu Mexican wave as the bat flew frantically from one end of the dormitory to the other.

In his deepest, most authoritative voice, Thomas called out, 'That's enough, now!'

To no avail – the bat was far too compelling. But after Thomas had walked around the dormitory, setting the sporting relics to rest, the boys lay down on their beds and mattresses, eyes wide open, mesmerised by the movement of the small black creature as it gradually slowed from exhaustion, finally coming to rest on top of a locker. Grabbing a towel, Thomas managed to scoop it up and take it to an open window.

He had always been fascinated by bats. It was the twitching nose, pointy ears and razor-sharp teeth he found disturbing – unchristian, he thought, like crows and ravens. For a second, the bat sat on the ledge, its sooty wings folded like a businessman's travelling umbrella, and then, with a silent flutter, the creature disappeared into the night, where it belonged.

It was now time for prayers and sleep. Each boy knelt by his bed and looked with sleepy eyes at Thomas, who set them off in unison.

Lighten our darkness, we beseech thee, O Lord;
And by thy great mercy defend us
From all perils and dangers of this night.
For the love of thy only Son, our Saviour, Jesus Christ.
Amen.

The boys curled up under their blankets as Thomas scanned the room for the dormitory's new addition. Squeezed into a corner at the far end, Regus lay on a thin piece of foam. His feet hung over the edge with his heels touching the floor. He too had covered his face with his blanket, but it was clear he was wide awake, every now and then cautiously lowering it to take in the activities around him. It was all new to him – the brick housing, the routine, the absence of familiar faces – strange and threatening.

In his six years at the William Westward, Thomas had seen many new children struggling to adjust, a process that sometimes took months. He felt a strong bond with them, for in the farthest recesses of his memory, he understood what it was like to be the new child in this very dormitory.

He leaned down and patted Regus on the shoulder. 'Good night, Regus, we'll see you in the morning.' In a louder voice, he added, 'Good night, everyone!'

With that, Thomas turned off the lights and made his way down to his car.

Later that night, Thomas knelt by his bed to say his own prayers – a habit that persisted from his dark days away at Koodoo Range Preparatory. The prayers had all ended 'Through Jesus Christ our Lord, Amen', and even now, he pictured a beam of blue light transmitted from him to Jesus then to God, far above, and then back down to him again. Without this triangle of light he could not allow himself to fall asleep – failure to imagine it signalled that the connection had been lost, and with it came God's displeasure. As a boy he persevered, sometimes for hours, becoming more desperate with each failed attempt at visualising it. In this way, throughout his troubled years at boarding school, his prayers became his heaviest burden: self-imposed manacles from which he could not escape. Yet somehow, each time he returned home, back to the safety and familiarity of his own surrounds, with the comforting presence of his mother just down the passage, he was once again able to secure this vital celestial link, often with consummate ease.

Finishing his prayers, Thomas glanced up at the Great Ones, one by one, and then turned to the picture of Father, bidding a silent good night to each. Every day, for Thomas, ended in precisely the same way.

16

Cottage-like, with Lovely Cape Dutch Gables and a Thatched Roof – Charming, Really

With the sun barely upon the horizon, and a fresh morning breeze biting at him, Teddington pulled the sleeves of his jersey over his fingers. Pacing nervously to and fro on the deserted pavement outside the Spin Doctor's office, he scanned the street for any approaching vehicles. He had spent a long night tossing and turning.

At exactly half past six, a monstrous Hummer glided to a halt next to him. The passenger window slid down with a slick electronic buzz. Teddington froze with trepidation.

'Hop in, Teddy-Boy!' a familiar voice instructed from within.

Then, as he opened the door and climbed inside, a strange sense of excitement rippled through Teddington. He had noticed this Hummer, with its metallic orange exterior and tinted windows, cruising the streets of Harare, but the thought of ever riding in it was beyond his wildest imagination. Never in his life had he sunk into such a large, comfortable leather seat. The dashboard looked like pictures he had seen of the cockpit of an aeroplane rather than anything belonging inside a motor vehicle.

If only his friends could see him now, he thought.

'Comrade Shuranyama, this is quite some vehicle you have here,' Teddington ventured, finally plucking up the courage to say something as they turned off Samora Machel Avenue onto Enterprise Road.

The comrade chortled as he looked across at Teddington. 'Thank you, Teddy-Boy. A big man, you know, needs a big car – doesn't he?!'

Teddington laughed nervously. 'But these days, finding enough petrol for a big car like this ... with all the shortages ... it must be quite a task.'

Comrade Shuranyama's whole body shook with laughter. 'My dear Teddy-Boy, it is precisely the high cost of petrol that enables us to drive cars like this. For those with connections, shortages have a habit of creating opportunities.'

A long silence ensued. Clearly, Teddington had not understood.

'I'll show you one of our filling stations and you'll see what I mean.'

Minutes later, the Hummer pulled up at a filling station in Greendale.

'This,' stated Comrade Shuranyama proudly, 'is one of them.'

Comrade Shuranyama could see that Teddington was still puzzled. Evidently there was petrol, but without the customary queues.

'People are prepared to pay if they come here – double the government regulation price – purely for the convenience factor.' He smiled at his passenger. 'My business partner, the minister you met yesterday, sorts out the paperwork. We also get petrol and diesel supplies from the State Oil Company at a tenth of the usual rate, subsidised by the state – for agricultural development on the farms we have taken over.'

He paused and gave a loud guffaw. 'Some of us have noticed that there is more money in reselling the petrol than simply farming. And besides, farming isn't all that important any more – nowadays, if the people need food, it gets delivered in aid parcels right to our doorsteps from America and Britain, all for free!'

While the attendant filled the tank, Comrade Shuranyama climbed out of the Hummer, called Teddington over, and unlocked a door at the back of the building. 'Some of my other cars,' he said, gesturing nonchalantly.

Teddington's jaw fell open at the sight of a car park full of luxury vehicles, twenty at least – all the latest Mercedes Benzes, BMWs, Volkswagens, Bentleys, Jaguars, even a gleaming Rolls-Royce in the far corner. Teddington knew very few people who owned a vehicle of any description – certainly, almost no one did back in Hatcliffe, where he came from – so a sight like this left him breathless.

Back in the Hummer, with the radio playing, Teddington wished the journey would never come to an end. Warmly enveloped in the leather of the passenger seat, he had almost forgotten his anxiety. The journey to Goromonzi district did not take long, no more than thirty minutes at the most. Comrade Shuranyama slowed the Hummer as they approached a narrow side road. At the junction, a green plough disk hung from the branch of a msasa tree; Tony and Patsy Willoughby – Cotswold Downs Estate it said in neat white letters. The Hummer turned up the road, passing a row of brick tobacco-curing barns along the way.

'Who are Tony and Patsy Willoughby?' Teddington asked cautiously.

'Well, Tony is the old fellow who's going to be doing the farming for you, and Patsy's his wife. Nice folks, really … if you manage them properly, that is.'

'Farming?' Teddington said with a look of surprise.

His companion roared with laughter. 'So, he didn't he tell you, did he – about the farm you're getting. You know, for locking half the MDC up in the loony bin. Well, Teddy-Boy, this is it!'

Teddington gulped. 'And, er, where do they stay, Tony and, er?'

'Patsy. Oh, we chased them out of the farmhouse and off the farm completely a couple of years back, but the old fellow came back and said they had nowhere to go. So we struck a deal with him. He carries on with the farming and lives in the manager's cottage at the back of the farm, and we keep half the profits from the farming, which will now be yours. He'll pay the workers for you, and keep everything in shape. It's a system we find works nicely. Here's your farmhouse, Teddy-Boy.'

Teddington couldn't believe his eyes when he saw his new home. It was quaint, with whitewashed walls, lovely Cape Dutch gables and a thatched roof. Although it had the appearance of a cottage, it was actually quite big, with three bedrooms, a lounge, a dining room, a kitchen and two bathrooms.

'Apparently, Tony Willoughby's father built the original part of the cottage over seventy years ago; old Tony was still just a boy then,' the comrade explained.

They left the Hummer in the driveway and walked up to the house. Two years after the Willoughbys' departure, signs of neglect had begun to show. The lawn was knee high, and the verandah's wooden arches had collapsed, with the dried boughs of a once magnificent wisteria still clinging to its beams. Comrade Shuranyama pushed open the front door, whose lock had been forced open by looters some time back. Giant cobwebs had sprung up in the corners of the rooms and a number of fixtures had been removed, including the kitchen sink, taps and pipes in the shower, and many of the light fittings, but to Teddington's elation, most things were intact. There was even some furniture: a couple of beds, a cupboard or two, a table and a very old sofa. Were it not for the presence of his new comrade, he would have shouted with joy.

Comrade Shuranyama was eager to get back to Harare. A Customs and Excise auction was scheduled to start at eleven, and a number of interesting vehicles were listed. Lots of bargains. He could not afford to be late.

Back in the Hummer, they proceeded directly to meet the Willoughbys, Comrade Shuranyama using the time to explain to Teddington how the relationship should be managed.

'Okay, so basically he'll give you anything you ask for, you just have to, how does one put it ... *motivate* him.'

'And how does one motivate him?' Teddington asked.

Comrade Shuranyama reached behind his seat and pulled out a panga. Its blade looked like it had recently been sharpened, though its handle was makeshift – just some old black plastic sheeting wrapped around the base of the shaft and bound with twine. Teddington recoiled with fright.

'I find this tends to focus his attention,' Comrade Shuranyama said solemnly, thrusting the panga into Teddington's hands.

'Basically, the process of extracting things from them is something of an art. The old boy is really quite a pleasant chap, and his wife's quite a dear, which makes it a lot easier. Of course, we could just throw them off the farm, but it's better to milk them for every cent before they go. I mean, who would run the place otherwise? One needs to be a bit strategic.'

He smiled broadly and slapped Teddington's thigh. 'So, say you tell him you want something. Something like petrol, or money, or beer, or meat, or to use his pickup ... anything you want. You'll see he'll probably refuse the first time you ask, particularly these days, now that they don't have that much left. So what you do is, you shout at him a bit, you know, call him a useless honky, a white colonialist pig, whatever you like. Don't hold back, he's heard it all before. Use the F-word a lot. You can even spit on him now and then. He hates that. It helps if old Patsy's around.'

With a snigger, he continued. 'She goes to pieces in seconds. What you do then is stare at her, and move your finger from one side of your throat to the other, slowly, and with your tongue hanging half out – like as if you'll cut her throat if old Tony doesn't cough up. Once she bursts into tears, it's generally all over. He capitulates in seconds. He'll give you whatever you want. If he still refuses – and usually he doesn't when Patsy starts wailing – but if he does refuse, you get the panga out and you threaten him with it. Wave it around a bit, take a few swings at him. You can even whack him a few times, but try not to kill him. You should try to see him as the goose that lays the golden egg around here, and it's a real nightmare in terms of all the paperwork and the media when you bump them off – trust me, I speak from experience. That said, it's probably not as bad as it used to be, especially since we've had the independent press shut down.'

Teddington stared at Comrade Shuranyama in disbelief. He did not know any white people personally – there weren't a great many around, these days – but those he had met in the past had always been pleasant enough. Then again, he quickly reasoned, if this is how people are behaving these days it would be a shame to lose out, especially if this was an official programme sponsored by the government to correct colonial injustices.

'Of course, the whole process of extracting things from old Tony works a lot better, I find, when for periods, maybe a month or so, you treat them quite nicely. Let them believe you care about them. Encourage them not to leave too soon. Once they start responding positively and relaxing a bit, it's time to start demanding things again. I'm a master at it, that's why they call me Hitler Jesus – sometimes the tyrant, and other times the saviour. Taking with the one hand, and giving – but only sometimes – with the other. Mainly taking, though. That's the whole point, isn't it?'

Teddington giggled nervously, and Comrade Shuranyama looked at him sternly. 'Funny, is it?'

Teddington stopped immediately. It did not seem that this giant of a man, this Hitler Jesus, was the kind of man one should joke around with.

Comrade Shuranyama continued staring at him, his expression deadly serious. 'Sometimes the funniest things you hear are funny precisely because they're true.'

17

Marie's Secret

It was after seven when Thomas eventually got out of bed. Later than usual. Through his window he could see his mother, who was dressed in Father's paisley dressing gown. Just as she did every morning, she placed a small square of worn tarpaulin on the lawn and knelt down on one knee. Then, lightly touching the grass to wet her fingers and palms with dew, she moistened her face and cleared the sleep from her eyes. Staightening up, she caught a glimpse of Thomas, smiling as she turned and walked slowly past the derelict aviary on her way to the msasa thicket with its concealed clearing.

At this time of year, with the rain falling every second day, the air was clear and crisp and the bush thick with new growth. Despite Father's liberal outlook, he had retained that quintessentially British colonial zeal for taming the bush and replacing it, wherever possible, with the civilities of an English garden – rows of roses, flowerbeds full of pansies, marigolds, dahlias, sweetpeas and petunias, all surrounded by perfectly manicured lawns. After his passing, the flowerbeds gradually became overgrown. Marie did not have the heart to dig them up, relying instead on the indigenous plants and grasses slowly to reclaim their rightful place. Only a small patch of lawn directly in front of the house remained. The rest had returned to its pre-colonial state, but for some giant pumpkin vines cultivated here and there by Marie and Leviticus.

Shortly after her husband's death, Marie Threscothic began to impart to Thomas her secret – if only, at first, to test if he might be receptive. Its origins had never been entirely clear. A nun, one of a circle of Anglican mystics, had singled out seven-year-old Marie from among her classmates in a small school on the outskirts of the English town of Sherborne. Marie's training had lasted several years. To Marie's knowledge, the mystical teachings had never been passed on to a boy. Only women, the sisters believed, possessed the requisite stillness and patience. However, after Marie's first glimpse of the silent three-year-old Thomas hidden in the branches of a guava tree, with a crown of finches orbiting his head, she allowed herself to think otherwise.

Now, having eaten a slice of bread with strawberry jam, Thomas looked from the kitchen window towards the msasa thicket. A Woodland Kingfisher darted to the boundary fence and into the undergrowth of the neighbouring farm. With a flash of brown wing feathers, a Namaqua Dove rose from the ground, flying low and fast. Mother must almost be finished, he thought. He left the kitchen and made his way to the edge of the thicket, just beyond the house. He paused. Peering through the trees, he could just make out his mother, seated on a bench that was bleached grey by the sun. The beams of its backrest had rotted away over the decades, leaving only a handful of twisted nails protruding. A Lilac-breasted Roller was perched on her foot, its head shifting anxiously from side to side, glancing up at her. On the bench, next to her thigh, a pair of African Hoopoes gazed up at her steadily, without moving. A Glossy Starling, its metallic blue-and-green plumage sparkling in the morning light, danced in circles at her feet. In the surrounding msasa branches, there were Whydahs, Fire Finches, and Canaries.

As Thomas watched, the birds one by one fluttered up into the trees before fading into the bush of the surrounding farmland. Then Marie stood up, her face glowing. With a gentle gesture, she summoned Thomas. It was his turn to call the birds.

Without a word, his mother slowly returned to the house. She and Thomas never uttered a word in the clearing, not ever, as birds are wary of the sound of the human voice. The rules were few and simple, all with the same purpose – to protect the birds. Furthermore, no record of the practice was to be recorded in writing; the best-kept secrets are those whispered from one generation to the chosen few of the next, far from prying ears and eyes.

It had been a constant source of concern for Marie that, apart from her own mentor, who was by now deceased, she knew of no other practitioner. With that in mind, after Father's death she resolved that she must at least test her intuition about Thomas. So it was that she woke him one morning before dawn and carried him out to the clearing, his ginger head resting on her shoulder, half asleep, half awake, his eyelids flickering with silent dreams. At the first sign of dawn, she had slowly raised his hand and placed it against her throat, so that he could feel the subtle vibrations as she called the birds with gentle cooing and clicking noises, interspersed with sharp, carefully timed, pishing sounds, thus arousing the curiosity of nearby birds – apart from crows and ravens, which ignored the calls. It was not the volume of the call that was important; the first bird whose interest was piqued uttered its own distinctive cries, arousing the attention of others. Distracted from their usual activities by these compelling sounds, once drawn to the caller's circle, no bird ever harmed another.

On that first day with Thomas, as the sky grew lighter above them, she saw him open his eyes in response to the soft flutter of feathers as a tiny Melba Finch landed on his head. He did not move as most children might have, and Marie fancied that she saw the suggestion of a smile on his face. With proper guidance, the value of this delicate interaction, she hoped, would reveal itself to her son over time.

While there may be something meditative and quietly enriching about the ritual of calling the birds, that was only part of it. The real value lay in the birds' intuition with respect to human emotions. In the same way as a horse may sense and react to its rider's confidence or apprehensiveness, or a cat or a dog to its owner's feelings, so too do birds.

Individual species, and more specifically, individual birds, Marie had come to understand, tended to sense and react to specific emotions – some to fear, others to anger, and yet others to self-doubt, or a combination of such feelings. It was their interpretation that had to be learnt, it was not something that could be taught. It could take years of patiently calling and watching to learn the birds' lessons, but with it came a subtle understanding of one's self.

Thomas sat on his mother's bench and breathed quietly for several minutes. To be calm was essential – a state of agitation or excitement might produce a reading that was valid only for that moment, ultimately misleading.

Drawing in one last deep breath, Thomas began to call his birds. Perhaps because his voice was slightly deeper than his mother's, the larger birds were often the first to respond – a Natal Francolin, a Helmeted Guineafowl or a Hamerkop. A solitary Crested Barbet usually followed, its scruffy cap of feathers giving it the appearance of a medieval jester. His favourites were a pair of Go'way birds – large, comical grey creatures, shaggy-crested, whose croaks and cries were curiously human.

The idea of 'reading' the birds was something his mother

constantly mentioned, but which he did not yet fully understand. Often, he thought he had reached the limits of his understanding. Yet he continued with the practice, for he loved the birds and could not imagine life without the morning ritual in the clearing with his mother.

18

The Hummer's
Real Purpose Revealed

Comrade Shuranyama drove on to the Willoughbys in silence before pulling up next to Tony's aging Nissan pickup. A man with sunken eyes peering from under ruffled grey hair appeared at the back door of a cottage that had previously housed his manager. He did not look at all happy.

Comrade Shuranyama passed the panga to Teddington.

'Let him see you with this right from the beginning.'

Alighting from the vehicle, Comrade Shuranyama shook hands with the older man and stared at him for a few ominous seconds before proceeding.

'Tony, this here is Comrade Teddington Chiwafambira. He's the new farmer who has been allocated this farm under the government's extra-fast-track land redistribution programme.' He frowned before continuing. 'From now on, if you and Patsy want to continue staying here, you'll have to co-operate with him. The current arrangement as regards your running of the farming activities and sharing of revenues can continue as before, except now you'll be sharing the revenues with Comrade Chiwafambira. Everything should be fine as long as you co-operate. It's up to you. Understood?'

'Yes, Comrade Shuranyama,' said Tony quietly, the fight in him now long gone.

Comrade Shuranyama gave a belly laugh and slapped Tony heartily on the shoulder. The old man stumbled forward. Instinctively, Teddington moved to catch him, but he instantly stopped himself.

'Cheer up, Tony,' coaxed Comrade Shuranyama. 'I'm sure you'll get along famously.'

As the Hummer pulled away, Teddington looked back at the manager's cottage. From behind a curtain in the cottage, he caught a glimpse of Patsy, whose grey hair was pulled back from her face. She pulled the curtain closed as soon as she met his gaze.

Teddington felt confused. There was an awkwardness about the situation that disconcerted him. Yet, to his surprise, he felt a thrill – he was owner of an unimaginably large estate – he had cattle, tobacco, workers, houses. He, Teddington Chiwafambira, was now a man to be respected.

'I tell you what,' Comrade Shuranyama turned to Teddington cheerfully, 'there's no point in leaving you out here on your own right now. That's no way to celebrate your reward! Let me drop you off in town. Collect your things. Round up some friends and get a minibus to bring you all out here.'

He reached over to Teddington's side and opened the cubbyhole. It was stuffed full of bank notes, thick wads held together by elastic bands.

'Take a couple of those to cover the transport costs, and when you get back here, you can test out old Tony's co-operation.'

He laughed and slapped Teddington's thigh. 'Get him to provide a few things for a party. Any problems, just tell him you want to use his phone to call me.' He handed Teddington a business card. David Shuranyama – Entrepreneur, it said.

With that decided, Comrade Shuranyama suddenly pulled the Hummer off the road without slowing down, and proceeded to make a wide U-turn through a field of tobacco plants that stood a foot taller than the bonnet. The huge vehicle thudded over furrow after furrow, flattening a tract of plants. Teddington steadied himself by holding onto the door handle.

'Damn! This is what these things were built for, Teddy-Boy!' Comrade Shuranyama shouted.

He kept his foot flat on the accelerator all the way back to Harare, and the journey was over in no time. By the time Teddington climbed out of the Hummer in front of a gawking crowd at a bus stop in Chisipite, his spirits had rallied and most of his uncertainties had dissipated. The wads of bank notes from the cubbyhole were too large to stuff inside his pockets. So he shoved them down the front of his underpants, pulling his shirt out to cover the bulge – common practice in these times. With nothing other than his newly acquired panga in his hand, he caught a minibus taxi and was home by two o'clock that afternoon.

19

The Children of
the Mazarodze Cannot Compete

Thomas returned from the clearing to find his mother and Leviticus hard at work with the wheelbarrow, harvesting pumpkins. A neat pile was stacked inside Marie's pantry, but most were packed onto the seats of the Datsun for Thomas to take to the kitchen at the William Westward. When he arrived at the gate, the sight of his ginger head amid ninety-three golden pumpkins drew a band of eager young helpers. From the car to the kitchen, a chain was formed to pass the pumpkins along, hand to hand.

'Why aren't you at breakfast?' Thomas asked the children.

'*Hapana* ZESA Mister Thomas! No electricity. No porridge. Three days in a row this time,' was the answer.

In lieu of breakfast bananas were distributed, after which the children prepared themselves for the day's activity. An athletics competition with the Mazarodze Children's Home in the nearby suburb of Eastlea had been planned. The old school bus was brought from its resting place next to the home's disused red-brick barn, itself a relic of the old Fairbridge Farm School days. The 'school bus' was, in reality, the horse of an ancient Mercedes truck with a bus-shaped trailer. That the bus still operated was due entirely to the unflagging efforts of Joseph Chiswa and the grounds manager, Robson Shambari, who spent countless hours scouring the city's scrapyards for spare parts, and even more hours underneath the horse installing them.

Taking seventy children at a time, the bus set off, with Robson behind the wheel and Betty Mukadota in charge of the carriage filled with the juniors. Thomas waited behind – on its return, he would take the seniors. An hour passed, with the seniors growing restless, flicking each other's ears and tossing pieces of straw, like javelins, at each other's hair.

Much to their surprise, the bus returned with the juniors still inside. Betty was in a sombre state. Some of the smaller children were in tears. As they disembarked, some children ran over to Thomas and clutched at his legs.

'What's the matter?' Thomas asked, but no one would answer him. He waited for Betty's bulky frame to descend the carriage's staircase.

'It was all fine when we arrived,' she explained. 'We went up that path to the main building to see if we could find any staff. When we could not find any, we decided to look in the dormitories … you know, those old buildings up at the top. That's where the problem started,' she continued, tears collecting in the corner of her eyes. 'We found some of the children in the dormitories, just lying on their blankets. They say they have not eaten properly for days. Some of them have arms and legs that look like sticks, one even had a swollen belly. We found a member of staff who says that there is no money for food. They have pleaded with the government to help, but there's been no response. The sports day is off … how can they run if they haven't eaten?'

An outspoken boy by the name of Tanaka, all of eleven years of age, spotted Baba Chiswa coming out of his office and led a small group to question him about the situation.

'Why is it, Baba Chiswa? Why is it that the children of the Mazarodze Home have no food or proper clothing?'

'Well, Tanaka, there's a lesson in this. In life there are always people less fortunate than oneself. One should always be grateful for what one has, and give where one can.' Words which he would later regret, for a commotion instantly arose. Something, it seemed, had to be done about the plight of 'the poor'. On Tanaka's suggestion, the smaller children bolted up to their dormitories to comb their lockers for any spare clothing. They came streaming down the stairs with an assortment of garments, well-worn and holey.

'Take us back!' they demanded.

Baba Chiswa knew he could not permit this generosity. The William Westward itself was critically short of clothing and food.

'Charity begins at home,' he cautiously back-pedalled, but it was too late. They would not rest, they protested, until this gross inequality had been addressed. Sensing that he could not win, Baba Chiswa came up with a plan. He told them to get back on the bus with as much clothing as they could spare. Robson and Betty looked horrified, but Baba Chiswa placated them with a solemn wink. Before turning the ignition, he flooded the engine. The children listened despondently to the drone of the starter motor winding up time and time again. As this was a bus that broke down at least once a month, the children were not at all surprised. With heavy hearts they wandered away from the bus and slowly walked back to their dormitories.

Back home, over a lunch of home-grown salad and roasted pumpkin, Thomas related the events of the morning.

Marie was silent for a few moments. Then, speaking slowly, as if weighing up various considerations, she enquired, 'But surely they too should have the right ... at least *sometimes*?'

'What do you mean?' Thomas asked, frowning.

'The right to give. Don't you see? These children have been the recipients of charity all their lives. Perhaps they too would like to have the chance to give.'

Thomas put his fork down. 'But what do they have to give, Ma?'

'Not much, I suppose.'

Marie stared out the window, catching sight of the wheelbarrow.

'What about their pumpkins?' she said suddenly. 'Couldn't they share them? We have a few more in the garden, anyway.'

'What an idea!' Thomas said, clapping his hands together, 'We'll take them to the Mazarodze home this afternoon.'

Marie continued to gaze out the window. 'This hunger we are seeing – I fear this is just the start of it. There are many years of this ahead.'

Thomas felt uncomfortable; these were heavy words.

'Each person will need to be resourceful, just to get by,' she continued slowly. 'You can no longer rely on others, or the government, or the church. They have nothing either.'

She stood up and began clearing the table.

'In fact, you should be growing your own food at the William Westward. We will go there with you this afternoon, Leviticus and I, to plant pumpkins.'

Half and hour later, Thomas, Marie and Leviticus had picked another thirty pumpkins and set off for the home. On arrival, Thomas quickly found Joseph and Betty to explain the plan. Both were in agreement. The younger children lined up next to the Datsun, with young Tanaka, the fiery advocate for social change, at the fore. Each took a pumpkin and skipped onto the bus trailer. They were off to feed 'the poor'. This time the engine took first time, and the bus arrived at the Mazarodze Home with much hooting and singing, arousing the attention of the children and their gaunt matron who came outside to investigate the din. Unable to contain themselves, the children of the William Westward clambered off the bus with their pumpkins, thrusting the heavy gifts into their recipients' hands with such gusto that some were bowled right over. Singing soon broke out, followed by impromptu dancing. The pumpkins were taken to the kitchen where some were cut into slices and placed into two huge pots of water that were soon simmering over an old cast-iron wood stove.

In three-quarters of an hour, a simple meal was ready. Despite Betty's efforts to get them to eat slowly, the hungry children could not be restrained. Blowing on the hot slices between frantic mouthfuls, they finished the meal in minutes before streaming down to the athletics fields with the William Westward juniors. The rest of the afternoon passed in a haze of excited cheering and leaping about. Every victor was applauded by all. No accurate score was kept.

20

The Arrangement, Tested

Teddington's arrest the previous day had been the neighbourhood's main topic of conversation, and speculation was rife as to the nature of the charges. A curious crowd gathered outside his house when Teddington arrived home, and he clambered on top of a forty-four-gallon drum. Elated, and at the top of his voice, he related the misunderstanding concerning the ZRP constables, as well as every detail of his time spent at the ministry. Waving a copy of the previous day's *Herald* above his head, he displayed the headline. A cry of resentment went up from the crowd – almost everyone in Hatcliffe was MDC.

'*Chiwafambira, unofunga kuti tiri kunyeba? Inhema!* It's a hoax!'

'Of course it's not!' he roared back. 'Those guys weren't right in the head, they needed help. *Vanhu avo vanopenga!* Hospital's the best place for them!'

Sensing a confrontation, Teddington shoved his hand into his trousers and yanked out the bank notes. 'Brothers! Let's drink!'

A cheer went up from the crowd, and his detractors' protestations were all but drowned out. Only a handful of people turned their backs in disgust and walked away.

'Let's go and roast some meat,' continued Teddington, 'at my farm out in Goromonzi!'

The crowd fell silent.

'What farm?' someone asked. 'Whose farm?'

'The farm I've been allocated! Come on, let's all go!'

One thick wad of notes was enough to conclude negotiations with a taxi operator for two minibuses to take him, and his friends, and their girlfriends, and some of their friends, out to the farm. With the remainder, Teddington bought several crates of beer for the journey. Cramming twenty-four jubilant revellers into one taxi, and twenty-six into the other, the drivers set off, with piles of foam mattresses and half-barrel barbecues loosely strapped to each roof. Teddington navigated from the front seat of the lead vehicle. Wallowing in his new-found status, he could hardly contain his excitement and quaffed no less than three quarts of Black Label beer on the short trip out to Goromonzi.

Once at the farmhouse, Teddington staggered about, leading a highly animated tour of his new home's interior. With most of the party staying behind to set up the barbecue, Teddington took a small group up to Tony's place. His manager's co-operation must be put to the test. Beneath his cocksure veneer, Teddington was dreading the encounter – but he had to go through with it. This was a system, it seemed, that only worked if one acted the part. To show weakness would be fatal. He settled into the driver's seat of one of the minibuses, and in a display of driving that elicited both cheers and screams, set about replicating the Harry-casual recklessness of Hitler Jesus, his new role-model. The minibus skidded to a halt, scattering gravel across the Willoughbys' driveway.

Tony and Patsy, startled by the sound of skidding wheels and ebullient singing, had come to the backdoor and were peering out through a chink. Limon, who had been their cook for more than forty years, abandoned his drying of the crockery and fled to the pantry. Many years back, his employer had been the fiercest taskmaster in the district, quick-tempered and impatient with his staff. Boss *Anovava*, 'the one who likes to shout a lot', they'd once called him – but now he seemed to exist solely for another man's convenience. Limon locked the pantry door behind him and crouched in the darkness. He did not want trouble. Nobody wanted trouble.

His head spinning with the various facets of Hitler Jesus's instructions, Teddington stepped down from the vehicle, panga in hand. Tony Willoughby bolted the door in fright as Teddington staggered closer. A small, rowdy crowd from the minibus hung closely behind him as he rapped on the door.

'Tony, come out! I need you to get some things for me!'

The house was silent. Teddington kicked the door and rattled the handle. Tony's face appeared from behind the curtain, exactly where Teddington had seen Patsy earlier that day. He was pale and his brow was furrowed.

'Tony, get out here, what's your problem!' yelled Teddington, tapping the window with the blade of the panga. His heart was pounding; he had to keep up the act.

With shoulders hunched, Tony opened the door and came out to face the crowd. He closed the door behind him and called out, 'Lock it, Patsy, and don't open unless I say so, whatever happens!'

'Tony, Tony … what took you so long, I was beginning to think our arrangement had come to an end!'

'I'm sorry, Comrade Chiwafambira, we weren't sure who all these people are. We were afraid.'

Running the flat side of the panga across the palm of his left hand, Teddington continued, 'We are celebrating the reallocation of this farm under the land redistribution scheme. We need you to provide us with some things. We must have ten crates of Black Label quarts, two crates of Coke, five bottles of vodka, two bags of groundnuts and, er, something nice for the barbecue. We need a goat. That's it, find us a goat. Bring it up to my house. Chop-chop, Tony! Half an hour.'

Tony did not offer any resistance, sparing Teddington from having to practise the throat-cutting routine in Patsy's direction, or having to spit on the old man, or call him names, or hit him with the blunt edge of the panga. Tony just quietly replied that he would do his best, and asked Patsy to let him in so that he could get the keys for his pickup. In seconds, he set off to fulfil his instructions. For all he knew, his life, and more importantly, Patsy's, probably depended on it.

Teddington was astounded at how smooth the process had been. His previous unease now seemed completely unfounded. He was the man – the system was working perfectly.

The minibus turned round and set off back to the farmhouse. Clearly amazed, Teddington's brother ventured, 'Do you think he'll bring the stuff?'

'He'd better … if he knows what's good for him,' Teddington said, talking tough to impress the present company. 'Or else I'll call Hitler Jesus to sort them out!'

Back at the farmhouse, the troop filed into the house. Those who had remained behind had hacked away the collapsed wisteria and set up the barbecue, using the broken wooden trellis to get the fire going. Teddington stood by the door and anxiously smoked a cigarette while taking regular swigs of Black Label lager. He propped his panga up against the door frame, where he would not forget it. What if Tony didn't deliver? Would the arrangement really work? He had guests to please, after all. He could see how things could become very embarrassing.

Less than twenty minutes later, a small cloud of dust could be seen following Tony's pickup along the farm road. He had been to the beer hall on the outskirts of Goromonzi town, and the back of the pickup was laden with crates. It was all there: the beer, the vodka, the Cokes, even the groundnuts. Everything, it seemed – but for one item.

'Tony, where's the goat, dammit! We can't have a party without the goat!'

Tony began to stammer.

'Where is the goat, Tony?' Teddington demanded to know, this time in a tone that meant business.

'It's coming,' Tony hurriedly assured him. 'I spoke to one of the workers here on the farm, and he'll be bringing one. He should be here in ten minutes. He lives just behind the barns, so he had to go and fetch it. I'm sorry for the delay, Comrade Chiwafambira. Really I am.'

Suddenly realising that this was an arrangement well worth maintaining, Teddington remembered Hitler Jesus's instructions on taking with the one hand and giving with the other. With a broad smile, he slapped Tony enthusiastically on the shoulder.

'I can see we are going to get on just fine, Tony. This is a very good start. I'll come by tomorrow and tell you about the party.'

Tony breathed a sigh of relief as he got back in his pickup and returned home. He spent the rest of the afternoon paging through tattered back copies of the *Farmer's Weekly*, not taking in a single word. His mind was a million miles away. He and Patsy ate their dinner in silence and went to bed at eight-thirty. Neither could fall asleep, and both were still lying awake when, at half past one in the morning, the sound of a minibus engine and the rasping skid of tyres fractured the silence.

There was a loud banging at the back door, and the sound of voices. Tony, in his pyjamas and slippers, turned on the light in the kitchen. He braced himself as he once again opened the door. This time, Teddington was nowhere to be seen. Indeed, he had collapsed on the sofa half an hour before, utterly satiated with Black Label, vodka and goat meat, in a state of near-catatonia. But in any case, whoever this was, they wanted more liquor. Any kind of liquor would do, they said.

Tony shook his head, explaining that the beer hall was closed at this time. A volley of abuse and nasty accusations followed as the group surrounded him. In the moments before his final collapse, Teddington had promised his visitors that Tony could and would supply anything, and Tony now felt them pressing closer and closer as they drunkenly demanded more liquor.

His head spun – he did not know what to do.

'Okay, okay,' he said, trying to make his way through the group to the back door, 'just wait here.' The group waited restlessly, but fortunately Tony did not take long. He emerged at the back door with several bottles of local Mukuyu Estates wine and half a bottle of Jameson whiskey.

'This is all I have. Please take these, I have nothing else at this time. Honestly.'

Delighted, the group piled back into the minibus. Again, Tony breathed a sigh of relief as the sound of the engine faded into the distance. If only he and Patsy could leave the farm and start a new life elsewhere, but it was not so easy. Even if they had somewhere to go, Tony knew that the laws obliged him to pay a termination gratuity to all the farm workers. It was not a large amount per person – certainly unlikely to last more than a few months, for each of them – but as there were almost a hundred workers, the grand total was an amount he simply could not afford at this stage, or at any time in the future, probably.

At seventy-three years of age, Tony felt tired.

21

Stevie's Inferno

As the William Westward horse and trailer rumbled back after the athletics meeting, past the Chapman Golf Course and the Hellenic Club, a flood of painful memories came over Thomas. He recalled his own dreaded bus trips back to Koodoo Range Preparatory School – a two-hour drive from Harare on this very same road – near the town of Macheke. As an Anglican boarding school for boys aged between seven and thirteen, Koodoo Range enjoyed a fair academic record and a fine sporting reputation, serving as a feeder school to the country's best-known boys' private senior schools. Father had set funds aside for the fees, and his will was amended to reflect his unequivocal intention that Thomas should be enrolled there as soon as he was old enough. Marie had tried to intervene. The boy was far too sensitive, she felt – but that served only to strengthen her husband's resolve. His sensitivity was precisely why he should be sent there, to toughen him up. He must be properly prepared for the harsh realities of life. As the late-afternoon shadows flitted by, Thomas's mind went back to the uncomfortable itching of a little boy's brand-new grey uniform and the green cap pulled over his ginger curls, as Marie had driven him out to his first day at school …

* * *

On arrival, the new boys were herded into the hall, to be distracted by a screening of cartoons while the parents were invited to the headmaster's home for a midday session of gin and tonics. Thomas did not find the cartoons at all amusing. In fact, he barely realised they were showing, so overwhelming was his sense of foreboding. Terrified, he asked the supervising master – a burly, hairy fellow who reeked of cigarette smoke – if he could go to the toilet.

The master looked at him scornfully. 'What do you need the toilet for? The oke's just started up the Tom and Jerry, man! Can't you wait?'

Thomas looked down at the floor tearfully and the master sighed. Not another bloody sissie, and deaf at that, he probably thought as he stared with dismay at Thomas's hearing aids. If it were up to him, the school would have a comprehensive entrance exam to weed these types out – make them jump backwards off the ten-metre diving board, or leave them out in the bush for a night or two with nothing but a pair of underpants and a boiled egg.

'Jesus Christ,' the master muttered under his breath, rolling his eyes in frustration. 'Okay, oke, go if you must, but come straight back here when you're done. You hear me?'

Meanwhile, at the headmaster's house, Marie was braving her way though an exchange of coarse anecdotes among hefty sunburnt tobacco farmers as they helped themselves to drinks from a silver tray portered about by the headmaster's flustered manservant, when suddenly a sense of disquiet engulfed her. She instantly put down her lime and soda, and made her way down the driveway, the gravel crunching under her feet. Following her instinct, she walked straight towards her car. Marie noticed a slight movement in the Bluebird's rear and there, curled up under a sack, she found Thomas hiding from the world, hoping to be taken home without anyone noticing. She lifted him up. Together they sat on the tailgate of the stationwagon with their legs dangling down. Marie did not really know what to say. She tried to explain that, often in life, change can be difficult, but it soon became clear that philosophical commentary was to no avail. She assured Thomas that she would not be far away, but they both knew this was not true – she would be a couple of hundred kilometres away, if not more, and the school rules only permitted the children to go home twice a term. In addition, telephone calls were not permitted, only letters, and no more than one a week.

Marie took Thomas's hand and led him back to the hall. There, the burly master managed a smile. 'Ja, ja, ja. Don't worry about anything. He'll be square once you've gone! Go have some drinks, Granny, seriously!'

She bent down, giving Thomas a kiss on his head. Then she touched his cheek and said, 'Remember, God will look after you, my little one.' With that, the boy's mother departed.

And so, for Thomas, a lifetime of God began in earnest.

Thomas's newly acquired classroom hearing apparatus consisted of a cream-coloured plastic microphone box that hung from the teacher's neck and transmitted a signal to a receiver hanging from Thomas's neck, which had wires attached to a headphone in each of his ears. Predictably, it did not take long for him to become an object of intense ridicule. In response to his wide-eyed look of constant surprise, he was instantly christened 'Wonder', which rapidly transformed into 'Stevie Wonder', and then finally just 'Stevie'.

Nobody knew his name was Thomas, and no one cared; they

called him Stevie or Threscothic. When he spoke, which was sel-dom – for his manner of speaking elicited shrieks of hilarity – his accent betrayed the influence of Mother and Father, and he there-fore sounded like a Pom. Being labelled a Pom at Koodoo Range Pre-paratory was the gravest of insults – Poms were deeply despised. For white Rhodesians, it had been the Poms who had betrayed them, it had been the Poms who had tried to hand 'their' country over to the blacks on a plate, back in 1965 – a particularly unpalatable action, given the number of Rhodesians who had valiantly shed their blood for Britain and her Empire in two World Wars. Small wonder that Stevie quickly learnt to keep his mouth firmly closed.

Stevie was neither good at sport, nor at school work, where his tendency to write certain letters backwards, or even upside down, was greeted with unrestrained mirth by his classmates and broad smirks from his teachers. On top of all this, the beatings were mer-ciless. You were caned for being late. You were caned for forgetting your garters. You were caned for talking after lights-out. You were caned for failing to comb your hair properly. You were caned for failing spelling tests. You were caned for walking across the cricket pitch in brown shoes and not takkies. You were caned for failing to polish your shoes. You were caned for losing your shoes. You were caned for losing your stationery. You were caned for having an un-tidy locker. You were caned for having an untidy desk. You were caned for peeing in your pants. You were caned for peeing in your bed. You were caned for failing to sweep the classroom properly. You were caned for talking in class. You were caned for having any kind of sweets or chocolate except on Tuck Day. You were caned for not finishing your food. You were caned for whistling. Sometimes you even got caned just for fun.

With no one and nowhere to turn to, Stevie followed Marie's ad-vice. He looked to God for help. Until his arrival at Koodoo Range, Christianity had been about fun activities and entertainment. At St Luke's Sunday School, back in Greendale, they had played 'Simon says touch your nose', and they had sung 'Silver and gold have I none said he' and 'If you're happy and you know it' to the enthusiastic strumming of a duo of buxom youth-group leaders, all pimples and smiles, who handed out copies from the banda machine, covered in sketches of Noah and the ark, Moses with his tablets, and Jesus walking on water – all for colouring in.

Where Christianity had previously been an activity or a hobby, like potato painting or Morris dancing, at Koodoo Range it became for Stevie a means of survival. God must be prayed to nightly, and constantly obeyed – that way Stevie could be assured of God's protection, without which he would perish. He began to read the Bible, starting at the most obvious place: right at the very beginning. Sometimes it took him an hour to read two or three pages. But he persisted. On Sundays, during the compulsory walks out into the bush that surrounded the school, he tucked his illustrated Children's Bible – which Mother had covered for him in transparent plastic – under his arm. Under the mistaken impression that someone might actually wish to steal it, she had written his name on the inside cover. It was stuffed with bookmarks that featured stirring pictures of brilliant pink sunsets and turquoise lakes and inspirational quotations from Helen Steiner Rice, or just cheerful sayings like 'Stand up and be Counted' and 'Every Cloud has a Silver Lining'. Using his index finger to follow the words, Stevie struggled to mouth their sounds. In this manner, he would subject himself to as much of the Old Testament as he possibly could, until, inevitably, his attention became distracted by the birds in the trees.

One Sunday, the image of Stevie ambling along the path through the bush with his Bible, looking just like a monk, so intrigued and amused the other boys that they laid an ambush. A band of observers hid behind rocks and trees next to the path, while one, a proper thug called Rory Johnstone who was eleven years old, climbed a tall msasa tree and perched himself over a fork with his shorts and underpants pulled down. A look-out let forth the secret whistle as

Stevie came into sight. Everyone fell silent, except for Rory Johnstone who made a disturbing succession of frantic straining sounds.
Just as Stevie was passing below him, a dark lump of pooh tumbled through the air, narrowly missing the corner of Stevie's Bible,
and splattered squarely onto his shoe. The other boys leapt out of
their hiding places, screaming and wetting themselves with laughter. Rory Johnstone almost fell from the tree. At first Stevie did not
know what had happened, but after a minute of finger-pointing and
jeering, he knew that he was once again the object of a cruel ruse.

After five months of relentless endeavour, Stevie reached page 368
of the Old Testament, yet, try as he might, he could not recollect
a single thing he had read. He had learnt nothing. Despite his determination and his sense of Christian obligation, he decided one
day, almost subconsciously, behind his own back, that it would be
impossible to ever get through the whole Book, let alone the Old
Testament, and he gave up.

Under the serene tutelage of Sister Norma Goodwin, meetings of
the school Christian Club were held on Sunday afternoons, on the
lawn under the jacaranda trees outside the sanatorium. The meetings were poorly attended – at most, ten boys turned up, among
them a bright-eyed child by the name of Simon Sinclair who was a
star at cricket and hockey, and a near-virtuoso on the piano. Stevie
admired him greatly and warmed to his lively temperament. He was
extremely excitable, and despite being in the Christian Club, was
uncontrollably naughty, somehow managing to separate real sins
from petty ones pertaining to school rules.

Stevie stayed behind after Chapel each morning and evening to
pray – everybody noticed this, but only Sinclair did not find it odd.
One day, Sinclair waited for Stevie outside Chapel. He offered to
teach him to speak in tongues – that very evening, in fact, on the
balcony after lights-out. Stevie was apprehensive at first; he was already a misfit – an episode of involuntary incantation in a language

unknown to anyone, including the speaker, would most certainly finish him off socially. He did like Sinclair, though, and so agreed to give it a go.

Stevie lay waiting nervously in his bed, when suddenly Sinclair whipped down the covers and shot him in the eye with a water pistol.

'Quick, let's go! Lunchie's on the prowl,' he whispered, referring to the pimpled disciplinarian dormitory master whose nose resembled the knobbly surface of a nutty chocolate bar.

Stevie was up like a shot, and the two ran through the dormitory in their pajamas, out onto the balcony. Kneeling behind a row of damp towels hanging from a rail, Sinclair explained how it worked.

'What you do,' he said, 'is to come up with a word, any kind of gibberish, and say it to yourself a few times, again and again and again, and then suddenly the Holy Spirit will just take over, and you'll be speaking in tongues. It's easy. Watch me!'

With an angelic moonlit smile, Sinclair closed his eyes and burst into a ferocious babble, like a robot singing in Chinese, thought Stevie. He gasped and leaned back to watch the spectacle, which went on for what felt like an age. It seemed all but inevitable that Lunchie would appear and haul them in for a lashing. Stevie's heart was racing.

Quite unexpectedly, Sinclair's babbling ceased.

'Right! Your turn,' he said enthusiastically.

Stevie was aghast.

'What! Me?'

'Yes, you. Go on, make up your word.'

Panicked, and under the proverbial spotlight, the best Stevie could manage was a restrained 'Blablublublub.'

'Excellent!' Sinclair whispered. 'Now keep going until the Holy Spirit takes over.'

Cringing, Stevie began chanting his half-baked gobbledygook like a reticent mechanic cranking up an old car engine, waiting for the spark of the Holy Spirit. He went on like that for at least a minute, but alas, no spark came.

'Did you get it?' asked Sinclair expectantly.

Stevie was stumped. 'Er … well, maybe … at one point I thought there was something.'

'Excellent! We'll try again sometime soon. Let's get out of here before Lunchie lynches us!'

Stevie scrambled into bed, hugely relieved to get under the covers and back to his prayers, but he did wonder why, unlike Sinclair, God never gave him any signs. To whom exactly was he praying? Was there really anyone or anything out there? He could see no signs, nor detect any response to his prayers. Was there something wrong with him, perhaps? Some of the boys at Christian Club spoke of the joy of being 'washed over by the Holy Spirit'. What did that mean?

One afternoon, Stevie found a moth-eaten old book in the Religion Section of the school library. *The Wounds of Christ*, it was called. In it, there were stories of people of great faith from the olden days who suddenly and spontaneously exhibited symptoms of the wounds of Christ upon the cross. Some people's hands had begun to bleed as if they'd been pierced with nails, just like Jesus. For months, if not years afterwards, Stevie was intrigued. He began to pray for this stigmata, as the book called it – a sign that his prayers were being heard after all. He would pray and pray and pray to convince himself that he had within him faith the size of not just one mustard seed, as required in the Book of Matthew, but ten thousand million mustard seeds. With great anticipation, he would flick on his torch to inspect his hands, but the result was always the same. There was nothing there, just his little pink palms and chewed fingernails – no signs of the cross at all.

After the tribulations of Koodoo Range, Marie enrolled Thomas at a government high school, Oriel Boys, in the suburbs of Harare. There were not many other white boys in the school, but that was fine. Thomas found a gentleness and tolerance among his black schoolmates that he had never experienced among the white boys at Koodoo Range – although high-spirited and full of humour, their pranks were aimed at having fun, not making fun of others. Thomas made few friends, preferring to return home straight after school. He managed to get seven O-level passes, and even attempted a year of A-levels, but gave up when he and Marie realised it was well beyond him. While pondering what to do with his life, he followed his mother's suggestion of a temporary post at the William Westward. Baba Chiswa took him under his wing and, as the years went by, all other career possibilities faded away. He did not earn much, but he and his mother did not need much either.

* * *

The aged Mercedes horse and its bus-like carriage chugged to a halt outside the William Westward, jolting Thomas from his recollections. Marie and Leviticus were waiting by the car, ready to leave, though Thomas insisted on being shown the home's new pumpkin patch. They walked over to the old red-brick barn. On the far side, Leviticus had cleared an area of bush with a panga, while Marie had dug several lines of shallow holes, each surrounded by a small moat for catching and holding water. In the centre of every one, Marie planted a single pumpkin seed – the humble beginnings of the William Westward's return to agriculture.

22

Tony Willoughby's Comeuppance

The mid-morning sunlight crept through the sitting-room window of what had once been the Willoughby residence. His eyelids flickering, Teddington woke to find himself stretched out on the old couch where he had collapsed just after midnight. He had a pounding headache and his mouth felt dry and furry, like a mouse's nest. He fumbled for the bottle of Black Label he felt sure he had left next to the couch. To his surprise, his fingers found it. Snatching it up, he took a healthy swig – and immediately sat bolt upright in horror. His eyes bulged as he gagged, spitting out a soggy cigarette butt. Suddenly, confusion and angst engulfed him. What were his new responsibilities? What must be done to maintain the status quo? He leapt to his feet and stumbled across to the main bedroom where he found his naked brother spread-eagled across the double bed, each of his arms flung across the bare back of a woman lying on either side of him. It had been a hell of night. Young women, it seemed, become quite impressionable in the face of new-found wealth.

'Zvito!' Teddington shouted.

All three occupants of the bed woke up with a start, the women scambling to cover themselves.

'What! What is it! Is something wrong?' Zvito responded.

'Get up, Zvito. I need to get a few things straight with Tony.'

Teddington made his way out of the house and looked out at the driveway. Both taxis had gone. Empty bottles and scuds lay strewn across the patio, and the charred remains of the goat skeleton smouldered in the embers of a makeshift barbecue. It was a real mess. Tony had better send someone down to sort this out.

Zvito and the women appeared from inside the house, gingerly at first, the panga in Teddington's hand causing some uncertainty. Without looking over his shoulder, the new owner set off purpose-fully in the direction of his manager's house. The amorous trio had no option but to follow, though the women struggled to keep up in their high heels.

They did not need to bang on the door this time. Tony had seen them coming and came over to meet them, out of earshot of his wife. Teddington shook his hand firmly and glared at him for a few uncomfortable seconds. Tony's left eye began to twitch.

'Tony, that nonsense with the goat last night. Okay, so it did come eventually, but I told you I had guests waiting.'

'I'm really sorry, Comrade Chiwafambira, I did my best to get it there quickly, really I did.'

'Well, all I'm saying is that it's a pity we got off to a bad start. A real shame. But let's see if we can start again. Send someone up to the house to clean up, Tony, and we'll be needing your pickup and some money. Five million will do.'

Tony despaired. That was a lot more than he could spare. Defeated, he went back inside the house and returned immediately with the keys and a wad of notes.

Teddington could not suppress his glee. 'Good man, Tony. I'll be back tomorrow and you can show me around the lands.'

23

The Law Clouds
his Lordship's Judgment

Yet another cacophony of cackles and sniggers consumed the court-room, packed as it was with podgy pressmen from *The Herald* and a handful of ZANU-PF little-wigs.

'My Lord, I implore you! No, I go so far as to beg of you, my Lord, to see the facts for what they are!' pleaded Scotsman Mandi-kuvadza, his hands raised in supplication.

'It is common cause, my Lord, that my client, the Movement for Democratic Change, had yesterday morning filed its own urgent application for the release of its members who have been detained at the Parirenyatwa Hospital. The application before this court today was brought by the Ministry of Health only this morning. It is clear to all, my Lord, that the purpose of today's application is purely to frustrate the application filed yesterday, and to hold these so-called patients purely for political gain. To grant the applicant's Order under such dubious circumstances would constitute a perversion of justice … in the extreme, my Lord!'

The Honourable Justice Vuroyi's mouth broadened into a smirk as he adjusted the fluffy grey wig that perched on his head like a rooster on its post.

'Mister Mandikuvadza, we have all heard the evidence, we have all seen the pictures, what more can I do! *Nyaya iyi haisi* Catch-22! What am I supposed to do about it? Counsel for the applicant has asked for an *Ex Parte* Order extending the period during which psychiatric evaluation of the patients may be undertaken, from seven days to ninety days. I see no reason to withhold such an Order. The law on this point is clear.'

The battle was clearly over, and Scotsman Mandikuvadza knew it all too well. Still, he could not restrain himself. 'With respect, my Lord, in all the years I have appeared before his Lordship's court, I have never once witnessed the law, as you call it, cloud his Lordship's judgment. Why start now, my Lord?'

The smirk disappeared from the judge's face. He raised his gavel and pounded it against its block. 'That, Mister Mandikuvadza, is contempt! By now you should know better. Two weeks, this time. Guards, take him down!'

With a sigh, the embattled advocate handed his files over to his assistant, who handed him the packet of peanut butter sandwiches brought to court as standard practice precisely for such eventualities. Scotsman Mandikuvadza, the firebrand of the MDC's legal team, clearly had no fear of incarceration.

'Order granted, with costs against the respondent,' grunted the judge as he tossed aside his gavel and strode off directly to his Mercedes Benz. He sped off in a great hurry, his wig still upon his head. Tee-off at the Royal Harare Golf Course was in fifteen minutes, and the Spin Doctor did not like to be kept waiting.

Veterans of countless protracted treason trials, electoral disputes, and writs *habeas corpus* for the release of many hundreds of activists held without charge, the MDC's legal team was not even vaguely surprised by the ruling. As with all other matters of a political nature, this too would be a war of attrition, the results of which were by no means certain. A further urgent application would have to be filed, this time to the Judge President, for an order allowing the 'patients' to be assessed by an independent psychiatrist. Someone would have to be flown in from outside the country, someone immune to attempts at interference. Drafting would start that very afternoon – the affidivits had to be ready for signature by morning if they were to be filed by lunch time the following day.

24

Inspector Rajiv Gupta
to the Rescue

It seemed improbable, thought Thomas, that not just one but two senior girls of such considerable size had managed to squeeze into the half-tyre seat of the slide. As the girls hurtled through the air, a fever of excitement gripped the crowd of children below. Baba Chiswa, always the aspirant engineer, had over the weekend rigged up a wire-and-pulley slide from the Fairbridge balcony to an old foam high-jump mat on the lawn, using a length of mining cable he had recently purchased at the closing auction of yet another mining company gone bust. With a hacksaw, he had fashioned a safe and comfortable rubber seat from an old car tyre – safe and comfortable, that is, if you were under twelve years of age. Landing heavily on the mat, the two girls rolled onto the lawn, shrieking with laughter. Matron Betty, hands on her hips, marched purposefully over to them. A firm set of rules for the slide was clearly required.

Thomas put his sandwiches down in his office before going through to congratulate the headmaster on the new installation. Baba Chiswa looked concerned. On the desk were two pink Department of Child Welfare files. The top one was open, and Baba Chiswa was paging through the contents.

'Thomas, there you are. Take a seat for a moment, there is something I wanted to discuss with you.'

Somewhat apprehensively, Thomas sat down at the desk.

'These are the files for Regus and Ruth that have come through from the Department of Child Welfare. Problematic histories, it seems. I need you to take special care of them, particularly Regus.'

'What is the matter?' Thomas asked.

'Well, it seems Regus has a history of running away and hiding. It says here his mother died from an HIV-related illness shortly after his birth, and he was raised by his father for a couple of years until he too passed away, also HIV related. Nearby relatives took custody of the boy, but not a day went by without him running away, back to his original home – to look for his father, he said. The relatives, it seems, did not have the time or the means to search for him every day, which is why someone eventually called Child Welfare. And they sent him here, to the other side of the country, so that he would not try to run away again. Trouble is, he's already gone missing. No one has seen him since breakfast yesterday.'

'What do you want me to do, Baba Chiswa?'

'Well, I'd like you to look for him this morning with Robson Shambari, and once he's found, can you keep a close eye on him please? And also speak to his teachers down at the school. And if that doesn't work, after lunch we can send groups of juniors to look for him.'

'Certainly, Baba Chiswa. I'll start looking right away.'

Robson and Thomas set off together on foot, scouring the perimeter of the property. They trudged up and down the old Fairbridge School maize and tobacco fields that were now overgrown with bushes and trees, and dotted with giant anthills, but there was no sign of the boy. After tea, they drove up to the shopping centre and spoke to the guards there, but no one had seen Regus.

Back in his office, Thomas pondered Regus's dilemma. Intuitively understanding the many reasons why a child might wish to run away, he had a sense that the headmaster's plan of sending out search parties might only cause Regus to retreat further. All the boy really needed was to feel included. Using a pair of rusty scissors, Thomas cut out a pair of square-framed spectacles and an oversized nose from an old cornflakes box. With these, he hoped to bring to life Scotland Yard's Inspector Rajiv Gupta. The William Westward needed his services for this unusual case.

After lunch, Thomas led the juniors out onto the lawn in front of the administration block, where he had positioned a blackboard on an easel. In bold letters, he wrote on the board: William Westward's Top Ten Most Wanted. Below, he listed the numbers 1 to 10.

Standing behind the blackboard, Thomas took out his cardboard spectacles and nose, placing them on his face to the amusement of all. With a piece of chalk, he wrote 'Mister Shambari' next to the first number. The children scattered in different directions, but as it was known that Robson Shambari could generally be found near the old tobacco barn that doubled as his workshop, most of them sprinted directly there, finding him dozing in the sun on his deck-chair, with a half-eaten roasted mealie in his hand.

The children eagerly gathered round the blackboard again. Thomas raised the chalk and wrote the name 'Regus' next to the number 2.

A few children scratched their heads and called out, 'Who's that?'
Several answers followed.
'He's the new guy.'
'The funny one who doesn't say anything.'
'The one who just stares at the ground!'

'Oh, *that* guy!' they all chorused.

Then they were off, scampering to the far corners of the grounds, peering under bushes and calling Regus's name. Thomas felt an almost imperceptible tug on his trouser leg. He turned to see the diminutive figure of Ruth, who had been keeping to herself ever since her arrival, now start to run in the direction of Paget Block towards the playground. She stopped to see if Thomas was following her; once certain that he was, she ran on, disappearing behind the jacaranda trees at the far side of the field, where she ducked down and hid. He strolled over towards her, hoping that he might win her trust. To avoid frightening her away, he stopped several yards from the jacarandas and waited, softly calling her name. She peered out from behind a jacaranda and pointed towards the guava tree on the fringe of the playing field before running away. Two small shoeless feet dangled from one of the branches. Gradually, the silent, motionless figure of Regus, hiding in the branches, revealed itself. A small flock of bronze mannikins bouncing from branch to branch gravitated around him, like tiny moons around a distant planet.

Standing under the tree, Thomas gently called Regus's name. The boy's downcast eyes flickered in response, but he was careful not to shift any part of his body so as to avoid betraying his position and unsettling the birds. Thomas took an apple from his pocket. Moving slowly forward, he carefully balanced it in the fork of a branch close to the boy.

From his own experiences in that very same tree, Thomas knew it was best to gain the child's confidence rather than drag him back to the dormitory, where he was likely to become an object of curiosity. Thomas walked back to the blackboard, certain now that Regus would not be going anywhere. The boy felt safe where he was.

At four-thirty that afternoon, Thomas returned to the guava tree. The apple had gone, but the two little feet had not moved from their position, and were still dangling from the branches. Sensing that the boy's resolve was fading, Thomas reached up and gently lifted him down. Without lifting his gaze – a habit that would continue for many years – Regus allowed Thomas to take his hand and lead him back to the dormitory, where he was handed over to Betty for a shower and some dinner.

Speaking to him in his own language, Betty softly asked him why he had run away.

It was his father, he mumbled. He was hoping to find him.

25

A Tug o' War
over the Village Idiot

After what he had witnessed three days before, right outside his General Store, Mister R Utsichingoka was convinced that never again could anything surprise him. Just after four that afternoon, a ZUPCO omnibus, identical to the one that had recently halted briefly outside his Zama Zama Growth Point Store, came to a standstill in exactly the same position as its predecessor. Save for the driver, as well as a band of six sturdy medical orderlies, three Fawcett's security guards, and two ZRP constables, this one was empty.

As the steel door swung open, the security guards and constables scrambled down, followed by the orderlies. Displaying urgency and purpose, they wasted no time in descending on the beer hall across the road, like an amateur SWAT team. They pressed themselves against the walls on either side of the entrance, ready for action. One of the constables unclipped a canister from his belt. He twisted open its lid and rolled the canister, hissing and spurting, beneath the makeshift curtain of bottle-top strings hanging from the door-frame. Clouds of gas began pouring from the tavern's windows.

Discordant yelps and wails from the beer hall threw the entire village into a panic. Men dropped their newspapers. Women threw down their hoes. Children abandoned their mischief. All but the newborn, the elderly and the infirm charged up to the roadside to take a look.

Blinded by teargas and discombobulated with drink, several men reeled out of the beer hall, spluttering and staggering. The orderlies and security guards pounced on them with consummate ease. Few resisted as they were dragged to the omnibus. With visible enjoy-ment, the driver stood guard over the door, keeping it firmly locked until another quarry needed to be squeezed inside the vehicle. In less than five minutes, some twenty-five had been bagged.

It was a turkey-shoot – or so the orderlies thought, until one of them put on his sunglasses, tied a folded handkerchief over his mouth like a cowboy, and burst into the beer hall. Seconds later the orderly emerged, dragging a partially clothed elderly man who was in surprisingly good spirits, despite his adverse circumstances. A cry of distress went up from the villagers as the man was yanked towards the omnibus door.

'You can't take him! *Musiiye akadaro chero ari Village Idiot tinongomu-da ari zvaari!'* they shouted. 'He's one of us. Let him go!'

A little backward perhaps, yes, and with a taste for the tipple, this captive was universally known and liked by the Zama Zama Growth Point community. For years he had brightened their days with his puppet-like jerks and jangles as he danced his jigs outside the beer hall, all elbows and knees. He was someone's grandfather. He was someone's uncle. He could not be detained.

A band of children and women grabbed the elderly man's arm, and tried with all their might to drag him back to the village. Sev-eral orderlies came to their colleagues' rescue. A tug o' war over the man ensued, with one side gaining a bit of ground, only to lose it seconds later. It was a fierce battle that threatened to tear the prize's arms from their aging sockets.

After several minutes, a shrill, ear-piercing whistle rang out, so loudly that every villager, orderly, constable and security guard instantly released their grip in order to cover their ears.

'Benedict Tsoko QC. Headman! Now what seems to be the problem here?' a loud voice demanded. All attention turned instantly to a middle-aged man with a policeman's whistle. He was dressed in a frayed dark suit, one sleeve of which had been torn right off.

Forcing his way through the crowd, an irate gentleman wearing brown trousers and a grimy Manchester United football shirt, cried out, *'Musaterere zvaanotaura!* Don't believe a word he says!' Without warning, the man snatched at the breast pocket of the barrister's suit, trying to rip it off. He would no doubt have succeeded, had it not been for the shrewd actions of the orderlies, who seized the moment to pounce upon the two quarrelling men and propel them both onto the omnibus – along with the all-popular village idiot.

Inside the omnibus, a number of detainees had come round from their gassing and began knocking on the windows, pleading to be released. The crowd outside grew restless. Sensing the odds were against them should the mood turn nasty, the older of the two constables called out, 'We've got enough, let's go, let's go!'

Seconds later, the engine gave off a throaty roar. The last of the orderlies scrambled up the stairs and the omnibus set off, the crowd scattering as the driver accelerated. A little way up the road, the brakes screeched loudly as the vehicle skidded to a halt. Directly in its path, a lone man cut a courageous figure. With his left palm raised, he signalled for the omnibus to stop. In his right hand, boldly displayed as a policeman might display his badge, was a muddied pocket Bible. Through the dust and the noise, his hoarse incantations reached the villagers, but not for long. One of the orderlies hopped off the omnibus and dragged the man aboard.

With its extra passenger, the omnibus set off at full tilt towards Harare.

Seated on the low wall that fronted Mister R Utsichingoka's General Store was one man who had kept his composure throughout, his attention quietly focused on twirling a partially straightened paper clip between two fingers.

With his view somewhat obscured by a haze of greasy fingerprints on the store's windows, Mister R Utsichingoka decided he had seen enough for one day. Sighing, he rolled down the store's steel grid and wandered home in the afternoon shadows.

26

Marie, Interrupted

Wearing her faded lime-green dress, the one she always wore for appointments, Marie was waiting at the gate for Thomas to return from the William Westward – pretending, or so he suspected, to be inspecting the pumpkin beds. Thomas felt uneasy as they walked into the house, where they sat down with a pot of tea in the lounge, the conversation stilted and superficial.

Marie paused for a moment, then looked up at Thomas.

'Mister Johnson from the church took me to the doctor today.'

An uncomfortable silence followed.

'Was everything okay, Ma?'

He felt afraid – he wanted to cover his ears, or run away to his room to hide.

'It should be fine, Thomas,' Marie said, 'but I need to have a little operation on Sunday.'

She lightly placed her hand on her left breast. 'There's a small lump right here, and the doctor wants to check up on it.'

'And then? What happens after that?'

'Well, if the doctor has a look at it, and it's fine, then that'll be the end of it. If there is something wrong, then he'll take the lump out, and everything else that's bad, and after some treatment, everything should be fine.'

'But it will be okay, won't it?' Thomas asked, reaching out for reassurance. He stood up from his chair to put his arms around his mother, tears in his eyes.

'I'm sure it'll be fine, Thomas. I'm sure everything will work out fine,' Marie said, resting her hand on Thomas's forearm.

The night before the procedure, neither Marie nor Thomas slept very well. Both tossed and turned, caught inside a cinema of dark possibilities from which neither managed to escape until dawn. Fumbling in the early-morning gloom, Thomas found his hearing aids on his side table, resting against the furry green foot of Edwin Swales VC. As soon as he put them in he heard the rasping croak of a crow that landed on his window sill, casting a shadow that danced eerily on his walls, in among the Great Ones. Thomas scowled; he had always regarded crows with distrust. They never came to the clearing when he and his mother called. Along with ravens, they were not interested, preferring to hang about the stench of the rubbish dumps rummaging through people's leftovers, or to steal biscuits from dogs and cats, or to chase other birds from their roosts.

Thomas caught sight of Marie on her way to the clearing. He dressed and ate quickly, then set off, pausing when he neared his destination. Responding to the uncertainty in Marie's voice as she called them, and to the anxiety – though subtle – revealed in her movements, the birds were far more animated than usual. A small flock of Carmine Bee-eaters, with rose-coloured chests and sky-blue crowns and undertails, seemed agitated as they sprang from Marie's knees to her shoulders and down to her feet again. Her attention, he knew, would be focused on the birds that came each day – her gentle pair of Hoopoes, the bright-eyed Glossy Starlings, the sagacious Purple-Crested Louries, the diminutive Blue Waxbills.

There were strange movements in the trees, which Thomas did not recognise. It was difficult to discern their shapes against the gnarled trunks of the msasas, except when a muffled hoot, or sharp swivel of a head, betrayed their positions. Owls. Certain birds, Marie had once told him, respond to specific physical states supposedly discernible in the human voice. Some are intrigued by pregnancy, some by puberty. Still others – usually owls – recognise ill-health. The presence of the owls was therefore to be expected on a day like this. Marie would be neither surprised nor afraid; acceptance, for her, was linked to awareness.

As Marie ceased her calls, the birds gradually flew off. She looked refreshed as she emerged from the clearing, nodding to Thomas to take his seat on the old bench in the clearing. He quickly began calling, but he was distracted, his calls lacking the necessary rhythm and intonation. Still, some interest was aroused. From high up in the branches came the penetrating trill of a Crested Barbet, like an old bicycle bell rung with a thumb pressed against it, dulling its chime. The bird flew down and landed at Thomas's feet, then bobbed around in circles, stopping every so often to tilt its head and inspect his face. A series of soft, inquisitive squawks signalled the arrival of the theatrical Go-away birds, which bounced down onto the bench, one on either side of Thomas, glancing curiously at him from time to time. As his attention wandered, so the birds withdrew.

Still somewhat unsettled, he returned to the house. They did not dilly-dally, the doctor had said to be at St Anne's Hospital in Avondale by eight. Thomas placed Marie's little suitcase on the back seat of the Datsun, and they set off as soon as they had said their goodbyes to Leviticus.

In less than twenty-five minutes they had reached the hospital. Thomas followed Marie into the reception area and held the overnight case on his lap while she filled in forms and signed them. Although the operation was scheduled for two that afternoon, a number of tests and procedures still needed to be performed. A nurse led them through to the ward. Eventually, when she drew back the plastic curtains around the bed, Thomas stepped forward to see his mother lying under the sheets in her nightdress – like a sick person. Tearfully he hugged her, promising he would be back that evening, after the operation.

'God bless you, Mother,' he said as he left.

'God bless you too, Thomas.'

27

The Liberation of the Comrade Sizemore Chinovhiringa Country Club

Despite the eviction of the majority of commercial farmers from the district, Taffy Jones had somehow managed to keep the Goromonzi Country Club going, with its nine-hole golf course and country cricket ground intact. He saw to it each day that the little pub was swept clean, its counters and glasses well-polished, and its fridges stocked with whatever beverages were obtainable.

The golf course was considered among the finest in the country. The manicured greens and neatly mown fairways enticed many an enthusiast from Harare, including a number of former commercial farmers who came largely for old time's sake, and to keep in touch. Membership had remained steady and, through shrewd administration, Taffy had even managed to add a new set of showers and an extensive locker room where the weekenders could keep their clubs.

It was a Sunday, so the club was crowded. By eleven, over

twenty-five golfers had played through, and several others were still on the course. Groups of middle-aged professionals – black, white, and Indian – had converged upon Taffy's pub in the convivial atmosphere that always accompanies the arrival of the first round of drinks. Some were settling into the sole item on Taffy's menu, Cornish pasty with chips.

At the bar, the beleaguered Tony Willoughby, eager for some measure of escape, however fleeting, from his unfortunate circumstances, was seated with his long-standing mate, Scally Barbour. They were there to celebrate. Completely out of the blue, Scally's compensation had arrived.

Scally, short for 'Scallywag', had farmed in the Goromonzi district all his life, until his abrupt eviction in the turbulent April of the year 2000, during the initial wave of informal land resettlement. Given twenty-four hours to clear off his land, he had crammed his truck with as much of the family's furniture, personal effects and workshop tooling as he and his bewildered staff had managed, hauling it off to his son's back yard in Harare. Late that afternoon, Scally returned and loaded up his most prized possession, the hastily disassembled centre pivot of his newly installed irrigation system. This was a time when most people still believed that the political fracas would pass – it would only be a matter of weeks before he could return with the pivot and continue farming as before.

A large crowd of chanting, dancing youths, numbering perhaps a hundred or more, had gathered at the front gates of the workshop yard, armed with badzas, spades and pangas. When the segments of the centre pivot had been loaded and secured, Scally's elderly mechanic unlocked the back gate, pulled it open and fled into the darkness. Waving their implements and screaming threats, the mob raced around as Scally tried to manoeuvre the truck through the gates. They struck at the horse and trailer with their badzas; the din was deafening. When it seemed that the truck would get through, they pelted the horse with a hail of rocks that shattered the windscreen and side windows. Bleeding from a cut that stretched across his ear and cheek, Scally, now fearing for his life, managed to shake off two assailants who had jumped up on the running board, with the apparent intention of hauling him out through the broken window. He shifted the horse into second and picked up some speed. An hour later, bleeding and sobbing, he dragged the centre pivot into his son's yard and collapsed into his wife's arms.

But that was not the end of it. The following week, a group of soldiers escorted by a police vehicle arrived, demanding to see Scally. The centre pivot, as well as the truck, was, they claimed, the property of one Brigadier Mazondo, the new owner of Scally's farm. The brigadier demanded their return, or a charge of theft would be laid. A police constable stepped forward to make an arrest. Scally did not have the stamina to resist and handed over the keys. The officer thrust a clipboard at him, with a printed sheet attached; headed 'Compensation Schedule', it listed, in barely legible writing, the words 'truck' and 'pivot'. Scally signed the form, and the truck and pivot drove off, never to be seen again.

Naturally, it came as something of a surprise to Scally when, earlier that week – and so many years after the event – a brown government envelope had arrived in the post, addressed to Mister Horace P Barbour, Esq. Inside was a letter, typed on a Ministry of Lands letterhead, stating:

> *To – Compensation for improvements to land – Erf 1437 –*
> *Reitfontein Estate*
> *1 x Truck*
> *1 x Pivot*

A cheque for the amount of two hundred thousand dollars was stapled to the statement. Scally had cashed the cheque later that day at the Newlands Branch of Standard Bank, before calling Tony to make plans to meet on Sunday at the club. With this compensation for the entirety of his life's possessions, Scally ordered two Cornish pasties with chips, and two Bollinger lagers. It was not enough though, and Tony had to chip in ten thousand dollars. Highly amused as he was, Scally's mood was nothing short of ebullient.

The barman, a newly recruited young man of somewhat surly disposition, served them the two lagers before turning on a small television set secured in an iron cage bolted to the wall above the bar counter. The characteristic drumming announcing the commencement of the ZBC's News was almost inaudible above the chatter of the golfers.

'This is the news read by Reuben Garwe. Today the President, His Excellency Comrade Robert Gabriel Mugabe, sent his condolences to the family of Comrade Sizemore Chinovhiringa, chairman of the Zimbabwe National Liberation War Veterans' Association for Mashonaland East. Instrumental in the establishment of the government's land resettlement programme in the Marondera district, Comrade Chinovhiringa died on Wednesday following a long undisclosed illness ...'

'That's the bloke,' Scally muttered under his breath to Tony, 'the one who shot that fellow, whatsisname, Connelly, in Marondera a couple of years back. Got away with it, too. Scot free. Poisonous bloody swine! "Long undisclosed illness", my arse. Like no one knows what that means!'

He rose to his feet, pushed back his barstool and cleared his throat loudly. The golfers' babble subsided. When he had the pub's attention, Scally raised his Bollinger in a toast, 'Gentlemen, to the untimely passing of Comrade Sizemore Chinovhiringa!'

An awkward silence ensued – no one knew quite what to do. Tony shifted nervously and glanced at the barman, who was now glaring at Scally with narrowed eyes, his head slightly cocked. Scally took a swig and placed his Bollinger back on the bar counter. Slowly, the babble resumed. Without removing his gaze from Scally, the barman threw his dishcloth down on the counter. Then, turning and exiting to the storeroom, he took his cellphone out of his pocket.

'Is that Comrade Teddington Chiwafambira? … Comrade, I've got some news for you. I'm down at the Goromonzi Country Club. There's some *varungu* making jokes about Comrade Chinovhiringa … No, its old guys, one of them is that *murungu* from your place … No, no, no, they don't look like they're going anywhere in a hurry. But be quick, Comrade.'

The barman's call filled Teddington with excitement. Abandoning his quart of Black Label, he leapt up from the couch. With no credit left on the cellphone he had appropriated from Tony, he hastened out to the driveway and jumped into Tony's pickup to speed down to the manager's house.

Fortunately, Patsy was out. Not that it really mattered, but Teddington still felt slightly awkward around her. Limon, the cook, let him in without asking any questions before shrinking back to the pantry. Quickly, Teddington dialled Comrade David Shuranyama on the Willoughby's landline. The comrade's phone rang and rang. Teddington glanced at his watch impatiently. Half past one; he must move fast to get on top of the situation.

At last, a deep chortle came through the receiver.

'Comrade Shuranyama. It's Teddy-Boy. How are you, Comrade? … Me, I'm good, very good, Comrade. But busy! You know, all this farming! Ha, I'm tired! … Comrade, there's some *varungu* making fun of Comrade Chinovhiringa at the Goromonzi golf club. Can you get here quick, Comrade? … Ah, at a wedding, that's nice! Very nice, hey! … But can you send some guys from the wedding? I'll be waiting at the farm with the pickup. But please, Comrade, they must be quick, you know how these *varungu* like to move around! Okay, *tatenda*, Comrade!'

An hour can be a painfully long time for a comrade waiting to take command of his first mission. Technically, of course, it was Teddington's second – if one included the incident with the bus, which had brought him instant praise and authority; however, as that was largely accidental, to Teddington – privately – it did not really count. He loaded some scuds onto the back of the pickup for the guys, and waited in the driver's seat, ready to go.

To be fair, the guys were quick. Less than an hour later, a minibus taxi had arrived, followed by a pickup laden with comrades dressed in suits – their ties now loosened – as well as some hangers-on, scruffy types who had come along for the ride. Now a man of some status, Teddington only shook hands with those in suits, the big men, not the riff-raff.

The three vehicles set off at a frightening pace, almost forcing Patsy off the road as she turned off to the manager's house. Within five minutes, the mob had arrived at the Goromonzi Country Club, where they stormed the bar, scattering the golfers who fled immediately without asking any questions. Fortunately, Scally and Tony were relieving themselves in the new locker room's ablution facility when they heard the shouting. Realising at once they were in danger, they managed to escape unnoticed across the putting green to Scally's wife's worn-out Hyundai. They sped off to Harare, stopping only to collect Patsy and a couple of suitcases.

Back in the pub, the excited barman showed Teddington to the locker room where he suspected Scally and Tony were hiding.

'Dammit!' Teddington shouted in a forced display of leadership, noticing the crowd looking to him for direction.

'Comrades,' he continued, uncertain as to what to say next, 'let us, ah, er …'

Then it came to him.

'Comrades, let us liberate this club! *Ngativatorereyi!*'

The mob responded instantly and enthusiastically. After all, most, if not all of them, had come along in the hope of 'liberating' something from its current owner. Instantly, they set upon the lockers, prising them open with pangas or smashing the locks with rocks to remove whatever lay within – golf bags, jackets, clubs, cricket bats, pads, boxes, wickets, watches, anything they could find. Others set upon the pub's fridges and pantry. Phone calls were made and more comrades invited. No one wanted to miss out.

At first Taffy Jones kicked up a fuss, protesting, 'Who are you to take this stuff?' and 'What right do you have to come into this pub?'

Frankly, he became quite a nuisance and had to be locked in his office – where he would remain for the next two days until fortuitously freed by another band of comrades in search of the pub's cash box.

Elated, the comrades split into two groups, according to their interests and talents. Some went in for cricket, with seven or eight heavily padded batsmen at the crease of Taffy's pitch at any one time, all swinging wildly. Others, perhaps the more cultured, senior comrades, preferred a spot of golf. At any rate, at sunset, all assembled at the front entrance for the renaming of the club. Using bitumen and a paintbrush that the barman found in the workshop behind the mower, Teddington had the honour of painting over the italic lettering of the word 'Goromonzi', and replacing it in bold dribbling script with 'Comrade Sizemore Chinovhiringa'. Cheering and singing broke out on its completion, and Teddington was showered with the spray of countless quarts of Black Label and Castle Lager.

After forty-two years of colonial oppression since its construction, the Comrade Sizemore Chinovhiringa Country Club had finally been liberated.

Behind the jubilant mob, two men crept off down the road, quietly heaving a wheelbarrow containing a large electric fridge. Its wheel jammed in a rut, and the fridge tumbled over with a clatter of bottles and dishes that were hidden inside it.

The excited crowd of comrades all turned around instantly. A torch flashed, and two caddies were caught in its beam.

'Thieves!' roared the mob, 'After them!'

28

A Nice Mazoe for Dumbo, Lots of Ice

Thomas was in quite a state as he started his car in the St Anne's Hospital parking lot. He dreaded going to church later that morning on his own; people would ask questions as to Marie's whereabouts. He did not want to go home either – it was sure to be a long and lonely day of worry. He thought of Darryl Mackay, an old friend from Oriel Boys' High School who lived with his mother in the near-by suburb of Strathaven. He could visit him, perhaps. Though they had little in common these days, there was no one else Thomas could think of.

He had not visited Darryl in months, and had some difficulty finding the house. When he did eventually get there, the Mackay's cook, Distan, greeted him as he opened the gate. Thomas entered the house through Darryl's side door. Empty beer bottles lay in clusters on the floor and table, and on a couch, nestling in an orange

Frisbee, was a green plastic bong, surrounded by several heads of marijuana. Heavy snoring emanated from Darryl's darkened bedroom. Thomas took a step towards the door, accidentally kicking over a glass with his foot. It fell with a crash.

'Who's that?' Darryl shouted. Wearing only a pair of underpants, he grabbed his knobkerrie as he leapt out of bed, staggering about in the darkness.

'Stop, stop! It's me, Thomas!'

Darryl flipped on the light switch. 'Jesus, Dumbo! What the hell're you doing, giving me a fright like that!'

The unfortunate portmanteau 'Dumbo' was the name assigned to Thomas back at high school, but save for Darryl, no one still remembered it.

'My mother's in St Anne's Hospital, so I thought I'd come and visit. I should've called first.'

'Jesus! Your old queen's in the hospital! Is she okay?'

'I think so … she's just got to have a small operation, that's all.'

'Operation! Holy shit! On what?'

'What do you mean?'

'Well, where's she going to have her operation? What part of her? Like, her head or her arse or something?'

'Er, I dunno, they didn't say.' Thomas shied away from the details.

'Well, I hope she'll be *kenge* soon, Dumbo, and back on her feet. Eh, d'you want Distan to make you a Mazoe?' he asked, pointing at a near-empty plastic bottle of orange concentrate. Without waiting for an answer, he leant out the window bellowing, 'Distan! DISTAN!'

There was no response. Darryl turned to Thomas to complain. 'Shit, Dumbo, the minute my old queen buggers off, that bloody oke goes AWOL! I tell you, these okes, give them half an inch, and they'll take a bloody light year!'

'How is your mum, Darryl?'

'Giving me crap, as usual. Check what I had to do to keep her out!' he said, pointing to where he had bricked up the passage leading to the main part of the house, almost to the ceiling, 'Ask Distan about her crap, he'll tell you!'

'And work? You still at the video store?'

'Crap as well, and my old queen won't let me use the car any more. I've got to cycle there,' he said gesturing towards the beat-up BMX Thomas remembered from high school. At twenty-five, still supporting a skirmish of teenage acne, Darryl was a scrawny, scruffy sort of fellow who spent most of his time on the couch, trawling the internet for adult sites on a computer assembled from discarded parts.

A call came from the driveway – Distan, it seemed, was still about. Instantly, Darryl leant out the window again, shouting, 'Distan, make a nice Mazoe for Dumbo! LOTS OF ICE!'

'Mister Sithole – your mother's surgeon,' the young doctor introduced himself, shaking Thomas's hand. 'The nurse will be here shortly to take you through to visit your mother.'

'Was the operation successful, Doctor?' Thomas's voice quavered with apprehension.

'Well … yes,' the doctor replied, looking directly at Thomas. 'I think it was successful.'

Thomas felt a wave of relief.

'Of course, we had to remove the breast, and I believe we managed to remove the entirety of the lump, but there will need to be follow-up treatment.'

'For what?' Thomas asked, frowning.

'For the cancer,' the doctor replied, looking slightly perplexed. 'But probably not chemotherapy, rather radiotherapy, but then again, you'll need to speak to the oncologist about that. I'm just the surgeon.'

Tears welled up in Thomas's eyes. Cancer, he knew, was an awful disease from which few people recovered.

When Thomas entered the ward, he saw his mother lying quietly on her side. He rushed over and grabbed her hand, and she replied with a tired smile.

'Is it true you've got cancer? Will you be all right, Ma? Say you'll be all right, please, Ma!'

'Yes, they did tell me that, Thomas, but they also said that, with the treatment, everything should be fine.'

'I'm scared, Ma. What will we do?'

'Don't be afraid, Thomas, everything will be as it should be.'

Even when ill, Marie was not one to lie around in bed. For the first couple of days after her release from hospital, Thomas hardly left her side, save to make her tea, or fix her a little lunch, or to visit the shops for groceries – but on her third day home, she got up at dawn and resumed her routine, finding respite in its familiarity. With Baba Chiswa's consent, Thomas stayed home for a few more days. Since Leviticus was not feeling well either, Thomas busied himself by weeding the pumpkin patch, and watering the plants with a long black hosepipe in the cool of the late afternoon.

To his relief, everything seemed to be returning to normal.

29

In his Dreams, Justice Lazarus Mushonga Sees Himself as a Kangaroo

A heavy mist obscured the striking vistas that greeted Justice Lazarus Mushonga each morning, ever since he'd taken up residence in the Mazoe Hills, some twenty kilometres outside Harare. Muffled too, was the rumble of the tractor as it moved through the deep green of his orange orchards. From the dairy above the main farmhouse, his herd of Jerseys lowed softly.

An eerie, unsettled feeling came over the judge as he stared out into the suffocating gloom – a feeling that had been his constant companion ever since moving to the farm. It was that darned urgent application, the one that appeared in the newspapers every day: the pressures, the expectations, the constant calls from ministers and other party officials checking on the progress of the matter, each providing 'friendly advice', which was often conflicting. Sometimes he felt he simply could not cope.

Day after day, for almost two weeks now, a different patient from G20 had taken the stand to defend his or her sanity so as to secure his or her release from custody. The state's cross-examination had been relentless, calling upon a slew of witnesses who provided an incredible litany of fabrications, most of it utter drivel, completely without substance by any reasonable standard. He had listened to the accounts of doormen, secretaries, secret lovers, hairdressers, barbers, acupuncturists, churchmen, postmen, event organisers, traditional healers, faith healers, doctors – you name it, he had seen and heard it all.

The 'friendly advice' was to accept each state witness's testimony with due solemnity, and to ask only those questions that might seek to substantiate rather than diminish their outlandish claims. He had tried, at first, in all honesty, but several days in, the sheer lunacy of it all had begun to haunt him. He would wake up in the middle of the night, shouting. In his dreams, he took on the form of a kangaroo – a tiny grey wig perched on his head in proceedings where it was clear that, far from someone else's sanity being in question, his own dignity was under review. The change in him was plain for all to see. He had taken to remonstrating with himself, often aloud while driving, and even in the toilet at the High Court – where he now frequently retreated from the incessant ringing of his office telephone. The 'friendly advice' became less friendly with every passing day, soon escalating to blatantly directive.

The judge finished his cup of tea, sombrely bade his wife farewell, and set off for town. The final patient was due to take the stand later that morning – the dreaded moment had arrived.

'All rise!' cried the High Court clerk. 'The Honourable Justice Lazarus Mushonga to preside.'

The packed courtroom bristled with excitement. With the hearings due to conclude that day, the judgment was imminent.

'Order!' called the judge, pounding his gavel in annoyance.

'My Lord, the State calls to the stand Patient Number 30, Mister Lennard Chavundukwe, formerly MP for Marondera West.'

Justice Mushonga could not bring himself to raise his eyes as Mister Lennard Chavundukwe was brought to the dock. After a series of questions from the applicant's lead counsel, all of which were answered with the MP's customary eloquence and clarity, the Attorney General himself leapt to his feet and gleefully launched into a lengthy, painstakingly well-reseached monologue on the subtleties of mental illness. A bout of cross-examination followed, with the Attorney General referring to statements that had been made by Patient Number 30 as far back as five years ago, and holding them as examples of inconsistency and progressive mental decline.

The state witnesses were called to the stand. Most had forgotten their words and improvised, with mixed results. It was evident from the rambling accounts and downward glances that some were reading from notes pinned to the inside lining of their trouser pockets. One, purporting to be a priest, relied for his answers on a blue-tooth device attached to his ear, which was partially concealed under a beret cocked to one side.

Finally, the judge could take it no more.

'Enough! God damn you all!' he cried, his hand shaking uncontrollably as he raised his gavel, 'I've heard enough!'

Silence fell upon the courtroom as the judge made his hurried exit. Losing his grip, his enormous file thudded to the floor, pages flying everywhere. He paused only for a second to look down at the chaos at his feet. Shaking his head once, he hurried to his chambers.

The Attorney General was already on his feet, his cellphone pressed to his ear. He quickly stuffed his notepad into his briefcase and strutted down the aisle of the courtroom. As he reached the door, his call came through. His voice sounded out crisp and clear over the silent courtroom, 'Kudzai, it's me. Put me through to the minister, would you?'

The Spin Doctor answered, his mouth stuffed with Colcom's steak-and-kidney pie. 'What's the latest, AG? When can we expect our judgment?'

'Boss, its Mushonga. We appear to have a rogue agent on our hands. Looks like the old boy's finally lost the plot.'

'Christ, what is it now?'

'He didn't look up once all morning. I'd barely got into my cross-examination of Chavundukwe when, guess what, he suddenly says he's had enough, gets up and leaves. Drops his file on the way out and just leaves it on the floor.'

'Jesus, what do you think has got into him? I mean, he's supposed to be the man for the job. Chimurenga credentials coming out his ears, I understand. Two years in Mozambique during the war, sat on all the ZANU committees for affirmative action, and all that stuff – you'd think he'd be able to handle this in his sleep. Just goes to show, you can't bloody trust anyone these days.'

'And there's more, boss. The clerks up at the High Court reckon the old boy spends five hours a day on the shitter. Arguing with himself, out loud, too!'

'Serious! It doesn't sound pretty. What d'you reckon is going to happen with his judgment then?'

'I honestly can't say. For all I know, he could let the lot go tomorrow. Frankly, I'm worried boss.'

'Well, we can't have that, can we! Having those guys locked up has been like Christmas come early. Do think we can reason with Mushonga, lean on him a bit? Maybe get the old man to give him a ring personally?'

'I don't know, boss. From where I'm standing, it looks like he's gone barking mad!'

A long pause followed, 'What did you just say, AG?'

'What do you mean, boss? I said it looks like he's gone barking mad.'

A smile appeared upon the Spin Doctor's face. 'Excellent. I've got just the answer. Tell me, AG, what do we do with madmen in this country?'

'Throw them into the Pari, Boss. G20.'

'Precisely! So what are you waiting for? Get an ambulance down to the High Court chop-chop and take Mushonga in. We'll see how much sympathy he has for them from the inside! And once I've got it into *The Herald*, let's call a mis-trial. Make them go through the whole darn thing all over again, that should buy us a bit more time. Oh, and next time make sure we use that Justice Vuroyi. Now, there's a fellow who knows where his bread and butter comes from. *Ndeumwe wedu*! I'll make sure he gets Mushonga's new place up at Mazoe as soon I've had Mashonga's Missus thrown out.'

'Consider it done, boss.'

'And in the meantime, let's start letting them go, in ones and twos, a few each month. You know, make it look like there's a proper process, all reasonable, and stuff. Keep the big fish till the very end, though, and Mushonga too. That'll teach him.'

30

A Purple Spiderweb

In accordance with the surgeon's instructions, Thomas took Marie to see the oncologist a week after her operation. Highly regarded within Harare's medical fraternity, Dr Anna Matarayika was both professional and friendly. She explained that, with a course of injections and ten weekly sessions of radiotherapy, Marie was likely to make a full recovery. Much relieved, Marie and Thomas left with a referral letter to be taken directly to a doctor at the Radiotherapy Unit at the Parirenyatwa Hospital. To their dismay, a queue ran from the reception area into the parking lot. Despite the noon heat, there was no option but to wait. Thomas searched for a seat for his mother, eventually locating six half-bricks that had once marked the border of a flower bed. Using his hands, he dusted the spiders and soil off as best he could, and stacked them, forming a primitive seat for her to sit on whilst waiting her turn. He fetched the umbrella from the

Datsun to shade her from the fierce sun. Had it not been for the fact that many in the queue were in poor health, some bandaged with dressings that were in obvious need of change, Thomas might have considered making his way to the front to ask if Marie could be attended to immediately on account of her age and frailty. But Marie would hear nothing of it; each must wait their turn, she said resolutely.

By five o'clock the queue had moved sufficiently to enable Marie to take a seat on one of the chairs inside. But just then, a nurse came walking down the line; the Unit was now shut for the day, she politely explained, and would reopen at eight the following morning. The queue dispersed. No one had the energy to complain.

The following morning, Thomas and Marie took no chances and left for the hospital at six thirty. A number of other patients from the previous day were already waiting when they arrived, and nodded a greeting. All waited in the same order as before, lined up outside the locked doors. When the young nurse opened the doors at eight, almost everyone was already back in the line. On a small wooden table in the corner of the waiting room lay an old *National Geographic*, dog-eared and stained. Thomas picked it up and paged through it. Global warming was the topic of the lead article. He recalled something from his schooldays about suspect gases in deodorant cans and fridges, which destroyed ozone; but besides that, this was a subject about which Thomas knew virtually nothing.

Over the next four hours, he read every word in the article and analysed, with difficulty, every graph and chart, scrutinising each picture and becoming more and more panicked with each page. This was, after all, the respected *National Geographic* – its reporters the ultimate authority on the state of the planet. If they said the world was getting hotter, and the birds and beasts would soon perish, and the seas would rise, and the rivers would flood, and the forests would become deserts, one couldn't but take them seriously.

Meat production, said the article, was a major cause – vast tracts of forests were slashed and burnt to create pastures for cattle and sheep, which in turn produced another suspect gas: methane, they called it. By the year 2042, the seas would be empty of fish. Thomas touched his mother's arm. They should not be eating meat, he told her. And they must stop eating sea fish – immediately. No more hake on Thursdays. Now that they knew the truth, they could not be party to the devastation. Thomas's mind was racing. He must clean out Father's old swimming pool and stock it with local river fish, freshwater bream and barbel.

The young nurse finally announced Marie's turn to see Doctor Ruzhowa. Thomas waited anxiously for almost an hour before his mother returned. He covered his mouth in horror at the sight of her. A spiderweb had been drawn with a purple marker, across the left side of her neck, almost reaching her cheeks. Seeing Thomas's distress, Marie smiled gently and told him not to worry, explaining that the Doctor had drawn it so that the radiotherapy could be accurately aimed. The machine was at the end of a long corridor, identified by a sign on the door: Radiation – Restricted Area – No Unauthorised Entry. Below the sign was the yellow-and-black nuclear symbol, unfamiliar and unsettling to them both. They entered cautiously, uncertain as to whether or not they were authorised to go inside.

A diminutive technician wearing huge spectacles looked up from his desk, where he was busy completing reports. He gestured to them to step forward. Marie handed over her schedule card from the doctor and the technician studied it, frowning with concentration. With a flourish, he signed the card with a fountain pen before leading Marie through to an adjacent room where the radiotherapy machine was located. Once again, Thomas waited for an hour. He was relieved, however, that the treatment had at last begun.

31

A Messenger Sends Leviticus Back to his *Kumusha*

Leviticus remained ill. What started off as a sore throat had turned into a virulent case of the flu. Despite two weeks of rest, a painful dry cough regularly woke him in the dead of night. Sometimes he moaned, sometimes he shouted with delirium – his dreams inhabited, no doubt, by visitors of ill-intent.

Marie and Thomas were alarmed, but Leviticus refused to be taken to the doctor. In a few days he would be fine, he said. Each morning, Marie gave Thomas several aspirins and some vitamin pills to take across to Leviticus, along with a bowl of porridge and a slice of pawpaw. At lunch time, she took him a plate of mashed potato and pumpkin, and for dinner, pasta or rice with tomato relish. Although only thirty-four years old, Leviticus had worked for Marie for fifteen years; apart from Thomas, he was her closest companion. But now, he was just a shadow of his former self, having lost an impossible amount of weight. Marie's face too, with the fading purple spiderweb creeping up from her neck, was gaunt with worry. With one in five of the country's population infected with HIV, Marie had little doubt as to the diagnosis.

Marie tried to persuade Leviticus to be tested. Without antiretroviral medication, his time was limited, and a test would be the first step in procuring the correct medication. He did not want to go, but Marie insisted; she, too, would have a test, she told him, and so they set off together to the clinic. Marie went first, the smirking nurse taking her for a vintage vixen – a throwback from the white mischief of colonial times. Leviticus followed reluctantly. When the results were released, he refused to discuss them with Marie. She did not push him; he had his right to privacy. For days on end he lay in his underpants in his darkened room, his ribs protruding as he wasted away, racked by bouts of diarrhoea and deep dry coughing.

Understandably, Marie was surprised when, one morning, Leviticus knocked at the kitchen door. He was feeling a little better, he said, and wanted to do some work. They wandered slowly across the lawn, stepping carefully over pumpkin vines that spread about the yard like the dendritic fibres of a gigantic organic nervous system. Out of the corner of his eye, Leviticus glimpsed a movement in the sand. He stopped for a closer inspection, seeing nothing at first, until the swivel of small black eyes betrayed the creature's position. Leviticus jumped back in horror. Its skin blending perfectly with the mottled reddish soil, a lone chameleon stood, dead still, a front leg poised in mid-air, like a mime artist waiting for its cue. With an expression of hopelessness and dread, Leviticus shuffled back to his house as quickly as a man in his state of emaciation could manage: to prolong contact with this mysterious creature would, he feared, only worsen his predicament. Marie bent down and placed her hand in front of the chameleon. It climbed onto her fingers, clasping them tightly with its feet. Its dark conical eyes rotated until it fixed its gaze on hers. It did not move for some time.

Back in his room, Leviticus packed his few belongings into an old suitcase. If death was coming, he told Marie, he must return to his *kumusha* – in Shona, 'the place where one comes from'. He must face his death in Hwedza. Marie pleaded with him. There were medicines that could save him, if only he would come with her to get them. But Leviticus would not listen. His mind was made up.

Marie tried to persuade him to stay at least until lunch time, when Thomas would be home. Reluctantly, Leviticus agreed, giving Marie a chance to fill a brown paper bag with fruit and vegetables to take home with him, and also to collect what little cash she had on hand in the house to give him.

The smile on Thomas's face when he arrived home from the William Westward instantly disappeared as Marie told him about Leviticus's imminent departure. His perfect world was once again crumbling around him. All three of them wept openly as they said their goodbyes.

Slowly, Leviticus made his way down the driveway and out the gate to wave down a commuter minibus. He turned back to raise his hand briefly to his erstwhile companions. And soon he was gone.

32

No More Radiation
for Marie

Marie and Thomas returned to the house in silence. Thomas sat down on Father's old wingback in the lounge, staring dejectedly out of the window. Glancing down, he noticed his mother's radiotherapy card lying on the table in front of him. Apart from the grandiose signature of the first attendant, there were no other signatures next to the dates of Marie's scheduled weekly appointments. Ten weeks had passed, the course should already have been finished by now. Marie's face became flushed as she came around the corner with the tea to find Thomas puzzling over her card.

'What are you doing with that, Thomas? Did I not teach you that you shouldn't go through other people's things without their permission?'

'There are no signatures here, Ma. Why didn't you go?' asked Thomas, panic rising in his voice.

'I did, Thomas. I did go. I went each time I was supposed to.'

'Then why didn't they sign it?'

Marie looked up at Thomas. 'They didn't sign it because the machine is broken.'

Thomas was speechless.

'The hospital says there's no money for the spare parts,' Marie continued, 'and in any case, the person who used to fix the machine has left the country. Doctor Ruzhowa is doing what he can, though, and he hopes to find a solution.'

'So how can we be sure you're getting better, if you don't have the treatment?'

'Well, I've been resting and eating well. You have noticed, haven't you?' Marie said, trying to lighten the atmosphere.

'That's not enough,' Thomas cried out. 'We must go this afternoon to sort this out.'

Down at the Radiotherapy Unit, the queue was twice as long as before. Scores of unhappy patients stood in the hot afternoon sun as the line snaked its way across the car park. Fortunately, because Marie had already been registered as a patient, they proceeded directly down the long corridor to the tiny technician with the large spectacles. He jumped up with a smile – after Marie's ten visits, they were by now on friendly terms. An exchange of pleasantries followed, after which Marie enquired as to the state of 'the machine', as everyone called it. The technician frowned, painfully aware that the fate of nearly all the patients hung in the balance, dependent solely on its repair. Speaking in a hushed voice that suggested confidentiality as well as embarrassment, he explained that the matter had been taken right to the top, to the beleaguered Minister of Health himself, and that all concerned had accorded it the highest priority.

Thomas's complexion became blotched. The technician's words seemed unacceptable and insincere. To be calmed by them would be to fail his mother. So he exploded, partly because he felt it was what one was supposed to do under the circumstances, and partly because he did not know what else to do.

'This hospital is useless!' he shouted. 'All you people are crap! Why can't you people do your jobs? Can't you see my mother needs treatment?'

'Thomas,' Marie said firmly, touching his arm. 'All those people out there need treatment, some more urgently than I. It is not this man's fault that the machine hasn't been fixed.'

Anger radiated from Thomas. He wanted to hoist the man up and leave him hanging by his collar from the fire-extinguisher hook, with his little legs and arms dangling helplessly – just like his schoolmates had done to him at Koodoo Range Preparatory. He stormed out the door. Marie apologised to the technician, and followed Thomas.

Using her umbrella as a walking stick, Marie moved slowly down the corridor, thanking the nurse as she exited. Thomas was waiting for her outside, his back to the queue. Without a word, they walked to the Datsun. The visit had been a failure. Thomas knew that the only alternative was to seek treatment in South Africa, but they did not have the money; only politicians could afford to do that – and the currency dealers, and those who made their fortunes from looting equipment from state-owned enterprises and derelict farms, or trading illegal gold and diamonds.

For everyone else, there was virtually no hope.

33

The Greatest Championship in the Country's History

You could set your watch by it. At precisely seven o'clock each morning, Cromwell Shimwa would commence his day by pounding against the wooden door of his padded cell. Two months prior, at the outset of his incarceration, he had swung the cell's chair against the door, causing panic and distress to staff, patients and prisoners alike. Matron Matambanadzo promptly ordered that the chair be confiscated, but this failed to quell the racket. Cromwell Shimwa, a young man of great ambition and little patience, would not be deterred. There was nothing passive about his resistance. With his palms and feet, he continued to hammer at his door. In addition, after some experimentation over a period of weeks, he had developed a blood-curdling howl – a kind of psychopathic yodel capable of driving any man, woman or beast to the brink of insanity. Anything to get the guard's attention. By quarter past seven, someone usually relented. With a jangling of keys, the mechanism of the lock could be heard turning, and the muffled sounds of Cromwell Shimwa's at first polite observations marked the commencement of his strategy's second phase. He had quickly learnt that launching directly into a full-blown complaint served only to shorten his day's only distraction, thereby diminishing his satisfaction. It was far better, he had established, to circle the issues calmly for a good twenty minutes or so, before raising the temperature.

By eight o'clock, a crescendo of torrid insults and alarming expletives would be released, swiftly switching to logic and reason, holding his audience just long enough each time to repeat the cycle. The record, set some two weeks before, now stood at an improbable four hours and fifteen minutes.

In the adjacent cell, Mister Lennard Chavundukwe had long since ceased to follow the intricacies of these exchanges. A lifetime advocate for social reform, he was no stranger to conflict, taking each encounter in his stride, and seldom, if ever, losing his composure. Indeed, it had not taken long for him to win the respect of the G20 staff. Disputes frequently broke out in the kitchen as to who would get the opportunity to take him his tea. His breakfast, served on a dented but highly polished silver tray, was hardly ever delivered without a fresh copy of *The Herald* and a crimson hibiscus bloom in a chipped teacup.

On this day, a well-meaning attendant with an unfortunate stutter had brought him a copy of the *Financial Gazette*, the business weekly. By noon, Mister Chavundukwe had dozed off, when, without warning, his door sprang open and a man was pushed in backwards, the attendants fumbling to loosen the strings of his straitjacket. The man spun around as the jacket was removed, and Mister Chavundukwe raised his eyebrows in surprise.

The door slammed shut as he rose to his feet with a smile.

'Justice Mushonga. Had I known you were coming, I might've had a shave!'

Tears welled up in the judge's eyes and his lips quivered. 'Lennard. My brother. My comrade. Can you ever forgive me?'

Mister Chavundukwe stepped forward and clasped the judge's hand tightly for a second before pulling him into an embrace.

'Lazarus, my comrade. I never doubted you would come to your senses. Eventually, that is! The only forgiveness you'll be needing is your own.'

'I couldn't go through with it, Lennard. Seeing you in the dock like that. Not just you, but all of them.'

'Take a seat, Lazarus. Let's not talk about it, not now. There'll be more than enough time for that.'

The two men seated themselves opposite each other at a small table. Reaching into the inside breast pocket of his robe, the judge extracted what seemed to be a book, from which emanated an unusual rattle.

'Perhaps you recognise this, Lennard?'

A smile flashed across the former MP's face. 'How could I possibly forget? I remember the very day the commander – Tongogara himself – gave it to you in that camp in Mozambique. It was the day he sent us off to England, to study.'

'Do you remember what he said to us that day?' the judge asked.

'Of course. I have never forgotten it: "Not all can be soldiers," he said, "some must study to be leaders after the revolution."'

'I tell you, Lennard, this last month, not a day has gone by when I haven't thought of that. What kind of leader had I become, I've kept asking myself.'

'Well,' said the parliamentarian with a wink as he snatched the miniature magnetic chess set from the judge's hand, 'we can only hope that your game has improved more than your leadership. Come on, Lazarus, let's play!'

Lennard Chavundukwe set out the pieces and leaned back in his chair.

'Nice in here, isn't it?' the judge commented.

Mister Chavundukwe frowned, 'How so, Lazarus?'

'Well, listen to it all, Len. That is the sound of no telephones ringing in your ear. No ministers telling you what to do. No one kicking your conscience around the turf like a football!'

'Hmm, well, my experience has been somewhat different.'

'Splendid company, too!' continued the judge.

'Relatively spacious, I suppose,' responded Mister Chavundukwe with a wink.

'Lovely fresh air!' said the judge, gesturing at the tiny barred window.

'Oh, yes! Firm mattresses, too. And you'll be surprised, Lazarus, that the food's not half bad, either!'

The two old friends chuckled.

'Right!' said Mister Chavundukwe, clapping his hands together. 'The rules are the same as we always used, and the winner is the first to take, hmm, five hundred games. Your move, Laz!'

Employing his characteristically conservative opening move, the judge moved his right-most pawn. The greatest championship in the country's history had just begun.

34

Swallows and Swifts Descend from the Night Sky

Disheartened by his mother's deteriorating condition, Thomas resolved that something had to be done. He left the house immediately after breakfast, and with Baba Chiswa's permission, he took Regus down to Cleveland Dam. The boy's usual poker-faced expression and frown seemed to relax at the prospect of a Saturday away from the William Westward.

Thomas had always liked fish – fascinated as he was by their propulsion through water, purely by wiggling. On arrival at the dam, he bought a fifty-thousand-dollar can of worms. Within minutes, he had two lines in the water, with multi-coloured floats bobbing about several metres from the shore. By mid-morning they had hooked five small bream and a sturdy barbel, which they kept alive in a bucket filled with water.

Wedging the bucket between Regus's feet so that the water would not slosh out, Thomas drove back home. Marie fixed them both a glass of Mazoe – which Regus relished, slurping loudly – and then they set to work with pitchforks, clearing away bougainvillea and hibiscus clippings that had, over the years, accumulated in the empty pool. Leaving a layer of soil on the bottom, Thomas turned on the hose, filled the pool, and released the fish into the water – all but one small bream, which he kept aside to cook for his mother. Just before lunch, Thomas delivered Regus back to school. With the suggestion of a smile on his lips, Regus alighted from the Datsun, watched by a group of gaping youngsters.

That evening, as the sun was setting, Marie went outside to inspect the new pond. She walked slowly, leaning heavily on Father's walking stick. An iridescent pink-and-orange hue spread across the horizon. The air was cool. She peered cautiously over the edge of the pond, clutching at the frayed sleeve ends of her beige cardigan. For a few moments she seemed serene, the weight of the day lifted from her shoulders, but as she turned towards the house, without warning, her legs gave way and she collapsed, falling like an apron from a washing line on a windless day.

'Ma! Ma!' Thomas cried out as he ran towards her. His tears fell onto her forehead as he cradled his mother in his arms, helpless and uncertain. In the fading light he saw her eyes flicker, and gradually open again.

'I'm all right, Thomas,' she whispered. 'I must have just fainted from the heat ... give me a second and I'll be up and about.'

She took Thomas's hand, breathing deeply to compose herself. Thomas helped her to her feet, handed her the walking stick, and they slowly made their way back to house, where she lay down on her bed. She smiled when Thomas brought her dinner on a tray – grilled bream and mashed potato – but she ate very little, and minutes later, she fell asleep.

Thomas washed the pots and plates and returned quietly to

Marie's room to pray. As he knelt at the end of her bed, the scale of the impending catastrophe struck him. Realising he must recruit help, he tiptoed to his room and carefully took down the Great Ones from his walls, where Father had placed them two decades before.

Very quietly, Thomas carried them to Marie's room; he hung them wherever he found nails on the walls, but decided to place Mother Theresa and Desmond Tutu on the little wooden tables on either side of her bed. Calling on the Great Ones to plead with God on his behalf, he prayed until late into the night, imploring God to heal his mother.

The following morning, Marie did not have the strength to get up. Thomas insisted she should see a doctor, a private doctor, where they would not have to wait in a queue for two days, but she was adamant that all she needed was rest. Hoping to raise her spirits, Thomas phoned Reverend Harold Hardcastle at St Luke's and asked him to visit Marie. Out of respect, Marie sat up when he arrived, though she was exhausted within minutes and had to lie back, propped up on her pillows. Reverend Hardcastle administered Holy Communion to her and to Thomas; this seemed to calm Marie, and she asked Thomas if she might have a word in private with the reverend. Thomas waited in the kitchen for nearly half an hour for the reverend to emerge, and then the two of them walked out to the reverend's antiquated parish Anglia.

'Your mother is asleep now, Thomas. I suggest you allow her to rest until dinner time.'

He got into his car and wound down his window.

'When the time comes, Thomas, I trust you will call me.'

Thomas nodded his head uncertainly, 'Sure, Reverend, thanks again for coming.'

Marie did not stir at dinner time. Thomas brought Father's wing-back chair through from the lounge and placed it next to her bed.

During the course of the night his mother seemed to have diminished in size – it struck him then, as if for the first time, just how old she had become.

At first light, she opened her eyes to find him beside her.

'I must see them, Thomas.'

'Who is that, Ma?'

'My feathered friends,' she smiled, 'who have been with me for so long and taught me so much. Please, Thomas, help me to the clearing.'

He sat his mother up and helped her into her dressing gown. It was a beautiful morning, but the air was crisp and Marie needed to be kept warm to aid her recovery. He lifted her into his arms and proceeded towards the clearing. Marie looked eager, her neck craned forward in anticipation. Thomas gently positioned her on the bench; he would have liked to stay with her, but he knew she needed to be alone. From behind the msasa trees, he kept a close eye on her stooped figure in the dappled early-morning light.

Softly, Marie began calling the birds. It was as if they had been waiting for her, lingering in the woodlands and stony outcrops nearby. The air was instantly alive with dazzling colours and the myriad melodies of birdsong. There were choirs of Golden Orioles, their far-reaching liquid calls as mesmerising as bamboo flutes. There were Rollers, Canaries, Bee-eaters, delicate Sunbirds and shimmering Starlings. Every kind of bird Thomas had ever seen, and dozens he had not, flew into the clearing and the surrounding trees. Marie continued calling until the final bird, a solitary Paradise Flycatcher with a radiant bonze tail, landed gently on her head. High above, a trio of swifts circled gracefully.

Marie slowly moved her head to survey the congregation perched silently on the ground, the bench, and the trees around her, some even on her shoulders, head, hands, lap and feet. In an instant, Marie realised that after seven decades of calling, interpreting and cherishing her birds, she had finally relinquished all human compulsion; she surrendered, left only with the fundamental verb, to be. She bowed her head in thanks. In response, each and every bird tilted its head towards her in union, and then, almost soundlessly, the birds departed.

Witnessing this, Thomas's faith was steadfast. His prayers must now be answered, and a miracle, he felt certain, would heal his mother.

Marie was sitting completely still, breathing slowly and deeply, when he came to fetch her. Her eyes were closed and her face bore an expression of contentment. Thomas touched her arm and she opened her eyes, her irises sparkling. He gathered her into his arms and carried her back to her room. She did not want anything to eat, but had a few sips of water before falling into a deep sleep.

At dusk, the dying rays of the sun filled the room with a soft warm light. Sensing that the day was coming to a close, she stirred and opened her eyes to find Thomas sitting attentively by her side.

'Thomas, my child,' Marie said softly.

'What is it, Ma? Can I get you something to drink?'

'No, my child … there is something I must tell you, Thomas – where you come from. It is only fair that you know.'

She raised her arm and pointed at the pink evening sky outside. Was she pointing east, Thomas wondered.

'I … I'm from Marondera?' he suggested.

Marie smiled and pointed again at the sky.

'From Rusape?' he ventured.

Once again his mother pointed.

'From Nyanga?'

'No, my boy.'

She fell silent and her hand dropped to her side.

'From the sky, or so they said – the ones who found you. A wonderful blessing to both of us. A little bird from the sky.'

With that, his mother closed her eyes and slipped back into a deep sleep.

Thomas felt troubled. She was probably confused, he told himself, from the illness.

Within minutes, darkness had enveloped the room. It would be hours before the full moon would rise, so Thomas got up to turn on the light. It did not come on, so he went through to the kitchen and tried the light there, but that too did not work. Yet another ill-timed power cut, courtesy of ZESA, he thought. Searching for a candle, he ran his hands along the top of the kitchen counter, but all he found was a waxy stub in small candle holder. Fortunately, the matches were in their usual place on the window sill. He lit the wick and a dim glow flickered.

Shielding the flame with his left hand, he returned to his mother's side. He placed the candle by her bedside, just making out the shape of her face – which shone with an unearthly whiteness – and the six faces of the Great Ones, who peered at Marie from their new positions. With a quiet hiss, the candle stub soon faded, and darkness enveloped the room.

Thomas dropped to his knees and began praying again, this time even more fervently than before. In his mind's eye he tried to visualise a beam emanating from his centre, radiating outwards toward the Great Ones, then up to God, and down to his mother. A combined stream of light that must surely save her. Yet each time he tried to complete this circuit he failed, sometimes by just a fraction. He tried again and again, praying more and more desperately, until finally, the elusive celestial beam found its mark. A red flash shone through his tightly closed eyelids just as a familiar buzzing noise emanated from the kitchen. God had spoken through his anointed agent, ZESA.

The lights had come on, but his mother had gone – her skin already cold and waxy.

Thomas heard an unusual whirring noise in the cloudless night sky – gentle but powerful, as if a multitude of whistles were calling him.

Despite an overwhelming feeling of emptiness, he felt drawn to this mysterious and compelling presence.

He stumbled slowly through the kitchen and out into the garden. The full moon hung, a giant teardrop in the pre-dawn sky. Descending from above was an immense flock of swallows and swifts, their wings swishing effortlessly through the cool air. They swirled around him in a spiral, their wing tips almost touching his face, ears and neck, drying his tears. The night air whirled about him like Marie's cool breath in the fevers of his troubled infancy. The moonlight danced upon feathers and shining black eyes, and then the flock rose slowly again, like an enormous shimmering ball levitating above the roof over Marie's room for just a second before being engulfed by the darkness again and disappearing.

Thomas sank to ground, exhausted. For nearly twenty years, he and Marie had been constant companions – their lives entwined, like the roots of two trees deep below the surface. Thomas could not picture life without her; he did not believe such a life could exist for him. Despite his unwavering faith and devotion, his God had failed him.

35

Sowing the Seeds of Promiscuity

A little more than a stone's throw away, under the same night sky, a peculiar figure had business to attend to – business both mysterious and mischievous in nature, if not downright lewd. Creeping around the edge of the village that lay beyond the silent playing fields of the William Westward, the figure moved stealthily through the undergrowth. The faint rustle of a plastic packet – stuffed with women's underwear, mostly stolen – sounded in the moonlight. The figure edged towards a two-roomed dwelling made of rough concrete airbricks roofed with a patchwork of tin sheeting.

Sighs and snores of varying volume and pitch could be heard from within. That, and the school shoes and workmen's gumboots lined up neatly outside the front door, provided the prowler with the assurance that this was exactly what he was looking for, namely, a stable, monogamous family household. Propped up against the gate post was a pale blue toddler's bicycle with rusty stabilisers on either side of the rear wheel and a tiny wicker carry basket strapped to the handlebars. Perfect – he could not have wished for better.

With a splendid moonlit view of the dusty path that ran steeply down from the nearby dwelling, all the way across the village, the man paused to roll himself a cigarette. Cupping his hand to shield the flame from sight, he struck a match and inhaled a pungent lungful, savouring it. In the distance, a goat bleated. Puffing quietly, the man plotted his route with precision.

Minutes later, he tossed down his cigarette and carefully extracted a pair of cheap pink knickers from the packet dangling from his forearm. *GIRLS – 13 to 16*, it said on the label, followed by a line of Chinese characters. That afternoon at the Zhing-Zhong store in Msasa, he had shoplifted a handful of them before pilfering a range of bloomers and oversized brassieres from the village's unguarded washing lines. Conscious of the pink hue beginning to colour the horizon to the east, he now tiptoed forward and dropped the knickers over the dwelling's gate post. Lifting the diminutive bicycle, he carried it several yards down the path to prevent its wheels from squeaking.

Once out of earshot, he mounted the bicycle with some difficulty, his back arched over the handlebars. Pushing off with both feet, he began coasting down the slope, the cool morning breeze rushing against his cheeks. A wicked smile appeared on his face as he picked up speed. This, after all, was what his profession was all about, wasn't it? Catching sight of a thatched mud hut coming up ahead, he reached into the packet and pulled out a fistful of second-hand underwear. With a newspaper boy's disregard, he tossed it towards the homestead. Bloomers and bras somersaulted through the air as he cycled on, some landing in a scotch cart, and others on the back seat of a wrecked car.

He barely had time to glance back as another homestead came into view. This time he flicked a giant bra across the yard, its capacious cups parachuting squarely onto the door handle of a brick ablution block, then swinging to and fro, risqué if not downright decadent. A mangy hound howled as the cyclist sailed past, but he did not care. With a protracted, strangely high-pitched 'Yahoooooooooo!' he fractured the pre-dawn peace – it was just about time for the villagers to wake up and take a look around, anyway. Everything was going entirely according to plan; the man had followed this exact modus operandi across the country for several years, though it was seldom that he did not need to improvise so as to avoid being exposed. Make no mistake, improvisation could be fun – in truth, the thrill of it was probably what had kept him in the trade for so long. But, as he kept reminding himself, this was a job: the more convincing the backdrop he created, the greater the likelihood of success.

Soon afterwards, with the village's homesteads draped with undergarments and the morning silence rudely interrupted by the baying of hounds and the crowing of roosters, the bicycle thief skidded to a halt on the path outside the largest dwelling. This was home, as everyone knew, to Mister Enoch Mutasa and his five busty daughters – a veritable bevy of teenage sirens, visions of whom permeated the slumbering imaginations of every male within a ten-kilometre radius. Propping the bicycle up against the Mutasas' water tank, the man paused to toss the last remaining pair of pink panties into the bicycle's wicker basket, where its presence would be most likely to cause panic, alarm and suspicion. With dawn only minutes away, he scampered to a rocky outcrop near the house.

There, comfortably concealed, he cleared his throat and yelled in an imp-like falsetto, 'Hey, you! *Tuma vana vasikana!* Send out your daughters!' followed by a series of high-pitched evil sniggers. Instantly, lights came on and anxious voices called out. Flicking wild dreadlocks from his face, the man withdrew into the undergrowth and casually sauntered home, leaving the village's collective imagination to ferment. It would be only a month or two before they'd start begging him to come back and fix things. Of that, he was certain.

36

Marie's Final Sentiment on the Importance of Faith

Joseph Chiswa slowed his Peugeot 504 to a standstill outside the Threscothic's gate. He had not heard from Thomas for two days, which was unusual. Despite his hooting, nobody came to open the gate and so he let himself in, driving cautiously down the narrow driveway. Again, no one answered as he knocked on the kitchen door, which he was surprised to find wide open.

'Hello!' he called out in a sing-song manner so as not to cause alarm. 'Anybody home?'

When no response came, he entered the house and walked through to the kitchen. As he turned into the passage, he immediately saw them – Thomas asleep on the chair with his head and shoulders leaning over onto the bed, and Marie, drained of all colour, lying in front of him. Touching Thomas's shoulder, Joseph shook him gently, calling his name till he woke with a start.

Thomas had little or no recollection of the next two days. There were many visitors to the house. Some of Marie's church friends called round, carrying pies in chipped Pyrex oven dishes. Others brought baker's boxes of sausage rolls. He mostly stayed in bed, not bothering to put his hearing aids in, so he could ignore anyone who entered his room. Reverend Hardcastle suggested that the funeral be postponed, but the general consensus was that it might be best for Thomas to get it over and done with as quickly as possible.

Despite his grief and confusion, Thomas's disciplinarian background and the remnants of his Koodoo Range exoskeleton enabled him to present some degree of composure at the funeral, even while holding back tears as he mumbled his way through 'All things Bright and Beautiful'. Afterwards, he stayed for tea and biscuits, faltering around the polite chitchat with the fifteen or so people who had come to pay their respects.

It was clear to him that he must get away, far away, from all these people. Surprising himself, he told a group – among them, Reverend Hardcastle and Joseph Chiswa – that he had accepted an invitation from a friend of Marie's. She had a cottage in the Nyanga highlands, where he would be staying until he felt a bit better. Heads nodded solemnly; a break would do him the world of good, they agreed.

As Thomas was getting into the Datsun, Father's friend and lawyer, Mister Channings, came over and handed him a small brown envelope.

'Your mother came to see me a few days ago. She asked me to give this to you,' he said, brushing a tear from his wrinkled cheek.

Thomas did not open it, not even when he got home. Later on, he walked to the bottle store in Msasa and bought himself a half-jack of Smirnoff vodka and another of Mainstay cane. He began drinking the vodka neat from the bottle, taking large swigs that had him gagging and retching all the way home. By the time he reached the gate he was drunk, and he hurled the empty bottle against the gate post. Finding relief in the sound of the glass as it smashed, he leant against the gate, swaying heavily as he imbibed glugs of neat cane until it too was finished. Thomas held the bottle by the neck and swung it at the gate post. Like a Molotov cocktail, he thought. It shattered, slicing his hand, but he did not care. He was pleasantly surprised at the numbness he felt as he staggered into the kitchen to collect some empty jam jars to throw at Father's old ham-radio tower.

Waking late the next morning, he found rubbery brown strips of congealed gravy under his fingernails, suggesting that he'd had a go at one of the steak-and-kidney pies in the fridge. He located its Pyrex dish, smashed to pieces against the kitchen's outside wall, the shards surrounded by flakes of pastry crust and lumps of gristle that crawled with little black ants.

Feeling like a stranger in his own body, he set off into town to collect Marie's ashes from the Doves Morgan Crematorium. A blur of white arms and legs, waving and pumping, startled Thomas just as he was about to pull out of the driveway. Darryl on his vintage BMX.

'Shit,' Thomas muttered. He was not in the mood for this.

'Hey, Dumbo,' Darryl called out, 'Dumbo, man! My old queen told me about your old queen. Shit, man, I'm sorry. She was a cool old queen. But you gotta admit, man, she was getting on a bit. Had a really good innings, my mum reckons. So maybe it's for the best, eh? Anyway, I'm really sorry, china.'

'Thanks,' Thomas replied.

The two stared at each other. Thomas could feel tears welling up in his eyes; it was nice of Darryl to cycle all the way across town.

'Eh, I got you something. Something to cheer you up, Dumbo!' Darryl grinned broadly, his eyebrows flicking up and down with excitement, 'Just don't take them all in one go!'

He handed Thomas a small plastic bank bag. Inside was a pile of tiny grey and brown twigs. Perplexed, Thomas peered at them more closely. A couple of them resembled dried toadstools, he thought, miniature ones.

'See what I mean, Dumbo!' Darryl gave a knowing wink. 'Just be careful, eh!'

'Listen, I've got to go.'

'Cool, man, eh, sorry again about your old queen. Cheers, man!'

Thomas pulled off in the Datsun. In the rear-view mirror he could see Darryl sitting on his BMX with one foot on a pedal and the other on the ground, waving at him.

At Doves Morgan, the receptionist brought though a little wooden box from the back. It had a sliding lid and a handle of white rope – disturbingly similar, thought Thomas, to the box Father had used for his fishing worms. On a black plastic strip stuck to its lid were the words 'The Late Marie Threscothic'.

Returning home, Thomas saw the brown envelope from the lawyer on the mantelpiece. He knew he could no longer avoid it, and tore it open. It was a letter from Marie, written in her characteristically small, slanted handwriting, and it was dated just a few days prior.

My dear Thomas,

Knowing that my days are numbered, I have spoken to Mister Channings, who has helped me prepare a will. Of course, I leave all that Father and I had in terms of worldly possessions to you, our dear son. There is our property, with the house and its furnishings, and the motor car (which at times may seem more trouble than it is worth).

Whilst you will no doubt need to be enterprising, I am quietly confident that you have what it takes to succeed, save for one thing, perhaps the most important thing – something that neither I, nor any amount of money could ever give you, and maybe my presence all these years has denied you. Certainly you have great faith in God, too much I fear sometimes, but the faith you really need, only you can find. That, Thomas, is a faith in yourself.

I pray that you find this.

All my love,

Mother

37

A New Suit from George Smith Men's Clothing for Eight Million Dollars

Ever since the golden goose had flown some weeks before, things on the farm had not been easy. Teddington's resentment towards Tony ran deep – for being at the Country Club that day, for precipitating his own departure.

After much deliberation, Teddington trudged up to the manager's house. It stood vacant now, although Limon, by force of habit and perhaps harbouring some hope, continued to come in each day to dust the ornamental gnomes on the mantelpiece, and to polish the verandah until the slate shone. Usually easily cowed, Limon offered some resistance when Teddington demanded to know where his employers had gone. But fearing destitution, he quickly relented and produced a telephone number.

Teddington anxiously waited for Tony to answer, but instead he heard a woman's voice at the other end.

'Patsy! How are you?'

'Who's that?'

'It's Teddington. I just thought I'd check up on you guys. To see how things have been going.'

'What is it that you want, Comrade Chiwafambira?' Patsy's voice sounded tremulous.

'Well, as I said, I was just wondering how you were doing, and also to see when you're coming back.'

'We won't be coming back, Tony's taken ill. It's serious this time.'

A silence followed. Teddington did not know what to say.

'Is there anything else, Comrade Chiwafambira?'

'Well, no, not really. But let me know if you change you minds. You know where to find me.'

Teddington replaced the receiver and turned to see Limon's head disappear behind the kitchen door, from where he had been eavesdropping. On the telephone table, next to the phone, stood a photo of the couple. They were seated on the verandah of the main house, beneath the wisteria; a boy, presumably a grandson, sat on Patsy's knee. Both grandparents were smiling. Patsy's dark hair reached well below her shoulders. A shadow of guilt suddenly fell over Teddington. He felt awful. He snapped the photo down so he could not see their faces.

As he walked outside, Limon softly called out to him, 'Master, will the other master be returning?'

'Which other master are you talking about?' he said coldly, closing the door behind him.

He was in too deep already, he told himself. There was no turning back now.

From the start, the labour force had regarded Teddington with suspicion. As the farm's new owner, he held their fate in his hands. Each time he drove along the dusty farm roads in Tony's pickup, he noticed their attempts to conceal themselves, hiding behind trees, watching silently as he went by.

He now spotted two men standing next to the workshop, loitering because there was nothing else to do. Like Limon, out of habit they still turned up each morning. With obvious reluctance, they approached Teddington as he called out to them.

'Where are the cattle?'

Awkwardly, the men shifted their weight from one foot to the other. The cattle, it transpired, had gone – taken by the farm workers. When Boss Willoughby left, the two men told Teddington, he owed the workers severance pay. Because he had not paid them, the cattle were taken, all but five.

Teddington's fury was instant. 'What? Who gave them the right to take my cattle! *Ndiyani akavapa mvumo yekutora mombe dzangu!*'

The police were summoned, men were dragged off from the compound, arrests were made, beatings were administered, but not a single beast was recovered. They had all been walked to the nearby slaughterhouse and sold for cash.

With the police at hand to enforce his orders, Teddington gave the rest of the labourers – a hundred men and their families – twenty-four hours to leave.

'All these people must bugger off. *Vanhu vese ava ngavabve!*'

The foreman stepped forward.

'Where must we go?'

'Each to his *kumusha*,' Teddington answered indignantly.

Many had no *kumusha*, the foreman explained, they were of Zambian, Malawian or Mozambican descent. Their grandparents had arrived as migrant labourers in colonial times, many decades before. 'Foreigners,' spat Teddington, 'are not our problem. *Vapambepfumi!*'

The women and children began to wail, pleading for mercy. '*Tino-zwireiwo tsitsi mambo!*' Teddington shook his head. His decision was final. Silently, the men loaded their meagre possessions onto scotch carts.

Hot and bothered, Teddington trudged back to his farmhouse. Soon afterwards, Comrade Shuranyama called to remind him that a proper suit and tie were required for the big event that lay ahead. Just the other day he had looked at a suit at George Smith Men's Clothing downtown. Armani from Italy. Eight million they wanted for it. It was damn nice, he thought, *Yakanaka*! Very fancy! – and he needed it too. Image was important these days to enhance one's position. That afternoon, he sold the remaining five cattle to the slaughterhouse, filled Tony's pickup with petrol, drove to town, and bought himself the suit. That night he stayed at his old home in Hatcliffe. He had no friends out at Cotswold Downs Estate. With Tony gone, the farm was no longer any fun.

38

Reborn from
the Rabbit Hutch

Thomas folded up his mother's letter and put it back inside its envelope. He did not know what to make of it. After all these years of religious instruction, and hundreds upon hundreds of hours of prayer, why had no one told him this before? It seemed that he had been tricked, his faith in God cultivated on false promises, under false pretexts. Regardless of the strength of his faith, he had never received a shred of evidence of the Lord's existence. Instead, Marie's companionship, the cornerstone of his life, had been taken away from him. He felt betrayed. There was nothing left for him to live for, no point in going on. Removing his hearing aids, he threw them down on the kitchen counter and, with a mallet, he struck each with one deft blow. Two cheerless little heaps of buckled plastic remained, bursting with disfigured springs, twisted tubes and microscopic wires. He was plunged into an absolute silence, which he found strangely reassuring.

His mind was made up. He had seen it at the cinema, so he knew it could be done. It need not even be painful – in fact, he might even enjoy it. His resolve was firm. He must finish himself off, with drink.

'Forty bottles of vodka and five crates of Chibuku scuds,' the bottle store's proprietor repeated in disbelief, as Thomas spread six bricks of bank notes on the counter. The journey home was difficult. The barrow's disobedient wheel kept veering off to the left, into grassy ditches. With a determined grunt, Thomas finally brought the barrow and its jangling contents to a halt outside the kitchen door.

Twisting off the plastic lid of a scud, he threw himself down on the couch in the lounge. It was Thursday evening, so he turned on the aging Telefunken, longing for the company of old friends. Finding nothing but a screen of electronic snow, he remembered that the Mucheches had come to say their final goodbye two weeks previously. Off to Manchester, Mister Mucheche had said, where his sister was a nurse. So there would be no more CNN for Thomas. Richard, Femi, Becky, Monita, Rageh, Christiane, Jeff, Jonathan and Halla – his friends, all gone. Their absence reminded him of how alone he felt. Every room in the house brought back memories that served no other purpose but to increase his sense of isolation. Believing he could bear it no longer, he moved the loaded wheelbarrow one last time, out to the old aviary. This was where he would live from now on, he resolved. Until the end.

With some difficulty Thomas finished the scud, and immediately started on a bottle of vodka, once again, neat. In his pocket, he found the little packet Darryl had brought him that morning. Wilfully disregarding Darryl's warnings, he tilted the entire packet – all the little dried sticks and flakes of tiny fungal umbrellas – into his mouth. Then he washed them down with a swig of vodka.

'Now what?' he asked himself cynically.

Covering one eye, he looked up at the night sky, scanning for familiar constellations; after some time and with limited certainty, he located what he believed might be the Southern Cross. Lying back on the asbestos roof of the rabbit hutch, his view of the sky was better. As he stared at the stars his mind seemed to clear. Constellations began to appear everywhere. In them, he could see dragons and whales and baobabs. It was extraordinary. If he closed his eyes he could create constellations at will on the backs of his eyelids, which moved and transformed as he wished. He felt confident and at peace. Then he climbed inside the rabbit hutch, pulling the roof over the brick walls once again. Engulfed in complete darkness, he saw himself with his mother surveying the garden with its tangled vines and abundant pumpkins for several timeless hours. Then they were relaxing in the lounge over cups of tea and egg sandwiches, enjoying the company of their friends on CNN. Best of all were the mornings in the clearing, where they took turns communicating with the birds that surrounded them. It was glorious.

Finally, Thomas fell into a deep sleep, curled up in the rabbit hutch like a foetus.

He awoke the next morning, deeply disorientated, rat droppings and spiderwebs clinging to his face. His knees and elbows were grazed where he had rubbed them against the walls and concrete floor of the hutch. Quickly, he opened another scud of Chibuku, slurping as the warm milky liquid dribbled from his chin in viscous strands. When it was finished, he started again on the vodka, craving the escape that he knew it would bring. By three in the afternoon, he was muttering curses at inanimate objects. He gathered up an armful of empty jars from under the sink and hurled them at Leviticus's house; these were followed by a plastic bottle of Handy Andy, a blue sachet of Sta-Soft, and all the oven dishes he could find. He finished off with the crockery, flinging it against the pillars of the verandah, smashing the windows of his room at the same time. It felt satisfying.

By five, Thomas was wild-eyed and cursing. Feeling hungry, he hatched a plan to catch the barbel and roast it over a fire. Even though the pool was only a third full, he belly-flopped into it, shrieking hysterically. Though he was winded, and his head was gashed, he threw himself again and again at the terrified creature, grazing his fingers against the walls. It was almost dark when the catfish succumbed to exhaustion. With its broad mouth gaping, Thomas snatched it up by the tail. He gutted it with his fingers and drove a skewer through the length of it. Then, dragging out his wooden bed frame from the house, he hacked at it with Leviticus's axe, chopping the wood into pieces small enough to throw onto a fire he planned to make in the cement bird bath of the aviary.

Lighting the fire proved his greatest challenge, as all the twigs and grass he collected from around the garden were wet from the recent rains. He went through two boxes of matches before returning to the house to look for something flammable, and returned to the aviary with his childhood companion, Edwin Swales VC. Like Abraham offering Isaac up to the Lord – though for opposite reasons – Thomas placed his beloved crocodile on the pyre. With a lump in his throat, he struck a match. Its tail caught alight instantly. A fierce blue flame leapt up the velvet ridges of the creature's back, and in seconds the stuffing burst into flames, showering orange lucky beans over the pile of wood. As the flames engulfed the crocodile's head, its olive-green plastic eyes began to melt. Molten crocodile tears streamed down its cheeks, and with that the broken bed frame caught alight.

Thomas held the skewered barbel over the fire, the flames licking its moist skin. It sizzled with a sickly aroma. Minutes later – the red hairs on his fingers singed – Thomas took a bite of the flesh directly off the skewer, burning his lip as he did so. The taste was appalling, the exterior charred, the inside still raw. But he ate it nevertheless, leaving only the head and bones.

Delirious from the day's alcohol, Thomas lay down on the ground by the fire. As the flames danced, throwing shadows across the aviary and the garden, he began to detect strange movements and sounds. He soon became convinced that he had company – a band of goblins, he surmised, eyeing him from the fringes of the firelight. He didn't fear them; if they decided to kill him, death would come as a favour.

Racked by alternate bouts of vomiting and diarrhoea, Thomas returned to his hutch and fell into a restless sleep. Over and over, a dream came to him where he heard a huge explosion and was engulfed by flames, only to feel himself plummeting thousands of feet through the air. Always, he awoke a second before he could determine his fate.

The following day, Thomas established a routine that would last for several weeks. Waking in his rabbit hutch – consumed with dread and self-loathing, his body twitching from the toxins – his craving for oblivion eventually became overwhelming, and he lifted the roof and crawled to the wheelbarrow to open a scud of Chibuku. By noon, he was roaring drunk. In the afternoon, he foraged across the property for food, crawling about on his hands and knees, bringing back a small green pumpkin which he baked whole in the coals. In the evening he lay by the fire, shouting accusations at God and insults at the goblins. When the flames died down and the cold wind began to bite at his skin, he fumbled his way back to his hutch. His feet cut and bleeding, and his heart black with anger and remorse, he curled up in the rabbit hutch, willing the end to come soon.

Within a week, the scuds began to putrefy. Though rancid in taste, Thomas continued to drink them, numbing himself with swigs of vodka. Doubled up in agony, it seemed likely that diarrhoea might finish him off before the alcohol did. Festering sores and rashes appeared all over his body, his knees, elbows, spine, ribs and hips rubbed raw against the hutch's walls each night. A patchy red beard had begun to grow on his chin, with wispy clusters glued together under a veneer of congealed Chibuku.

As his bottles of vodka dwindled, like a calendar countdown, a new idea consumed him. Using the whitewashed pebbles lining the driveway, he began to construct a message in Marie's clearing, in front of her bench, where the grass was short and clumpy. It must be large, he decided, visible from space – that way, God could not fail to notice it. It was a tedious task, transporting handfuls of pebbles all the way from the driveway to the clearing. By the end of the first day, he had only managed to complete three letters: ELI. Determined, Thomas continued for days, adamant that his epitaph should be complete before his end came.

After forty days and forty nights, he awoke to find that only one bottle of vodka remained. Harbouring the assumption that he would expire once the last drop had been drunk, he rationed himself, taking only a few sips during the day – just enough to keep him going, to complete the final question mark. At dusk, he stooped to place the last stone, and stepped back to contemplate his parting statement: ELI, ELI, LAMA SABACHTHANI? The last words uttered by Christ – 'My God, my God, why have you forsaken me?' – the guttural foreignness and seeming blasphemy of which had fascinated and terrified Thomas ever since Koodoo Range Preparatory. He poured the last drops of the vodka down his throat. Defiant, he was ready to go.

Throughout the afternoon, storm clouds had gathered, dark and brooding. The air prickled with electricity. In the nearby lands, cattle began bellowing. It started with a heavy drop that hit Thomas on the chest as he shook his fists at the skies. Then, bursting like an enormous dyke, the rain came down in torrents, bringing with it the blackness of night. Thunder and lightning raged across the sky. Still, Thomas held his ground. He picked up the pebbles that he had so painstakingly positioned, hurling them into the tumultuous night sky, shouting insults until his voice was hoarse.

For hours, the storm raged. Jagged bolts of lightning, splitting and multiplying as they neared the earth, drew closer and closer, striking at the msasas on the fringe of the clearing. Then, without warning, it ceased – but only over the clearing – while continuing to rage on all around it. Thomas found himself in the eye of the storm. He snatched up the last pebble and hurled it high into the darkness above, screaming with every remaining ounce of strength, 'You lied!'

The pebble reached the pinnacle of its trajectory high up above in the dense cloud. For a fraction of a second it was stationary before plummeting down, gathering speed as it hurtled towards the earth. It struck Thomas in the middle of his forehead, just above his eyebrows. He stumbled and fell back with his arms stretched out, dropping heavily onto his mother's bench, the palm of each hand pierced by the misshapen nails protruding from the backrest of the bench. Slumping forward, he collapsed to the ground, unconscious.

When Thomas awoke the next morning, the air was cool and refreshing, the sky a pale shade of blue. A flock of mousebirds fluttered overhead, their long grey tail feathers floating in the air behind them. In the centre of his forehead, a dark blue bruise had formed, like an eye. Raising his hands, Thomas was startled to discover his wounds. Was this the sign he had awaited all these years, the stigmata he had prayed for, finally bestowed upon him in recognition of his faith? Overwhelmed, he sat himself on his mother's bench to think. A war was raging in his mind. It was true that God had taken his mother, thus betraying him – but it was also true that God had granted this sign, shown to only a handful of people throughout history. With uncharacteristic decisiveness, Thomas resolved what he would do with God. No more would he grovel about on his knees each night, begging for one thing or another. He and God would respect each other and forgive each other. They would be friends, or they would be nothing.

Feeling a tap on his shoulder, Thomas jumped up with fright, expecting some celestial being – a messenger, the Archangel Michael, perhaps. Instead, it was the boy from the William Westward, Regus, still searching, it seemed, for his father. Without looking up, but appearing to sense Thomas's exhaustion, the boy produced half a biscuit from the pocket of his shorts. Overwhelmed, Thomas took it and put it in his mouth. It was like manna from heaven as it melted on his tongue. Without a word, Regus turned and disappeared into the msasas. Thomas called out, but the boy had gone. A sudden sense of urgency came over Thomas. There were people who needed him, children at the school, Baba Chiswa, Betty, Robson, and, God forbid, even Darryl. There was no time to waste. Slowly, Thomas made his way to the house. He was appalled at the mess he had created; he had to clean it up, restore it, just the way it would have been were his mother still alive.

Grateful that the electricity had not yet been disconnected, he scrubbed himself in a hot bath, shaved his patchy beard, trimmed his tangled locks in the mirror, and clipped his nails. Wincing with pain at each dab, he treated his sores with gentian violet. He searched his mother's pantry and found a tin of Cashel Valley peas, which he ate calmly with the decorum of a gentleman, despite his hunger. After that, he continued with the clean-up. Every fragment of broken crockery and glass was collected from around the house in a large cardboard box, and carried to the back behind the aviary. The vodka bottles and scuds were lined up next to the box. The walls of Leviticus's quarters were hosed down. The house was swept, and what remained of the furniture neatly arranged. The broken windows in his room were temporarily boarded up with sheets of cardboard and Sellotape.

Late that afternoon, Thomas began the back-breaking task of digging a large hole behind the aviary. Into it, he tossed the broken crockery, the vodka bottles, the scuds, and all the other garbage, and scooped shovelfuls of earth over it. A testing chapter now buried beneath the ground.

He was reborn, in a manner of speaking, from the rabbit hutch.

Earlier that day, Regus had made his way from the clearing, back to the William Westward. For the first time in years, his urge to run away was quelled. He had found Mister Thomas, who had been missing for so long and was thought not to be coming back. It was he who must deliver the news. Slipping into the gates of the home, his heart pounding with fear and excitement, he approached the children playing on the fields and scrambled onto a large boulder where everyone could see him. A small crowd of children soon gathered, for Regus too had been missing for some time. Even Betty and Baba Chiswa came out from the administration block to check on the commotion. Raising his head high, the lost boy uttered, to cheers of joy and celebration, those four words now immortalised in the chronicles of the William Westward's brief but colourful history.

'Mister Thomas, he alive!'

39

Comrade Teddington Chiwafambira is Awarded a Medal for his Actions

Without question, it was the proudest day of Comrade Chiwafambira's life. Bristling and itching in his brand new Armani suit, with some difficulty he fastened the top button of his Polo shirt just as the Rainbow Towers Hotel came into view. In the mirror of the passenger seat visor, he adjusted his tie, taking pains to puff out the double Windsor knot that Comrade Shuranyama had so kindly tied for him earlier that morning as they'd sipped their Johnny Walkers around the pool.

A band of curious cleaners and gardeners stopped to observe the Hummer as it came to rest outside the hotel's grandiose entrance. As Teddington opened the door and stepped down, a rumour spread among them, *'Uyo ndiReserve Bank Governor!'*

He responded with a smug smile, delighted that he might be mistaken for someone of such high standing and influence in the Party. A valet took the Hummer's keys. The two gentlemen sauntered past reception, pausing for a second to see if they might recognise anyone in the hotel's extensive foyer. Affably, Comrade Shuranyama raised his hand in greeting at a well-known local businessman drinking Coca-Colas with some Chinese traders, their communications confined to the exchange of cigarette boxes with dollar figures scrawled across them.

A notice board on an easel caught Teddington's eye. La Chandelle Restaurant – World Class French And International Cuisine, it said, and below it, in white lettering, Mashonaland East War Veterans' Association Luncheon.

Teddington pulled back his shoulders to compose himself, fiddling once again with his tie.

Down the carpeted corridors, they could hear the lively chatter of several dozen comrades. As guests of honour, the two men had purposely intended to be the last to arrive. Comrade Shuranyama opened the restaurant door, and within seconds the assembled diners fell quiet.

'*Tinokukorokotedzai Comrade David Shuranyama na Comrade Teddy-Boy Chiwafambira!* And a warm welcome to Comrade David Shuranyama and Comrade Teddy-Boy Chiwafambira!' announced a man at the door who had eagerly been awaiting their arrival.

A torrent of clapping and whistling ensued, interspersed with cheers and enthusiastic calls: '*Changamire!*' '*Pambere naHitler Jesus!*' 'Teddy-Boy!'

The two comrades raised their hands in acknowledgement before taking their seats. Starter plates of sautéed chicken livers were brought out from the kitchen, and the speeches began with a vitriolic diatribe aimed at sell-outs, Tony Blair, homosexuals, and most importantly the MDC, lapdogs of the West, agents of imperialism.

The liquor began to flow, and many found it difficult to maintain the sombre composure expected as the lengthy obituary of the late, great Comrade Sizemore Chinovhiringa was once again recounted.

Many lost their concentration, and separate conversations broke out across the restaurant, threatening to drown out the elaborate eulogy, the last third of which had to be summarised into a couple of sentences – stirring, but unheard over the din.

A sudden hush fell as the speaker left the podium; the younger veterans, those in their twenties and thirties, had come for the awards, not the farewells. The much-revered vice chairman of the association's central committee rose and made his way to the microphone.

'Comrades!' he commenced, '*Handisi kuda kukudyirai nguva yenyu* … we all know why we are here today, so I will proceed without delay. The new chairman of the Mashonaland East Branch, Zimbabwe National Liberation War Veterans' Association, is …'

Suspense mounted. Everyone had their suspicions, but you could never be sure.

'Comrade David Shuranyama!'

The room exploded in applause as every man leapt to his feet. Comrade Shuranyama was a popular choice – he had led many missions that had greatly benefited the members.

'A toast to Comrade Chairman Shuranyama!' someone cried out.

Everyone scrambled for their glasses and bottles.

'To Comrade Chairman Shuranyama!'

As the excitement died down, waiters streamed out of the kitchen, carrying plates of stuffed trout and new potatoes in a creamy lemon sauce.

The vice-chairman of the central committee tapped his glass with a butter knife, calling for silence.

'Comrades. For his role in the liberation of the Comrade Sizemore Chinovhiringa Country Club, the association wishes to honour Comrade Teddington Chiwafambira. Comrade, come forward to receive your medal!'

Teddington straightened his tie and stood up to tumultuous applause – the club had become a popular weekend entertainment venue. He made his way through the tables to the podium, where the vice-chairman shook his hand warmly. With a flash, *The Herald* photographer on hand captured and immortalised this momentous occasion for the whole nation to share. Teddington bowed his head so that the medal on its blue-and-white striped ribbon could be hung around his neck. Made of bronze, the medal was heavy, bearing a stylised figurine and some writing around the rim. From a distance, it looked quite artistic.

Overwhelmed with excitement, Teddington barely tasted his stuffed trout. In no time at all, the plates had been cleared away, and the members stood about in groups across the restaurant, drinking and making conversation.

An elderly man hobbled over to Teddington on crutches. He wore a charcoal jacket, faded and tattered, and no tie. His left trouser leg had been stitched at the knee. A sense of unease came over Teddington as he watched the man's slow approach.

Mumbling, the man asked, 'Where did you train during the Struggle?'

'What?' Teddington leaned forward, battling to hear over the din.

'Where did you train? *Wakafunda kupi semusoja? KuMozambique here?*'

'Goromonzi.' Teddington replied curtly.

'There were no camps in Goromonzi. What kind of veteran are you? What is this medal?'

Teddington looked down at the bronze medal around his neck. A puzzled frown appeared on his forehead as he read, STORK MARGARINE 5 KM FUN RUN 1996 – with a stick figure of a runner in mid-stride in the centre.

Looking up, Teddington found himself caught in the gaze of the older man, at which point, miraculously, his cellphone rang.

'A mission ... give us an hour, Comrade. Marondera, you say ... okay, give us until four o'clock. We'll be there as quick as we can. Don't let them out of the farmhouse until we get there, you hear me!'

Teddington clicked the fingers of his right hand, his forefinger pointing at the disabled veteran – like he had seen Comrade Shuranyama do, like Comrade Shuranyama had seen on the DStv action channel.

'I have to run. Another mission's come up.'

The old man nodded knowingly and turned around. Teddington watched as he hobbled away towards the door.

40

The Spirit of the Late Jimmy Moverley-Smith Lives on Inside his Hearing Aids

His skin still speckled with gentian violet, a somewhat gaunt Thomas walked through the gates of the William Westward at seven the following morning. The children abandoned their hopscotch, their hide-and-seek, and in some cases, even the remainder of their breakfast. A joyous mob came scrambling across, bowling Thomas over with a barrage of hugs. Joseph Chiswa arrived and pulled him up. With a lump in his throat, he silently squeezed Thomas's hand, holding it firmly for several seconds. Behind him stood Betty Mukadota, who enveloped Thomas in a warm embrace. Not one for the limelight, Thomas was relieved when it was time for the children to line up with their satchels for the march to school.

His snug office with his familiar little desk pleased him greatly – a quiet retreat, yet not too far from the community to which he belonged. Thomas did not hear the gentle knocking on the door.

It was Robson Shambari. He had come up from his workshop as soon as he heard that Thomas was back. A hands-on, practical kind of man, Robson was not one for emotional talk, preferring instead the Shona tradition of talking in parables to convey his condolences.

'A stone's journey down the river may be difficult, but with time, its edges will become smooth, like a pebble,' Robson ventured awkwardly.

Thomas touched his ears to indicate that he had no hearing aids. Robson picked up a pen and scribbled on a scrap of paper: Where are they? Thomas took the pen from Robson. Lost them, was his answer. Can you get new ones? Robson wrote.

Thomas shrugged and rubbed his thumb and forefingers together. Robson nodded. He again took the pen and wrote: No one ever dies completely.

He passed the paper to Thomas and quickly left the room.

Robson frowned as he trudged back to his workshop, pondering the problem of replacing Thomas's hearing aids. He knew it would take money, lots of it – and foreign currency, as well. Perhaps he could find some second-hand ones, even just as a temporary measure. He scanned the classifieds section of *The Herald*, but rather predictably there was no mention of hearing aids.

As he turned the page, he caught sight of the Births and Deaths column. A small notice caught his eye: 'MOVERLEY-SMITH, James Alexander (Jim) – passed away peacefully 20 November 2004 aged 103. Will be sorely missed by staff and residents of the Athol Evans. Farewell Jimmy.'

Taking a chance, Robson called the Athol Evans Hospital Home for the Aged. Yes, was the answer, old Jimmy had been deaf – deaf as a post, actually – and yes, he did have hearing aids, which Robson was free to take.

Robson jumped into his green Renault 5 and sped across town.

A signpost indicated the turnoff to Athol Evans. Someone had defaced it with graffiti. Home for the Wild, it now read.

Five minutes later, Robson was the owner of an ancient pair of hearing aids, large and cumbersome, but intact and apparently functioning, despite being varnished with a layer of orange ear wax. All they needed were new batteries, which he purchased from a Zhing-Zhong store downtown.

Using paint stripper, he wiped away Jimmy Moverley-Smith's stubborn ear wax and handed the hearing aids to Thomas to put to the test. Though far more conspicuous than the previous set, they did the job, definitely improving his hearing. Thomas's face lit up. Certain tones, however, seemed subject to a peculiar amplification: Thomas found his own voice sounding much deeper, more manly perhaps, as if the former owner's spirit lived on, hidden inside the plastic casings. This was disconcerting at first, but after a while, Thomas began to like it.

After lunch, a band of children dragged Thomas down to the vegetable garden that Marie and Leviticus had started. With the constant attention of the senior children, and abundant water from the school's borehole that had been restored by Robson and Baba Chiswa after twenty years of dormancy, the beds were flourishing.

The real surprise, however, was still to come. Pulling Thomas by the hand, the children rounded the back of the old tobacco barn, and there she was: a red Massey Ferguson 398 tractor – old perhaps, but functional. Self-sufficiency was the only way the home would survive, Baba Chiswa had reasoned, and any surplus produce that might be sold could cover the costs of clothing, school fees and salaries. He had thrown his entire life savings into the project. A crop of maize would soon be planted.

In just a few short weeks, Thomas's health had recovered – his sores healed, and weight regained. Using his entire salary, he replaced the broken windows in his bedroom and purchased some plastic bowls and plates, as well as a set of tin knives, forks and spoons.

Since his own bed was in ashes in the aviary, and Marie's double bed was too large to fit through the door of his bedroom, he took up residence in his mother's room, surrounded once more by the Great Ones. Although comfortable, Thomas was constantly reminded of Marie. The evenings, so quiet and lonely, were hardest for him.

There was, however, something else that bothered Thomas. His mind kept going back to it. How could he possibly have come from the sky? What was he? Angel, fallen angel, or alien? Aware of the home's policy of refusing to provide details of the former circumstances of adopted children, unless there were compelling reasons, Thomas felt reluctant to draw Baba Chiswa into the matter. Plotting and scheming in his office late one afternoon, he resolved to raid the headmaster's safe to steal his own file, which he assumed would still be there with all the others. The key, he knew, was in the top drawer of Baba Chiswa's desk.

The following afternoon, when Baba Chiswa had gone down to the barn after lunch to give Robson a hand with the tractor, and Mai Rutivi was out running errands, Thomas carried out his plan. He found what he was looking for near the top of a large pile of files. His eyes widened as he examined the cover, with its hand-written details:

Name:	*Thomas*
Surname:	----------
Place of Origin:	*Fell from the Sky?!*
Date of Arrival:	*10th June 1983*

After quietly closing the safe, Thomas returned the key and walked quickly back to his office with the file stuffed under his shirt.

As he locked his door behind him, his heart was pounding. The file was stuffed with various papers, mostly concerning the adoption process undertaken by Colonel Reginald and Marie Threscothic in late 1983, as well as a multitude of medical reports from ear, nose and throat specialists, child psychologists, occupational therapists, and radiologists.

None of it was of much interest to Thomas, who only wanted to know where he came from, and was not interested in his condition on arrival at the home. Hastily, he flipped through the medical reports until he found what he was looking for: his admission form. The details were scant. The identity of his biological parents was marked as unknown. The only information was his estimated age on arrival, recorded as three years old, and the name of the person who'd brought him in – one Hennie van Aswegen. The records stated that he had been found in the Sengwa Basin, Kariba. Intrigued, Thomas searched for a telephone directory. There was an H van Aswegen listed, with an address on the other side of town, near the Harare Showgrounds. Thomas did not even bother taking down the telephone number; with Jim Moverley-Smith's hearing aids, telephone calls were virtually impossible, and besides, what would he say to the man?

Thomas decided to visit Hennie van Aswegen in person, and resolved to set off that very minute. Looking up, however, he noticed through the window several children, large and small, streaming excitedly from the dormitories and sprinting across the playing field. At the far end of the field, Baba Chiswa, Robson, and the dormitory master, Gilbert Mashoko, were waging a valiant battle; with arms outstretched, they were trying to block the children's advance. It was obvious where the children were going. Beyond the school's boundary lay the village with its small community of subsistence farmers and their families, who all led a more or less traditional lifestyle. Conscious of his responsibilities, Thomas locked his office and ran down to help his colleagues contain the exodus. However compelling, his own plans would have to wait.

41

The Chess Player's Dilemma

Wearing tartan sports jackets, and both clean-shaven, the men faced each other with an intensity that bordered on dementia. A sudden burst of ululation echoed down the corridors of the asylum but failed to break the chess players' rigid gaze, firmly focused, as they were, on the board between them.

A minute later, Lennard Chavundukwe glanced at his watch. 'That's funny. Old Cromwell usually only makes his noises in the morning.'

Lazarus Mushonga glanced coldly at his opponent. 'Shush, Len, for goodness' sake, I'm concentrating!'

Without warning, the door sprang open. The imposing frame of Matron Matambanadzo blocked the doorway.

'Right, Chavundukwe, you can go!'

'What?'

'You heard me. Grab your things. You and that animal next door, Cromwell Shimwa, can go. The judge stays, though.'

Both men frowned and stared intently at one another. Several seconds of silence ensued.

'Chavundukwe, I haven't got all day!'

'Just another two days, Matron, please. We're in the middle of something,' the erstwhile parliamentarian pleaded.

Beatrice Matambanadzo blinked a few times as the words sank in.

'Suit yourself, Chavundukwe, stay as long as you like. But it's two hundred thousand dollars a night, and I'd prefer if you paid in US dollars, so let's make it one US dollar a night. Tell your wife to bring it next time she visits,' she said, slamming the door behind her. The muffled sound of her shouting continued down the passageway, 'And don't go telling anyone I didn't offer to let you out!'

The two men glanced at each other with eyebrows raised. This was an unexpected turn of events.

'Honestly, Len, you didn't have to stay on account of me.'

'What! And let you snatch the championship by default? Never, Lazarus. Never. Your move.'

At this crucial stage, the parliamentarian's game tally of four hundred and ninety-four had trailed the judge's by just three games. The final straights were ahead. It had been an epic journey. The parliamentarian had been the first to reach a hundred, his opponent distracted by recollections of events leading to his incarceration. Deeply competitive, however, the judge had fought back, easily gaining the lead to two hundred. From then on it was neck and neck, neither taking a lead of more than ten games at any stage. Night and day they'd played, over many months, stopping only to sleep and eat.

A ferocious banging on the door startled the opponents. The judge's knee knocked the board and both gasped in horror, though fortunately the chess pieces had largely remained in their squares.

At the door's narrow observation window, a heavily bearded face appeared, framed by a mass of hair, utterly without style and completely unkempt. The man's eyes looked wild.

Lennard sprang up and walked to the door. 'Is that you, Cromwell? My goodness, what's happened to you?'

'You coming?' the man barked, flecks of spittle visible in his unruly moustache.

'In a bit, Cromwell, in a bit, I've got a couple of things to do.'

'You old codgers are all the same, barking mad you are. And you hope one day to govern this country! It's a bloody joke. I swear if I get half –'

'All right, Cromwell, all right, that's enough,' the older man interjected.

'Suit yourself, old man, you can damn well suit yourself,' was Cromwell Shimwa's retort as he disappeared from sight, a torrent of expletives flung at each and every orderly, nurse and patient he passed along the way. A sustained volley of abuse persisted for several minutes until the wailing of a police siren could be heard, before abruptly stopping.

'Your turn, Len,' said the judge.

'Indeed it is, Laz, indeed it is.'

At 4.17 the following morning, after twenty minutes of unbroken concentration that had left a bead of sweat hanging precariously from his nose, the judge finally shifted his bishop, placing the parliamentarian's king in checkmate. The marathon series had at last been clinched. Both men sat back in silence, covering their faces with their hands as they struggled to comprehend the enormity of the series: nine hundred and ninety-eight games of chess, played all day and most of the night, for nearly nine months.

With conflicting emotions – including some measure of disdain for the victor, which it taxed his self-discipline to repress – Lennard Chavundukwe stood up from the table with a sigh, partly relief, and partly frustration and disappointment. Methodically, he folded his few items of clothing on his bed and formed them into piles which he placed carefully inside his little suitcase. Slowly, he walked across the room to collect his coat from its hook, where it hung next to that of the judge. He put it on but remained standing, his back to his companion, fighting back tears that welled up in his eyes.

'You know we'll do our best for you, Lazarus, through the lawyers and any other channels.'

'Yes, Len, I know you will.'

Lennard brushed his cheek with his palm and took a deep breath before turning round again. 'It's been a pleasure, Laz.'

The judge smiled. 'Len, the pleasure's been all mine!'

With some degree of formality the men shook hands. Lennard raised his eyes to meet Lazarus's gaze. Neither could hold their tears back as they abandoned the handshake in favour of a warm embrace, slapping each other's backs as they drew apart. Lennard composed himself for a moment before knocking on the door for the orderly, who unlocked it and waited politely outside as Lennard picked up his suitcase.

'So long, comrade.'

'So long, my brother.'

With that, the door closed, leaving Judge Lazarus Mushonga alone with his thoughts.

The former parliamentarian walked quietly down the deserted corridors of Ward G20 to the main entrance. The senior orderly, Boniface Mazingi, jumped up from behind the reception desk and straightened his thick-rimmed spectacles. The departure of Lennard Chavundukwe from the ward was a particularly sad occasion for the staff. He would be sorely missed.

'Excuse me, sir, Mister Chavundukwe. The night staff asked me to call them before you left. Would you mind, sir?'

'Not at all, Boniface, I'd be glad to have the chance to say goodbye.'

A junior orderly scampered off to the staff canteen.

'Sir, could I not try to arrange a taxi for you? Is there no one coming to collect you?'

'That is very kind of you, Boniface, but no, it's late now, and I would not want to disturb my wife. I'll walk. My home is not far from here.'

A group of nurses and orderlies lined up at the main entrance. Lennard shook hands with each one, thanking them for their kindness and consideration over the duration of his stay.

'Sir,' a young nurse said, 'you were the best patient we've ever had in here.'

Lennard chuckled, 'Miriam, in all the mental asylums in which I have been detained, *you* have been my favourite nurse!'

Longing to feel the cool breeze on his face again after so many months in the asylum, Lennard strode out towards the main gate. As he wandered through the city's dark and empty streets, he felt an exhilarating rush of freedom. At dawn, he stood patiently outside the gates of the Botanical Gardens. It had long been his practice to take a stroll there before work.

Just before six, the gatekeeper came wandering down with the keys.

'Mister Chavundukwe! Good to see you again, sir! *Makorokoto madzoka Sekuru!*'

'Shadrack. Good to see you, too!'

As the gate swung open, the former parliamentarian stepped inside, pleased to resume his old custom.

'Habit,' he muttered to himself, 'forms character – and character, destiny.'

42

Mister Onias Chikorobho's Goblins Become Too Hot to Handle

There were goblins in the village, three of them – nasty, pesky, lewd creatures with insatiable sexual appetites. Lusting for teenage girls, so it seemed. The curious children of the William Westward clambered to get a glimpse of the three *zvikwambo*. Even Thomas was curious; could these be the creatures that had peered at him from the perimeter of the aviary? he wondered.

Rumour had it that the goblins' owner, one Onias Chikorobho, had inherited them decades before from a deviant older brother who had used them as *mubobobo* – supernatural powers supposedly capable of rendering a man invisible, or otherwise allowing him to be intimate with a woman without her knowledge or approval. If Mister Chikorobho's version of events were to be believed, the goblins had since been put to good use, defending his family, striking out at his enemies. Lately, however, the three *zvikwambo* had become too hot to handle – even he could no longer control them. All had been well until one fateful night, not long ago, when the goblins had staged a mutiny and had begun acting outside their instructions. Without warning, it was whispered, they had turned on Mister Enoch Mutasa's unsuspecting teenage daughters. The nights were filled with bawdy groans and howls and wicked high-pitched goblin sniggers.

Clearly, something had to be done. In desperation, Mister Chikorobho approached the police. A diligent young ZRP constable was dispatched to the village on a bicycle, where he took detailed statements from the Mutasa family and their close neighbours, in a small black notebook. Every witness interviewed was hopeful for a swift end to the nightly menace that had not only tormented the entire village, but had fostered a wave of immorality – adolescent romances flourished, all forms of dangerous liaison thrived, older deviants lurked behind trees and bushes, ready to leap upon unsuspecting victims; whatever mischief occurred, the goblins could be blamed. It was a scourge such as had never before been seen in these parts.

The following morning the young constable returned to the village, bearing disappointing news. Such matters, his superior officers had said, fell beyond police jurisdiction. They must be handled by the headman. Though fearing rebuke, Mister Chikorobho set off for the headman's house at once. Yes, he admitted finally, he had lost control. Fortunately, the headman was a wise man of advanced years. He had seen this kind of thing before. Whether the rumpus was caused by *mubobobo*, *zvikwambo*, or residents with goblin-like motives, he could not be sure, but one thing he did know, those responsible must be purged or the blight would continue.

'Bring me a *tsikamutanda*,' he ordered, hoping that the man's special powers might detect and subdue or banish the goblins.

The headman's minion returned a few hours later with a dreadlocked man in his mid-thirties. Looking into his bloodshot eyes, the headman regarded the *tsikamutanda* with some suspicion. He did not look like a *tsikamutanda*, but who could tell these days? The headman asked some pointed questions, and narrowed his eyes while listening intently as the *tsikamutanda* responded with a flamboyant account of previous successes. His experience seemed satisfactory. When the headman gave him the details of the task at hand, the man's eyes lit up with excitement and anticipation. He slapped one palm over the other – a demonstration of decisive action to be taken. *Zvikwambo*, he said, were his speciality. He could not wait to get among them. Still not convinced, but under pressure to attend a meeting in the nearby town of Ruwa – to negotiate the price of a second-hand bar fridge in good nick – the headman decided to go ahead and engage the *tsikamutanda*'s services. What, he enquired, would it cost to drive out the goblins?

The *tsikamutanda* frowned and took a moment to think about this. Then, suddenly and dramatically, his tone changed. This was a serious matter, he said, and dangerous, very dangerous indeed. Two *zvikwambo* could be a real handful, but three were a different game entirely. They ganged up against you, he explained. Although small in stature, they could be infinitely cunning and utterly merciless. His price, therefore, would be three heifers – one for the capture of each goblin. The headman whistled in disbelief. With inflation up to 10 000%, prices really *had* escalated. Mister Chikorobho, who would have to pay the fee himself, almost collapsed. His eyes swivelled in their sockets as he felt himself sway. It would be cheaper for him to burn his house down and move back to his *kumusha*, leaving the goblins behind. In any event, he did not own so many heifers.

Sensing that he had pushed it a little too far, the *tsikamutanda* scratched his chin with the air of a man doing his level best to help under very challenging circumstances. Sighing, he reduced his asking price to two heifers. Mister Chikorobho winced with pain, stammering that he only had one. The *tsikamutanda*'s eyes glinted for a second as he formulated his final offer: he would accept one heifer and one goat, but this was as low as he could go. With a heavy heart, Mister Chikorobho shook the *tsikamutanda*'s hand – a deal had been struck.

The headman rushed off for his meeting, and Mister Chikorobho led the way back to his house with downcast eyes, followed by the headman's assistant and the beaming *tsikamutanda*, who held a carved teak drum under one arm. With his other hand he carried a plastic packet filled with bark, roots, leaves and herbs – along with an assortment of women's underwear.

As the solemn procession passed through the village, word spread like wildfire. The *tsikamutanda* was here at last. People from all around dropped their hoes to catch sight of the action. Someone ran up to the William Westward to pass on the message, igniting a frenzy of excitement among the children, almost all of whom were Christians; as orphans, they had received little exposure to traditional culture, and so creatures of this ilk piqued their curiosity without arousing fear. Down in the village it was a different thing entirely, though. All knew to beware: '*Uchenjerere zvinokuruma!*'

By the time Thomas arrived outside Mister Chikorobho's house, a large and very nervous crowd had gathered. The *tsikamutanda* had warmed his drum near an open fire, making the cowhide taut and its tone crisp, all the better for drawing out the goblins. On his instruction, Missus Chikorobho lit a new fire on the open hearth in the kitchen, and then fled the house. The crowd watched silently as smoke poured from the chimney of the two-roomed brick dwelling with its thatched roof.

Flicking back his dreadlocks, the *tsikamutanda* gathered up his drum and plastic packet and entered the house. The crowd fell silent as the sound of his ritual drumming and singing became louder. As different shades of smoke poured from the chimney, everyone surmised that he had been adding the appropriate concoctions of herbs and leaves to the fire.

Suddenly, there was a howl and the clattering of cooking pots and pans. The crowd gasped in horror. The door of the house burst

203

open, and out came the *tsikamutanda*, his trousers and dreadlocks ablaze. Panic spread through the crowd, and some trampled willy-nilly through Missus Chikorobho's maize and pumpkin fields in a frantic stampede. Hollering and shrieking, and wildly slapping his flaming head, the *tsikamutanda* dived head-first into the sandy soil of the cabbage patch. As if possessed by the devil himself, he rolled around in the soil until the flames were extinguished.

Mister Chikorobho gingerly approached him and doused him with a bucket of cold water before running back to the safety of the crowd. Drenched with water and covered in soil, his dreads some-what tamed, the *tsikamutanda* sat up in the cabbage patch.

The crowd again fell silent, waiting and watching – the atmos-phere tense. Had the vulgar trio of imps been banished? All eyes were on the *tsikamutanda*. Sensing his credibility was at stake, not to mention his exorbitant fee, he raised his arms slowly above his head. In his hand was a small leather pouch where the roguish fiends were presumed to be imprisoned. Gaining confidence, he shook it like a victorious *Makepekepe* midfielder holding the PSL Cup up to a packed Rufaro stadium. Spontaneous singing and dancing broke out in praise of the valiant *tsikamutanda*. He stood up before them, and for a moment it seemed he might even take a bow like a famous Italian tenor – until the crowd realised that the real casualty of the afternoon had been his trousers, which fell to his ankles, ex-posing his surprisingly diminutive manhood.

Instantly, he became an object of ridicule, until Missus Chikorobho provided him with a cloth to wrap around his waist like a woman – embarrassing for some, perhaps, but all the *tsikamutanda* cared about at that stage was his fee. Pushing his way across to Mister Chikorobho, he demanded his dues for a difficult job, well-executed. As he departed the village, leading his newly acquired livestock, he strutted past Joseph Chiswa and Thomas. Then it dawned upon Thomas: he had met this man before.

'Cuthbert! Cuthbert Kambazuma! Is that you?'

The man glanced across at them and winked.

Spellbound, Thomas stepped forward and shook the *tsikamutanda*'s hand. 'Well done, good work!' he said.

'Trust me,' Cuthbert laughed, 'when I say it was absolutely nothing!'

43

The Boy who
Fell from the Sky

Thomas had seldom seen the children more excitable, as they made their way back to the William Westward. It was as if they had spilt out of a Bruce Lee film. Dramatic impersonations of the flaming *tsikamutanda*, hot on the heels of bands of juniors, dominated the rest of the afternoon – 'cops and robbers' abandoned in favour of '*tsikamutanda* and *zvikwambo*'.

Back in his office, the file in his drawer reminded Thomas of his task. It was only three o'clock, he still had time to take a drive out to Mister H van Aswegen. Making an excuse about having to check his savings account balance, Thomas set off.

There was a huge chain and padlock on Mister van Aswegen's gate; the lower part was covered with fencing wire dripping with strings of canine slobber from the pack of Alsatians, Boerboels and Ridgebacks that snarled and barked from behind it. A heavy-set figure appeared, wearing veldskoens and a light-blue safari suit, a forest of grey chest hairs at the V of his neckline. He'd clearly just arrived home, as he was holding an old elephant skin briefcase. Despite his oversized seventies-style sunglasses, he raised a hand to shield his eyes as he looked down the driveway. With one leg out the car, Thomas stood up and waved. The man sauntered over to the gate and unlocked it with an indifferent expression.

Thomas drove the Datsun inside. The dogs leapt up as he opened the door and the man's gruff voice sounded out, telling them to get down.

'Mister van Aswegen?' Thomas asked.

'Ja?'

'My name is Thomas. I have a file here … It says here that you dropped me off at the William Westward Home twenty years ago.'

The man's eye's narrowed, and for a second he seemed a bit unsteady.

'Er, ja. Okay, man. Listen, er, why don't you come in for a drink?'

Thomas followed him along a path of concrete squares that ran across the lawn to the front door. Although well maintained, the garden was by no means ornate, just neat and tidy, with the leaves swept up and the lawn recently mown. Inside, the walls were decorated with hunting trophies, like a taxidermist's reception room – buffalo, sable, roan, kudu, nyala, eland, and even a white rhino – all somewhat dusty and cobwebbed, and all testament, Thomas would learn, to his host's illustrious career as a professional hunter. Right at the end of the living room, mounted above Mister van Aswegen's bar, was the head of an enormous elephant, its tusks raised defiantly.

'What can I get you, er, Thomas, isn't it? My name's Hennie, by the way.'

The thought of alcohol made Thomas feel ill. 'Do you have Mazoe?' he asked.

Hennie nodded, fumbling with the ice tray, which slipped from his grip and fell to the floor with a crash.

Thomas bent over to gather up the ice cubes before they melted, but Hennie stopped him.

'Don't worry, Fibian will sort it out. He's back on at five.'

He slid open the glass doors and ushered Thomas towards some garden chairs on the verandah. Hennie looked nervous; it was clear he seldom entertained. 'So,' he said, 'still got the red hair, I see.'

Thomas nodded.

'And they fixed your ears up, eh?'

'Yes … I've got hearing aids, though,' he said, as if Hennie had not noticed. 'But I can hear okay.'

Hennie took a long sip of his lager. 'I'll never forget that day. You were standing there at the edge of the lake, naked, just in your birthday suit, red hair down to your shoulders. You hardly came up to my knee – and you didn't say a word, nothing! I couldn't bloody believe it. Like *The Jungle Book* or something.'

'Where was that?'

'Up at Lake Kariba. At Sengwe. You see, we were hunting. We were taking a Spaniard oke on an elephant shoot.'

'What was I doing there?'

Hennie shook his head, 'I dunno man, I dunno what you were doing. I guess they found you, and they kept you. Well, that's what they told me anyway.'

'Who?'

'The Batonga. There was a village there near the shore. We went to speak to them. My tracker translated. They said they found you in a wicker basket. They gave it to me. Still got it, actually.'

Hennie jumped up and went through to the house. He appeared a few seconds later carrying a dusty baby basket, painted white, with a small dirty-looking pillow inside.

'Here it is.'

Thomas took the basket and inspected it closely. He turned it over and found a faded gold sticker that read Barbours, the name of

Harare's largest department store.

'What was I doing in the basket?'

'Floating on the lake, so they said, with some serious injuries. They told us that they'd found you, a little newborn baby, on Independence Day, the 18th of April 1980, the very day when Rhodesia became Zimbabwe. It seemed as if they thought you might have been part of the settlement – a peace offering from the British,' he laughed. 'They'd obviously grown quite attached to you, said you brought them good luck. Whatever it was, they didn't want me to take you.'

'Then why *did* you take me?'

'Dunno really, I thought maybe you had some relatives. Maybe the doctors could do something with your hearing. Anyways, I couldn't just leave you with a tribe of two-toed Batonga fishermen, could I?'

Thomas did not answer. For a second, he wished he had never been found. He took out his file, and pointing at the cover, he said, 'Says here I fell from the sky.'

Hennie took another sip of his lager. 'I wrote that,' he said. 'I wrote that because it's probably true, you did fall from the sky.'

'How can it be true?' Thomas frowned.

'The Batonga told us they heard the sound of an aircraft and an explosion. Maybe the plane was shot down – there were still a lot of guys out there with rockets and stuff, back then. They ran to see, and all they found was you in the basket, and a bent propeller which they brought out to show me. I asked the authorities, but they had no records that day of a plane anywhere near – whoever was in it was getting away quickly. The war was over that day, there were fears of reprisals, many people left. Who knows what the story was.'

There was a pause as Thomas contemplated Hennie's account. He had no preconceived ideas or hopes, so was not disappointed. Perhaps he was even slightly relieved, the riddle of his otherworldly beginnings solved. His true origin would remain a mystery, but it no longer mattered to him. His birth coincided with the birth of the new country – its first arrival perhaps, its first new citizen, spared the prejudices of the preceding generation. There was no direction home for him; there was only his own path forward.

Hennie got up and opened himself another Bollinger. Checking to see whether Thomas was watching, he quickly poured himself a capful of whiskey, which he tossed down his throat with a well-practised jerk. He was not usually one for conversation, though if truth be known, now that the difficult part of the conversation was over, he was glad for the company.

Hennie had been married once, but it did not last, and he had never had any children of his own. That week, when he had taken care of the small, ginger-haired boy who could neither speak nor hear, was the closest he had ever come to fatherhood. He still remembered stopping off at the OK Bazaars in Kadoma to buy the boy a pair of blue shorts, some underwear, a couple of khaki T-shirts, and a pair of veldskoens. Each time he turned his back the boy would strip off his clothes and wander outside, his eyes following the Bulbuls and Barbets in the thorn trees around their motel rondavel. Hennie had reluctantly dropped him off at the orphanage, wishing he could keep him for a bit longer, maybe even for ever – but it wouldn't have been right.

Returning to the verandah with his Bollinger and another glass of Mazoe for Thomas, Hennie was curious to know what had happened since he had left Thomas at the William Westward on the 10th of June, 1983. He listened intently, sipping at his lager. There was an awkward silence following Thomas's mention of his mother's passing.

'So, you've got no one now? No relatives, I mean,' said Hennie.

'No, I suppose not.'

'Like me, eh.'

'But I've got some friends among the staff. And we've got some new projects. So I keep busy.'

210

'I was going to ask … how are you okes weathering the storm there?'

'What storm?' Thomas asked.

'You know, the cock-up with the economy. It can't be easy.'

'Oh, that. We're really struggling. We've decided to grow all our own food now, so we've got a tractor, and now we just need a pump.'

'A pump,' Hennie said, his eyes lighting up. 'I've got a pump for you. It's a hydro-ram. Works on its own. Doesn't need fuel or electricity – perfect for this bloody country! I bought it for a cottage I had at Nyanga, but I ran out of bucks and had to sell the place before I installed it, so it's like brand new, even though it's twenty years old.'

'How does it work without fuel or electricity?'

'Dunno, really. I think it uses water pressure to push the water out.'

'Are you sure you don't want it?'

'I've got no use for it, and if it can help you okes, you should take it. It's hard times for everyone. We'll put it in the car when you go.'

'Thanks a lot, Mister van Aswegen.'

'Hennie, please. You make me feel like an old toppie otherwise.'

'Okay. Thanks, Hennie.' Thomas hated calling older people by their first names – it seemed disrespectful and overly familiar.

Leaving the glasses on the verandah, Hennie and Thomas walked through the lounge, past stuffed animal heads and mounted tiger fish.

'Do you still hunt?' Thomas asked.

Hennie stopped and turned around.

'No,' he said, 'I haven't shot an animal since that elephant over there.' He pointed at the head mounted over the bar. 'Funnily enough, it was the day after I took you to that place, way back in '83.'

'Why did you stop?'

Staring at the elephant, Hennie said, 'Don't know, really. When that one went down, we went over to look at it. It was the finest

211

animal I ever saw, and I didn't feel like shooting another one. I'd rather see them alive.' He glanced across at Thomas. 'Let me get that pump for you.'

'What did you do when you stopped hunting?'

'I bought Luna Park. You know the roller coaster and stuff at the Show Grounds?'

'Sure, I know. Everyone did.'

'Ran it for fifteen years. It was quite a hoot at the time, you know, with all the kids and stuff.'

Briefly, they smiled at each other.

Thomas waited by the Datsun as the older man rummaged in his garage. With a loud grunt, Hennie lifted a metal cylinder; struggling to maintain his balance, he stumbled across to the Datsun. He carefully placed the pump in the boot and fetched an assortment of rings and seals from the garage, which he positioned next to the pump.

'Don't try to lift this thing on your own, boykie,' he warned.

Just as Thomas was about to get in the car, Hennie called out, 'Stop! Stop! I've got something else for you.' He quickly walked back to the garage and came out with a battered generator in his hands. Before Thomas could protest, he had opened the boot and wedged it in next to the pump.

'Those Kawasakis go for ever, man. With ZESA all buggered up these days, you'll need it. Take it, I've got another one for myself.'

They shook hands. Hennie's grip was firm.

'It was good to see you, Thomas. Please come again, whenever you have a chance.'

Thomas smiled and then reversed the Datsun down the drive and onto the street. With a quick wave out the window, he set off. Hennie had walked out onto the tarmac behind him, and in his rear-view mirror Thomas watched him, his hand raised in the air, becoming smaller and smaller.

44

An Unused No 5 Y Blake's Hydro Ram

Excited about the hydro ram pump and the generator, Thomas drove to work early the following morning to show them to Baba Chiswa and Robson. He found the two men in solemn conversation in the headmaster's office. Baba Chiswa was at his desk, holding up a letter. With a sigh, he handed it to Robson. Rising from his chair, he walked across to the window to clear his head.

'You know what that means, don't you, Robson?'

Robson nodded his head sombrely.

'What is it?' Thomas asked.

'It's a letter from the Ministry of Education, saying that school fees will triple next term. What are we supposed to do?'

There was a silence as all three contemplated the William Westward's unfortunate fate. Half the children would no longer be able to attend school; this was exactly what the headmaster had feared for so long.

'Well, maybe we can produce enough crops to cover the school fees,' Thomas suggested. 'I was given a pump yesterday … maybe that will also help.'

'A pump?' said the headmaster. 'What kind of pump?'

'A pump that does not use fuel or electricity. It functions purely on water pressure. It's called a hydro ram. Come and have a look.'

They all walked over to the Datsun, glad of the distraction. Thomas opened the trunk.

'Well, what do you think?' he asked enthusiastically.

Joseph Chiswa shook his head. 'It's a good pump, but they only work in mountainous areas, like Nyanga. It's too flat around here to build up the necessary water pressure.'

'Bet you could sell it for a heap, though,' Robson suggested. 'A hundred bricks, maybe.'

'And what's that there?' Joseph Chiswa said, pointing at the Kawasaki generator.

'Oh, that. It's a generator … the same guy also gave that to me. I thought we could put it in the workshop in case we need it one day.'

The headmaster looked suspicious. 'And who is this guy that gave you all these valuable things?'

'Oh, no one really, just an old friend of the family,' Thomas hastened to respond.

That afternoon, Robson and Thomas drove through to the city's industrial sites, to a place that sold pumps, both new and reconditioned. An enthusiastic young man by the name of Bobby Terrence came out to look at the hydro ram.

'Holy shit! A Number 5 Y Blakes Hydro Ram! Jeepers!' he exclaimed. 'Do you have any idea how valuable these things are?'

Thomas and Robson shook their heads. Excitement was building. They were definitely onto a good thing here.

'Guys, these things are like hens' teeth, they're so rare. And it's unused, you say?'

'Totally unused,' Thomas confirmed.

'I actually can't believe this! These things go for five hundred years without needing repairs, just pumping away, day and night.'

Robson took this as his cue. 'Okay, then, how much are you prepared to offer for it?'

'Who, me?' Bobby seemed surprised. 'No ways, man, you're asking the wrong guy. A pump like this is for guy with a weekend cottage in the mountains. These days, no one's got money for that, not in this place!'

'So you don't think we can sell it?'

'No, man. Definitely not here.'

'Well, where then?' asked Thomas.

'Maybe down in SA. The guys there will throw long tom at you for this thing!'

'How does one get it down there?'

Bobby stuck his thumb in his mouth and pulled it out slowly with a sucking noise.

'Guys!' said Bobby with a grin. 'I tell you what. Lemme phone this oke I know in Jo'burg. I'll ask him what he thinks.'

They followed Bobby into the workshop. He sat down at an old steel desk. Gesturing to Thomas and Robson to take a seat on the plastic chairs opposite him, he managed to get through to his Johannesburg pump connection.

'Holy shit, Charl, ninety-eight thousand rand for a new 5Y, you say! And an old one that's unused – how much you reckon for that? … forty-thousand! Holy moly! Jeepers creepers! … And where's the best place to take it in Jo'burg? … Stewarts & Lloyds in Booysens. Okay, man, you're a star. Thanks, man, thanks, hey!'

Bobby pulled a grubby school exercise book from his desk and tore out a page to write the address and telephone number of Stewarts & Lloyds in Booysens, just outside Johannesburg. He handed the sheet to Thomas and Robson and saw them out, giving them a double thumbs-up as they drove off.

Back at the William Westward, Robson phoned the number in Booysens. A manager told him that there was generally a good re-sale market for such pumps, but that he would have to see it before he could make any offers or referrals. It was a lot of money, forty-thousand rand – enough to cover the increase in all the school fees. It was clear that someone had to drive down to Johannesburg with the pump and sell it. Seeking distraction from the monotony of his evenings alone at home, and as the only holder of a valid passport, Thomas stepped up to the plate. Baba Chiswa was hesitant at first, but on reflection reminded himself that Thomas was no longer a child. 'If he wants to go, he must go. He's an adult now,' he told his wife that evening.

With his motel booking, petrol and visa finally secured, Darryl took Thomas to a currency dealer to buy some rand on the par-allel market; forty-three million Zim dollars, the man wanted, for just one thousand rand – practically every cent Thomas owned. The mathematics baffled him, the risks seemed high, but the pump must be sold to raise school fees, he reminded himself, reluctantly handing over a shopping packet full of bricks.

45

MUTENGESI!

Tony Willoughby's pickup, its bumper dented from one of Teddington's recent moonlight joy rides gone wrong, snaked its way through the dusty potholed streets of Hatcliffe township. It being a Saturday, the pedestrians going about their weekend business made it difficult for Teddington to gather any speed. His rotund sadza-belly pressed impatiently up against the steering wheel.

It was an embarrassment, he muttered to himself, a man of his standing with a vehicle like this. He needed a twin cab, an Isuzu, and it wasn't as if he hadn't tried to do something about this. Over a month ago, he had filled in forms for an agricultural 'soft' loan from the Reserve Bank, meaning he would get the Isuzu for free to help him with the farming. Their first response had been prompt, with someone calling to ask what colour vehicle he wanted. Silver, he had said, with tinted windows. They phoned again a few days later to clarify the delivery address, but since then, nothing. Comrade Shuranyama had mentioned that the Reserve Bank was up to crap these days, and Teddington had to agree. Couldn't get their act together any more. All one could do was wait, but it was a damned nuisance, and he had phoned regularly to tell them about it, too.

As Teddington turned the corner of the lane where his one-roomed dwelling was located, a frown darkened his face. 'Jesus, what now!' he muttered.

A large mound of earth, taller than a man, had been dug up from the dirt road directly in front of his house. A small crowd stood around, passing buckets down into the hole.

Teddington brought the pickup to a halt and wound down the window. 'What's all this about? This is private property!'

No one responded. No one even looked in his direction, save for a small boy in dusty rags who shot him a few nervous glances before running off. From within the hole, a tin bucket was passed upwards, muddy water sloshing over the rim as an elderly man took it and walked away down the lane, struggling with its weight.

Teddington jumped out. Who were these people to ignore him? 'What is this then? *Chiyi ichocho*? A burst pipe?'

The silence continued as, one by one, the people steadily passed their buckets down to a man inside the hole who was covered in red mud, wearing only a pair of shorts.

'Come on, man! That's my house there. This is private property. If there's a burst pipe, call the municipality!'

Breaking the silence, his brother's neighbour stepped forward from the crowd. Teddington could see by her expression that she was not happy. 'A burst pipe would be a pleasure. This is a well. There's been no water in the taps for three weeks, so we had to dig it. But what do you and your comrades care? War veterans! Ha!'

Teddington squirmed uncomfortably. 'Just remember, that's my house!' he warned before turning to set off to his brother's place up the road.

The door was open to let the breeze run though. In the back yard, he could hear his nieces and nephews playing. He walked in without knocking. His father stood up from a wooden chair.

'What are you doing here, Teddington?'

'Baba, good to see you! *Mandifungawo nhasi baba!*'

'You're not welcome here. We saw you in the paper. Go back to your war veterans and your ZANU pals. *'Enda hako handisi kuda kukuona!'*

'What's the matter? I thought you'd be proud. This is a revolution. You don't understand.'

'I do understand, Teddington!'

'No, you don't. We must be vigilant – the British want to take this country back. If you're not with us, *uri kushandiswa!'*

'I'm your father, Teddington, not a puppet.'

An uncomfortable silence ensued.

'Look around you, Teddington. Do you see you brother Tafara?'

'I was going to ask, where is he?'

'Taken. He's been missing for a week,' was the solemn reply.

'Taken by whom?'

'By your mob, the Green Bombers, ZANU youth.'

'I'm not with the Green Bombers, that's for the youngsters.'

'It's all the same to me.'

'But it's not! *Handisi!* Our structures are different.'

Teddington's father sat down and looked away. He didn't even bother to respond. The conversation was over, and Teddington knew it. Indignant, he strode back to his house. Fortunately, the crowd of water-bearers had dispersed; he had little patience today. With some difficulty, Teddington managed to climb over the mound of soil. He was out of shape, not used to physical exercise these days. A shock awaited him as his room came into view. All the windows had been smashed, and the outside walls were charred. A petrol bomb – Teddington recognised it instantly. He had seen them used in the high-density neighbourhoods outside Marondera to frighten

219

opposition activists, teachers, doctors, nurses and other such troublemakers. Some of his comrades favoured them; they were, no doubt, effective. Whoever had thrown this one, though, was a total novice: they had missed the window entirely and succeeded only in burning the outside walls.

'Idiots,' Teddington muttered as he pushed open the door. His belongings were strewn across the floor. The bed had been taken, probably for firewood, and his wooden cupboard had been smashed to pieces with axes and the kicks of angry boots. Right across the wall, freshly painted in red, was the word MUTENGESI! glistening accusingly.

Teddington was horrified. They – his family and his neighbours – had branded him a traitor. He rushed back to the pickup and sped away, articulating his defence, regurgitating revolutionary slogans, all to himself. But the words in his head were a jumble, his arguments did not make their usual sense. He found himself adrift in an ocean of ghastly realisations.

By the time he reached the outskirts of Harare, he had pulled himself together. If they did not appreciate the work he did, and his important position, that was their problem, he told himself. There were others, he reminded himself, who did appreciate him. It took no more than a few quick calls to arrange a gathering at the Comrade Sizemore Chinovhiringa Country Club. In the cubbyhole, he had several bricks for the booze – soon, thankfully, all this would be forgotten. Racing to get to the club, an old saying of his father's came to mind: The path of least resistance makes a man, like a river, crooked. Try as he might, Teddington could not silence the voices in his head.

46

A Brigade of Earthly Angels in Flowing White Robes

Nothing could have prepared Thomas for the wholesale swindling going on at the border post. As he turned off the ignition in the car park on the Zimbabwean side, a man in a blue short-sleeved shirt and navy shorts came over to the car with a clipboard, demanding that Thomas open the boot. An official, it seemed.

'What's this?' he said sharply, pointing at the pump.

'It's an old pump. I'm hoping to get some spares for it down in South Africa.'

'No, no, no. That's exportation. This pump doesn't look used, it's just dirty. There's a duty of fifty million on that. You can pay me right now if you wish to proceed.'

'What? Fifty million!' exclaimed Thomas 'I don't have that much money.'

'How much do you have?'

'Maybe ten million.'

'And rands? Surely you have rands if you are going to South Africa?'

'I've got some rands, but I need it for my trip or I can't go,' pleaded Thomas.

'Okay, ten million dollars and two hundred rand, and you can go on.'

Crestfallen, Thomas handed over the money. The official put the notes under the clipboard. On a grubby sheet of A4 paper he wrote: Received Z$10 million and R200 – Duty on Pump. Signing it with a nondescript squiggle, he handed it to Thomas before taking off at a brisk pace.

Inside the Immigration building, Thomas produced the sheet of A4 paper to confirm that he had already paid duty on the pump. The immigration official screwed up her face. 'What's this?' she said.

'I already paid one of your guys in the car park for the duty on the pump I'm taking with me to South Africa.'

She scowled at him, shaking her head. 'There are no immigration officials in the car park.' Outside, she took a glance at the Blake's Hydro Ram and then flicked through her schedule of duties. 'That will be five thousand rand,' she said nonchalantly.

Thomas's spirits slumped; the children's opportunity of continued schooling was rapidly disappearing. 'I don't have anything near five thousand rand,' he said.

'Okay … I'll do you a special favour. Pay me three hundred rand right now, and I'll let you go.'

Thomas had no choice but to pay the money and hope that the pump could be sold, so that some of the proceeds could be used to buy petrol on his return. The official looked around before stuffing the notes deep into her bra. She gave him no receipt, only a gate pass, and then strutted off back to the Customs building.

Daunted at the prospect of losing his way in the notoriously large city of Johannesburg, Thomas set off at four the following morning from the motel where he had stayed overnight.

He made it through to the Booysens branch of Stewarts & Lloyds by ten-thirty, marvelling at the vast concrete skyline of Johannesburg's city centre. He told the receptionist that he had come to see a Mister Charl Meyer about a pump. Mister Meyer came through – a small quiet man in his mid-fifties, with a neatly trimmed grey moustache. He took a look at the pump and confirmed it was likely Thomas might find a buyer.

'Don't you want to buy it?' Thomas asked anxiously.

'No, that's not our business. We sell new machines and spare parts. We don't deal in second-hand equipment.'

'But it hasn't been used, it's not really second hand,' pleaded Thomas, searching for a loophole.

'Well, it would be difficult to convince someone it's new, I mean, just look at it!'

Tears welled up in Thomas's eyes. 'Please, sir, you have to help me. If I don't sell this pump, I can't even get back home to Zimbabwe. I'm desperate, sir, really.'

He told Charl Meyer about the problem with the school fees, and how they were trying to keep the William Westward afloat by growing their own food. Mister Meyer was stuck between a rock and hard place. He really wanted to help. Everyone knew how bad things were in Zimbabwe, it was always on the TV, but if he bought the pump, the payment would have to come out of his own pocket. The company would not pay for it.

'Okay, I'll help you,' he finally said with a sigh. 'I'll give you two thousand rand for it. Honestly, that's the best I can do.'

Thomas tried haggling, but Charl Meyer shook his head; this was a favour, he reminded Thomas. It was a far cry from the forty thousand rand they had been hoping for, but at least he would be able to get home.

'Thank you, sir,' Thomas said quietly as he put the money in his wallet. He listened carefully to the directions to the N1, but to no avail – five minutes later he was hopelessly lost. In the distance, he could see the sun glinting off the tin roofs of thousands of informal dwellings. To make matters worse, the Datsun's engine began to overheat. The arrow of the temperature gauge had entered the red, and soon afterwards the engine cut out. Thomas pulled the car off the road, where it rolled to a halt with a hiss beneath a large tree. He jumped out and opened the bonnet. Clouds of dark smoke poured out, covering his face in a layer of soot. He recoiled, spluttering and coughing. With his eyes smarting, he did not see a dark-blue VW Golf screech to a standstill next to the Datsun. Two men leapt out. Ruffians. Each with a pistol. They shouted at him in a language he did not know, and one struck him on the side of the head with his gun. Thomas fell down onto the gravel. While the man rifled through Thomas's pockets and extracted his wallet, his accomplice opened the boot, removing Thomas's suitcase.

'Get up!' they shouted. 'Take off your clothes!'

Uncertain as to whether or not he had heard correctly, Thomas did not react immediately. His assailant fired a shot between Thomas's feet, spattering gravel onto his shins. Thomas hastily stripped off his shirt and trousers and handed them over, along with his plastic Bata flip-flops.

With a squeal of tyres the men tore off, leaving Thomas cowering, naked but for his underpants. Before he had a moment to think, another vehicle drew up.

'Please, God, help me, please,' he repeated to himself as he hid behind the tree.

'Don't be afraid,' came the sound of a reassuring voice, 'we are here to help you.'

Thomas poked his head around the tree. A brigade of earthly angels – it seemed to him – wearing flowing white robes, were alighting from the back of an antiquated pickup. Each carried a shepherd's staff. Some wore head pieces of animal fur, and beaded anklets. Thomas was shocked. Never before had his prayers been answered so promptly.

They were Shembes, so they said – followers of Isaiah Shembe, who, almost a hundred years prior, had formed a church fusing Christianity with elements of Zulu tribalism. Saturday was their Sabbath, they told him, a day spent out in the open, worshipping God and celebrating miracles. They had seen Thomas's assailants make off, and had stopped to help.

A tall, well-built man offered Thomas his hand, introducing himself as Njabulo Mkhize. Turning to his brethren, he called out in Zulu, and a young man came forward with a white robe and staff.

'You can wear this,' Njabulo Mkhize offered, adding playfully, 'if you look like one of us you'll be safe from those tsotsis!'

Thomas pulled the robe over his shoulders. His sooty countenance appeared an almost comical attempt to blend in as they helped him up onto the back of the pickup. The Datsun was secured with a strong chain to the rear of the pickup, and one of the men sat in the driver's seat to steer the car. The group burst into song as they set off, crouching in the pickup's open back.

Heavily laden, and with the Datsun in tow, the pickup slowly made its way to an informal settlement – Lawley, it was called, home to these Shembe men. A dusty hamlet on the fringes of Johannesburg's seemingly endless urban sprawl, it was a poor community of many different languages and cultures, where pit latrines sufficed for toilets, and corrugated iron shacks were the norm. The mood on the pickup was jovial as it snaked its way around the muddy potholes of Lawley's untarred roads. It was not long before the vehicle stopped and the men offered a hand to Thomas as he climbed off.

Njabulo Mkhize's wife came out to greet them. Told of Thomas's misfortunes, she invited him in immediately. Inside, the corrugated iron walls were decorated with sheets of canned food labels showing pictures of pilchards and corned beef. The Mkhize's son was sent to the local spaza to buy a soft drink and some biscuits for Thomas, as well as a block of ice, to be wrapped in a cloth and pressed gently against the lump on Thomas's head. Water was warmed over a paraffin stove and poured into a bucket, which was handed to Thomas together with a cloth and some soap, so that he could wash.

In the meantime, Mister Mkhize and a couple of the men replaced their white robes with overalls and lifted the bonnet of the Datsun. Despite overheating, its engine had not seized, and with some repairs to the radiator, it seemed Thomas might be on his way the following morning. Word rippled through the Shembe community, and enough funds were raised for fuel to get Thomas back to Harare.

That evening, Thomas and the Mkhize family enjoyed a meal together, mutton stew with pap, which, despite his reservations about red meat, Thomas ate with visible relish, not only to convey his gratitude, but also to satisfy his hunger. He told his hosts about the problems faced by the William Westward. He also told them about his mother's passing, and his desperate days in the rabbit hutch. Finally, he showed them the scars on his palms. Mister Mkhize took his hands to study them more closely. He nodded slowly. He was familiar with such things, he said. After dinner, Missus Mkhize laid some cushions on the floor and gave Thomas a blanket. Exhausted, he fell asleep immediately.

They woke him up at four o'clock the next morning. With no clothes to wear other than the Shembe robe they had lent him, Thomas hovered around, embarrassed. Mister Mkhize read the situation quickly and placed his big workman's hand on Thomas's shoulder.

'You can take it with you. And the staff too,' he said. 'You will remember us each time you see it.'

Just as Thomas was about to reverse his car, Mister Mkhize thrust a small jar of Vaseline petroleum jelly into his hands. 'Take this too, it has been blessed. Rub some of it on yourself. We use it for protection.'

Thomas immediately dabbed some onto his arms, and smeared it onto his skin. He followed Mister Mkhize's pickup through the narrow lanes of Lawley, back to the highway, where he paused in the dim morning light to raise his hand in gratitude. The roads were quiet, and by dawn he had passed through the city and was on the open road home, without once looking back.

If Joseph and Vera Chiswa were surprised at Thomas's Old Testament attire when he arrived at their doorstep late that night, they were even more surprised at the calm manner with which he recounted the unfortunate details of his trip. While his voice carried a hint of bitterness over the loss of funds that would otherwise have been used for school fees, Thomas did not appear overly troubled by the violence with which he had been relieved of the money. A change, clearly, had come over him.

'One month,' Thomas said, as Joseph walked him out to the Datsun to say good night.

'What for?'

'To help you find the school fees,' Thomas replied.

He no longer wished to be a passenger in his own life, unsure of his destination. He wished to be a person of consequence in his community, like Baba Chiswa, like Njabulo Mkhize. Someone people could rely on. Joseph Chiswa smiled at his young friend's determination.

47

A Frosted Emperor
Pays the School Fees

With only a week until Christmas, the William Westward was abuzz with excitement. In no small measure, this was due to Betty Mukadota's vision of turning the msasa, encased in its jungle-like delicious monster at the front of the administration block, into a giant Christmas tree.

A Christmas-decoration competition was announced, with wonderful prizes from the Eastlea Dairy Den, sponsored by Baba Chiswa. There were three prizes in the junior category and three in the senior category. If you won first prize in your category you could choose any ice cream on the Dairy Den blackboard, including, most importantly, the Bee Sting, a mouth-watering combination of chocolate flakes, honeycomb, crunchie, and vanilla ice cream – depending, of course, on the availability of ingredients. If you came second, you were eligible for the milkshake; chocolate, cream soda or strawberry.

If you came third, you could savour a waffle with a scoop of ice cream. Joint entries were permitted, but these were limited to two to a team. As there were no funds for materials other than wire, wood glue and string, the rules of the competition required that all decorations be made from objects found by the children, either in the surrounding woodlands and fields, or in the yard behind the Spar supermarket in Msasa, where the manager had kindly agreed to allow the children to rummage around for an hour each morning for offcuts of tinfoil, cardboard and cans.

The children took to the competition instantly; the prizes were irresistible. The older boys poured into Robson's workshop by the dozen, and jostled for the use of his wire cutters and pliers in the creation of an array of angels and reindeers. The older girls focused their attention on crafting strings of tinsel and ornate lanterns holding off-cuts of candles to light up the tree, while the younger children, armed with scissors, set upon a pile of old Christmas cards and magazines sourced by Vera Chiswa, using wood glue to create bright collages and Christmas-themed shapes.

In accordance with the competition rules, before lunch two days before Christmas, the children deposited their decorations on the tables in the prep room below Paget dormitory, each item being identified by a paper name tag. The judging panel – Joseph, Robson, Betty and Thomas – took their clipboards and gave each decoration a mark out of ten. The process was difficult; many entries were truly exceptional, forcing the panel to reconvene in the headmaster's office to tally the scores and decide on the winners.

At one-thirty, the doors of the dining room burst open and the children gathered excitedly at the rear of the prep room, where they waited in line. When silence fell, Betty Mukadota stepped forward and announced the winners. The applause was deafening, everyone swept up in the victors' joy. Perhaps the greatest surprise of the day was the award of third prize in the junior category to the unlikely duo of Regus and Ruth – since hitherto, neither had ever seen a

Christmas tree or a Christmas decoration. More comfortable in the outdoors, they had shied away from the crowded yard behind the Spar and did not even page through Vera's magazines. For several days they had quietly searched the woodlands and rocky outcrops of the neighbouring pastures, climbing high into the trees, collecting seed pods of unusual colours and shapes. By making two holes in each pod, they had strung them together at equal intervals on a piece of twine, then curled them into a helix. The result was quite startling – a garland of exquisite pods to drape around the neck of the delicious monster. Quite overwhelmed following the announcement, each privately wondered what a waffle looked and tasted like.

Ladders were fetched from the workshop, decorations were hung from the msasa's branches, and tinsel was wrapped around the delicious monster. By four o'clock that afternoon, the transformation was complete. The result: an enormous exotic African mobile with a Yuletide theme. The participants stood back to admire their collective creation.

Baba Chiswa called Thomas to his office and thrust a thick wad of bank notes into his hand. 'Ice cream money. You, my friend, get to take the winners to the Dairy Den!'

The ordering process was protracted, the merits of every available ice cream debated to the extreme. The ice-cream man became exasperated, but managed to remain polite. Fortunately, there were no other patrons save for a well-dressed young man enjoying a chocolate-and-vanilla cone. In his top pocket, Thomas spotted a thin fold of US dollar bills; after his trip to South Africa, Thomas had a new awareness of the value of foreign money. Diffidently, he approached the man, briefly making chit-chat about the children's indecisiveness before getting down to business. 'Excuse me, but I couldn't help noticing you had some forex in your pocket. Not easy to find these days.'

The man's face lit up, his manner reassuringly unguarded.

'Brother Moth has been good to us this year,' he said with a grin.

'Brother Moth?' Thomas said, assuming this to be some form of acronym relating to the First World War.

The man raised his arms to either side and flapped his hands. 'Moths – the ones that fly around at night!'

'You serious?' Thomas gave a cautious smile.

'Serious,' replied the man. 'You know, when I was growing up on a farm in Ruwa, the farmer had a friend from Germany who came each year to collect moths. As a boy I used to help him catch them. He still writes to me now and then with a list of moths that he wants. I catch them and send them to him by courier. In return, he sends me money.'

'What does he do with them?'

'I don't know – mounts them in cabinets for his wall, I think. But he pays me very nicely!'

Surprised at his own audacity, Thomas asked the man for his telephone number.

Without hesitation, the man wrote it down on a piece of paper, which he handed to Thomas. Holding out his hand, he said, 'Noah Chipangura.'

'Thomas Threscothic.'

There was something instantly likable about Noah's openness, and Thomas invited him to join his table with the children, caught by now in an epiphany of ice creams, milkshakes and waffles, each mouthful appreciated with theatrical groans of appreciation.

Half an hour later the Datsun departed, its passengers deeply content.

Thomas did not waste time in getting across to Darryl's house that evening, after dropping off the children. The issue of the school fees had been pressing heavily on his mind. He could not lay his disastrous trip to South Africa to rest until he had proved to himself that he had it within him to solve this problem.

He found Darryl in a haze of Madison cigarette smoke, slouching on the couch watching a video.

'Hey, Dumbo, what's up, man!'

Thomas shook his head. 'Why do you have to call me that, Darryl?'

'What?' Darryl asked, nonplussed.

'You know exactly what. It's been going on for ten years. Don't you think it's enough now? The fact that you're still stuck on it says more about you than about me ... and that's not saying much.'

'Easy, Dumbo! Don't be so touchy.'

'My name is Thomas. If you don't want to call me that, then we don't have to be friends. I'll go right now.'

Darryl blushed and sat up. 'Okay, sorry man. Thomas. Hey, do you want a drink?'

'Yes, thanks. Just some water.'

Darryl stood up and pulled back the curtain. At the top of his lungs he shouted out the window, 'Distan!'

Thomas shook his head. 'And I don't know why you have to treat him like that. Can't you fetch me a glass of water yourself?'

'But that's his job, that's what my mom pays him for.'

'No, I don't think that's what your mom pays him for,' Thomas said. 'I'll fetch my own water.'

When he returned to the lounge, Darryl had turned off the TV and cleared the pizza boxes and old magazines off the couch to make room for him to sit.

'I need your help, Darryl. Can you look on the internet for something?'

'Sure. What?'

'I need to find someone out there who is interested in buying moths.'

'What? Is this some kind of joke? No one buys moths,' Darryl replied, glad of an apparent prank to break the tension.

'It's not a joke. I met someone who sells them for US dollars.'

Darryl stared at Thomas for a second. He seemed deadly serious, more serious than Darryl had ever seen him before.

He booted up his computer and ran a Google search, typing in 'moths sale'. The results were startling. There were several websites that sold moths from all over the world. They found sunset moths from Madagascar, white moon moths from India, and giant Atlas moths from the jungles of south-east Asia with wing patterns that resembled maps. Most importantly, they found moths from other countries in Africa: Tanzania, Togo, Kenya.

Overcoming his fear of the telephone, Thomas called Noah Chipangura. He told him he had business to discuss, it could not wait for tomorrow. Noah agreed to meet him, and Thomas drove to his flat in Eastlea with a proposal – if Thomas could find a buyer, would Noah help him to catch moths and prepare them for export? In return, Thomas was offering an equal split of any profits.

With a smile that flashed two rows of perfectly white teeth, Noah agreed. To get the ball rolling, Thomas asked for a list of the names of the moths that Noah had been collecting over the years. He took the list back to Darryl's house and prepared his first email ever.

Dear Sir/Madam

We have been collecting a variety of moths in the Mashonaland region of Zimbabwe for over ten years, at the request of collectors from Germany. We are skilled in the capture and packaging of these moths such that they are almost always in good condition on arrival by courier at their destinations.

The moths we have collected include the following:

1. *Frosted emperor – Bunaea Alcinoe*
2. *Ruby polyptychus – Afroclanis Calcarea*
3. *Death's head hawk – Acherontia Atropos*
4. *Oleander hawk – Daphnis Nerii*
5. *Sundowner moth – Sphingomorpha Chlorea*

6. *Streaked ermine – Estigmene linea*
7. *Msasa moth – Pachymeta Robusta*
8. *Carnegie's emperor – Imbrasia Carnegiei*
9. *Hieroglyphic moth – Mazuca Strigicincta*
10. *Beautiful tiger – Amphicallia Bellatrix.*

Should you wish to purchase any of the above moths from us, please email us a list of your requirements and the prices you are prepared to offer.

Yours faithfully,
Thomas Threscothic

Taken aback by Thomas's decisiveness, Darryl obediently sent the email to the addresses on four of the websites. Before he had even sent off the fourth, a response came from the first recipient, a company in Tampa, Florida, called Fly 'n Things.

Thomas
We are interested. However, having never seen a moth from Zimbabwe before, we would like to see one sample of each of the ten you have named, for which we will transfer into your nominated bank account US$3 per specimen as well as the courier charges. Please send your account details and the courier costs and we will do the transfer immediately, and expect the samples within the following week. If we like the samples we will put through a substantial order for the specimens we want and negotiate prices, etc.

What do you think?

Yours
Mike Chiappini

Thomas had not expected things to move so quickly. Telling himself to keep a cool head, he asked Darryl to send a reply agreeing to the proposal and saying that bank details would follow.

'Hey, my mum's got a US dollar bank account overseas. If money gets put in it, she can give you Zim dollars at the parallel rate,' said Darryl. 'I've got the details, I'll send them to the oke tonight.'

'Shouldn't you ask your mum first?'

'She never asks me when she uses my stuff, so why should I?'

At eight the following morning Thomas dropped in on Noah, who seemed delighted at the news. They would go out that night, Christmas Eve, he said, to search for the samples, but he warned Thomas it could take a week to get them all. Later that morning, Darryl called. Two of the remaining three companies had also responded with a request for samples. Armed with a torch and a butterfly net constructed from the frame of one of Father's old fishing nets, lined with a long tube of mosquito netting, Thomas followed Noah into the woodlands behind the William Westward, just after sunset.

It was a dark and cloudy evening, with flashes of lightning on the horizon. Thomas was fascinated to watch Noah checking the underside of huge boulders, examining the trunks of trees, eventually hanging his torch from a low-hanging branch to attract his quarry. Whenever he came across a moth, Noah artfully bagged it in his net and then gave the handle half a twist, trapping the moth inside the netting. Then, quickly, he worked his arm inside the netting and snatched the moth up in one fell swoop, to prevent it fluttering its wings to shreds. He held it by its thorax between his thumb and forefinger, giving it a gentle squeeze, ensuring that the insect did not suffer as it died. Folding a small sheet of brown paper into a triangle, he then placed the moth inside and turned the edges down to prevent it falling out. He stored these small parcels inside an old Tupperware ice-cream tub.

Thomas couldn't help feeling some degree of concern. 'Noah, are these moths very rare?' he asked.

Noah laughed. 'These ones, no. In any case, not as rare as the children you told me about who need food and education. There are some species I have seen only on one or two occasions that certainly are rare, but not these ones. I wouldn't do this, otherwise.'

Thomas was satisfied, at least for the moment, with this. After all, Noah was the expert. They'd stop immediately, he resolved, if he found out that this was in any way threatening a species. With only five specimens in the ice-cream tub by the time the rain came down, they took cover in the administration block.

Night after night for the next week, Thomas and Noah searched the woodlands with their torches and nets. In the afternoons while on playground duty, Thomas sat at a desk under the jacaranda trees, identifying and labelling the specimens caught the previous night by matching them against pictures in *Moths of Southern Africa*, by Elliot Pinhey (1975) – a rather moth-eaten edition that Thomas had located in the Harare City Library.

From the safety of his guava tree, Regus closely observed the process. In his silent wanderings around the grounds at night while the other children were asleep, he had been trailing Thomas and Noah with their torches and nets, keeping out of their sight. One morning, when Betty came down to chat with Thomas, Regus edged over to her. Without looking up, he tugged on her skirt to catch her attention. As she turned around, he muttered a few words in Ndebele to her for her to translate for Thomas.

'He says he knows these creatures,' Betty said, pointing at the moths in their triangular brown envelopes. 'He knows where to find them in the night, sometimes even during the day. He wants to help you find them.'

Thomas looked at the boy and smiled in agreement. That night, he fetched Regus from his dormitory just before lights-out. The boy followed Thomas and Noah into the woodlands, keeping a polite distance behind them. When they stopped, Thomas showed him pictures of the moths they were looking for. Regus nodded. Noah gave him some brown paper and showed him how to fold it into envelopes. Thomas offered him his torch, but Regus did not take it; he was happy, it seemed, to search by moonlight.

Regus disappeared for several minutes, without making a sound. Once Thomas thought he could hear a rustle in the branches above him. Then he caught a glimpse of a small white T-shirt on the perimeter of the recently ploughed mealie field. When at last the boy returned, he had a handful of folded envelopes, containing several large specimens; Noah and Thomas were astounded. Regus had collected more moths in thirty minutes than they had managed the whole of the night before.

Within days, Regus had become an integral member of the moth team. It was not long before he had learnt the names of all the specimens, both scientific and common. He took great pride in his labelling, copying Thomas's words letter by letter, for he had not yet learnt to write.

Such were the humble beginnings of the Brother Moth business, which developed a reputation among its clients for honesty and prompt delivery. Within a month, Brother Moth had raised over a thousand US dollars. The school fees were promptly paid, and in the ensuing months new uniforms and shoes were purchased for all the children – something that had not happened in twenty years.

Baba Chiswa looked on with great pride as the lines of children departed for school in the mornings, all immaculately dressed – a fitting tribute to the Msasa Technical School's motto, Reaching for the Stars. Spare parts were procured for the tractor, and a pump was purchased to ferry water from the borehole to the fields, where maize, potatoes, pumpkins, cabbages, tomatoes, carrots and beans were flourishing. Produce that was not served to the children in the William Westward's dining hall ended up on shelves in the supermarkets and stores of Msasa, providing a visible, easily explicable source for the home's new-found prosperity; those in the know had made the decision that the Brother Moth business was best kept secret. *The Herald* even ran an article on the William Westward, 'Children's Home Sails Triumphant In Stormy Seas', which included a fine black-and-white photograph of a beaming Baba Chiswa standing in front of the freshly whitewashed walls of Paget Block. Thomas smiled quietly to himself as he read the article. It was a golden era for the William Westward.

48

Thomas's Hidden Titan, Unleashed

It might not have been an argument in the true sense of the word, but it was the closest the headmaster and Thomas had ever come to a disagreement. For several months, Joseph had watched as the fortunes of the William Westward rose and rose. Brother Moth had been a resounding success – Thomas, he felt, should be rewarded. After all, Noah Chipangura, by then a much-loved member of the William Westward community, was taking home his half of the profits. Thomas, on the other hand, benefited only through the certainty that he would receive his salary. But Thomas wouldn't hear of it. After much debate, a compromise was reached. One tenth of the William Westward's profits from Brother Moth were to come directly to Thomas.

'But what will I do with it?' Thomas asked.

'I could think of many things,' Joseph replied. 'For a start, the price of petrol is formidable. Buy yourself some clothes. Maybe save up for a proper television. I don't know, you'll think of something, I'm sure.'

The following Saturday, with three bricks of bank notes stuffed into his pockets, Thomas set off for Sam Levy's Village in Borrowdale, the country's last bastion of Western consumerism. There, the race-horse set of Harare's dwindling white elite – by then sans horses – clung to the vestiges of a long-gone lifestyle, rubbing shoulders with the well-heeled housewives of the city's black elite and members of the reigning oligarchy. For everyone else who visited the Village, the experience of sauntering down the supermarket aisles, or window shopping along the boutique-lined walkways, was a crash course in ten-digit mental arithmetic and controlled hyperventilation.

Wearing creased khaki trousers and one of Father's faded short-sleeved Hawaiian shirts, Thomas stood out like a sore thumb. He could feel the amused gawks of the more refined patrons bearing down on him. Thomas was an outsider, just as he had been at Koo-doo Range, as he was almost everywhere, apart from the William Westward, and he did not like it.

In the window of a bookshop, a thick blue paperback stood out from a shelf of nondescript airport novels. On its cover, in big red letters, was the title: *Your Hidden Titan Unleashed*, with a one-line synopsis underneath: *Taking the future into your own hands and winning.*

Glancing around to see if anyone was watching, Thomas lifted the book from its shelf cautiously – as one might a family portrait standing on the piano in someone else's house. He leafed through it and came across a chapter headed 'Command your health, wealth and psychology'. Intrigued, he bought the book right there and then.

The chipped faces of cream-coloured mannequins, blotched with the smudges of a thousand fingerprints, stared at him sternly from the clothing shop next door, daring him to enter. He did so, though with some reluctance. He had never before bought his own clothes; Marie had always taken care of that. A young, stylishly dressed man approached him.

'Can I help you, sir?'

'Yes. Please. I'm looking for an outfit.'

'What sort of outfit?'

'One like that,' he said, pointing at a mannequin in the window.

'You serious?'

Thomas nodded. 'Do you have my size?'

'That depends. What is your size?'

'I don't know, quite small, I should think.'

The experience of standing in the changing booth, wearing what felt like someone else's clothing, gazing at himself in a full-length mirror for the first time in several years, was quite surreal. There had never been mirrors at home, save for a decorative one that hung in the living room. It had Jesus painted on it, with a halo and some doves. Father had forbidden mirrors; they could bring one no happiness, he said. Looking at himself that day in the clothing shop, Thomas had to agree. He purchased the mannequin's outfit, along with a pair of brown veldskoens, and fought the urge to break into a run as he headed for the Datsun.

Back home, Thomas threw himself down onto Father's Parker-Knoll with his new book. Within minutes he was gripped, a spell cast over him. It was several hours before he looked up, such was his excitement. He could not wait to start living the rest of his life as the ultimate master of his own existence, to unleash himself from the manacles of his limiting beliefs, and to adopt a strategy and goals that would see him soar like an eagle beyond his wildest expectations.

Every word he read made perfect sense. Talent wasn't a prerequisite for success, said the book; instead, it was all about vision, focus and perserverance. You should use energising expressions in your everyday speech – phrases like 'absolutely awesome' and 'to-tally psyched' – broadcasting to the world your go-getter attitude. It was vital to constantly repeat 'power affirmations', such as 'I am cruising on a highway of health and wealth' and 'Nothing can di-vert me from my goals'. Most importantly, you had to think big and dream big – anything is possible if you decide what it is that you truly want, visualise yourself doing it, and then commit yourself completely to achieving it. A myriad of examples were given of 'Av-erage Joes' from 'Armpit Alabama' who'd really made something of themselves out there. It got Thomas thinking: there was no rea-son why he too couldn't be an astronaut or a Nobel Laureate or an Olympic medallist or an Oscar nominee – no reason at all. Anyone, the book told him, could be a billionaire. All those sports cars he'd seen on CNN, he could have one; an Aston Martin, he thought, or no, a Bugatti rather – he liked the sound of it – and why not?

Thomas hardly slept at all that night, his mind spinning a tom-bola stuffed full of aspirations and accolades. His discovery was too compelling to be kept to himself. Next day, when the children re-turned from school, he herded them into the prep rooms and had them record on scraps of paper their personal goals, their career ambitions, even their financial aspirations.

A frenzy of excitement whipped through the corridors of the Wil-liam Westward. Little Tanaka, all of eleven years of age, declared that he would one day be Secretary General of the United Nations. Fights broke out in the corridors as children stole ideas from one another. It was pandemonium, and it went on for weeks, fuelled by Thomas's relentless recent convert's belief that nothing was impos-sible. At first Baba Chiswa thought it was all just a bit of fun, but along with the heightened expectations of grandiose future posi-tions, certain children became ungovernable. Several refused to go to school – professing uncommon talent, they demanded more respect from their peers and teachers alike. Some, it was rumoured, were even planning to run away – Hollywood became a major discussion theme, as did the much-abridged biographies of Forest Whitaker, Eddie Murphy and Oprah Winfrey. Finally, the headmaster put his foot down.

'These kids are lucky to have clothing, Thomas, and food. Two months ago they were on the brink of starvation, and now they won't go to school unless someone takes them in a Ferrari and brings them back in a space shuttle.'

'But, Joseph, it's only through the conscious renunciation of self-imposed limitations that they'll achieve the unthinkable.'

'Yes, Thomas, it's not that there's no merit in what you are saying, but this is Zimbabwe. We have the world's fastest-shrinking economy and the lowest life expectancy. Most of the children will be lucky to find any employment at all when they grow up, and many will not make it to the age of thirty. Perhaps you could conduct your exercises with that in mind. Give them realistic expectations to aim for, like becoming teachers or nurses, and having families.'

'But, Joseph ...'

'I'm not asking you, Thomas, I'm telling you. This has got to stop!'

Thomas was undeterred by Joseph Chiswa's caution – resistance, he had read, was to be expected. At home he devised a programme: 'From Zero to Hero', he called it. He took to strenuous exercise, running and weight-training, using a broomstick from which he suspended a bucket filled with sand at either end. He also embarked on a high-protein diet of grilled bream, which he got from the flourishing shoal in the swimming pool. He even took himself for a proper haircut, visiting an elderly Portuguese barber in Newlands. With growing confidence, Thomas felt ready for another trip to Sam Levy's Village. So, it was just a few weeks later that he dressed up in his new clothes, checked his hair in the Jesus mirror, and set off.

There was a commotion at the Eastlea shops as Thomas drove by. Scores of people had gathered, some with wheelbarrows and scotch carts piled high with old furniture and twisted sheets of corrugated iron. Some even had livestock – cows with mangy hides and protruding ribs. Groups of children ran around, snotty-faced and clothed in rags.

Thomas pulled over and got out of the Datsun, but kept his distance. On the pavement, the crowd had encircled a distraught man, forty years old, perhaps, dressed in tattered overalls. He stood on the raised concrete of the pavement, shouting and sobbing. The crowd drew back in horror as he fished around in a dirty white plastic packet with his hand, and pulled out a small snake.

'Put it down! *Isa pasi!*' they cried.

Holding the creature by its tail, the man dangled it over his head.

A street performer, Thomas thought. He had often seen them downtown – tightrope walkers, acrobats, jugglers and storytellers – but he had certainly never seen a performance involving a snake.

Gazing resolutely at the sky above, the man dropped the snake into his mouth, and with some difficulty proceeded to swallow it whole. The crowd reached fever pitch. Expecting the man to pull the snake from his sleeve and take a bow, Thomas was alarmed when he began to clutch at his throat as if he were choking. This was a most elaborate act, it seemed. Feeling somewhat uncomfortable, Thomas took a few steps back towards the car. The man started gasping for breath and was sweating profusely. Within minutes he had fallen to the ground, his limbs limp.

Thomas had seen enough. He jumped inside the Datsun and continued on to Sam Levy's Village in Borrowdale. From the car park, Thomas made his way to the brick walkways, ambling about incognito in his new sunglasses. He peered into shop windows as if he was a serious buyer. For a while he actually enjoyed himself. He felt confident and comfortable, even hoping to run into someone he knew, to test his new self, to see if he could hold his own. But there were few people about – just older women with worried expressions and tired sun-beaten ex-farmers, whiling away the vacant hours of a life lived in town.

It had only been half an hour, and Thomas did not want to go home just yet, not after all the hype he had attached to the outing. He sat down at a café on one of the walkways. There were waitresses in attendance, a couple of white ones even, something Thomas could not remember seeing for a number of years. One, in particular, caught his eye. Her dark hair was in a bob and parted to one side, just like Becky Anderson, he thought. Remembering that he was now master of his own destiny, having nothing to fear, Thomas raised his hand to call her over. Presenting the broadest of smiles to exude self-confidence and an air of authority, he drew upon weeks of vocabulary training as he put his best foot forward.

'Hi. What a stunning day! Fantastic, isn't it?'

'Um, I s'pose so,' said the waitress warily.

'Gorgeous! In fact, gorgeous – just like you!'

Clearly embarrassed, she took a step back from the table. 'Um, can I get you something?'

'A cup of tea would be awesome, darling!'

The waitress dashed to the far end of the café to place the order. Thomas kept his eyes on her, mesmerised. She huddled among the other waitresses, within earshot of the proprietor, recounting her tale. All eyes turned towards Thomas as a quartet of giggles reverberated softly across the room. The proprietor tossed his chocolate-smeared dishcloth onto the counter and made his way to Thomas's table.

'Everything all right here?'

'Super,' replied Thomas. 'Just waiting for my cup of tea.'

'You realise that these waitresses here are schoolgirls?'

'No, I didn't realise that. Commendable, though, earning a little extra on the side.'

The proprietor placed a hand on Thomas's shoulder. 'Listen here, chum, commendable or not, we like our customers to respect that fact. Do you understand?'

'Yes,' said Thomas quietly.

'So, no funny business, chum! Okay?'

'Okay,' Thomas answered, blushing again.

Thomas's hidden titan, finally unleashed, was now in full retreat. He gulped back his tea and, generously leaving several hundred thousand dollars on the table, he returned swiftly to the Datsun and drove home, still feeling flustered.

On the way, he noticed a small queue of cars outside a filling station in Newlands. Instinctively, he joined it – drivers could ill afford not to. He drew up beneath the massive gum trees that stood sentry to the dilapidated headquarters of what had once been a foreign Christian mission. The air above was filled with the croaking of pied crows that, for as long as he could remember, had roosted in these trees. He did not like them. To add insult to injury, a white-and-grey dropping splattered across his windscreen. Thomas jumped out in frustration, shaking his fists and cursing. A pitiful squawk pleaded from below. Barely clothed, with stubby black feathers and hatchling's fluff, a baby crow huddled between his feet, looking up at him, calling meekly for help. Sighing, he picked it up. He had no option but to take it home and feed it. Louis, he named it, short for Louis Cyphre, the sinister character from the film *Angel Heart*, who had terrified him as a teenager. The sound of hooting caught Thomas's attention – the queue ahead of him had disappeared. It was his turn. He wanted to fill his tank, up but they were only allowing five litres per customer. It wasn't his day.

As Thomas set off once again, his mind drifted back to the embarrassing encounter in the café. He played the events over and over again in his mind, cringing with each recollection. Why were his intentions so misunderstood? Would he spend all his life as an outsider, destined to inhabit the no-man's-land between two cultures? He pulled over at the Eastlea Dairy Den for an ice cream, more to postpone his return to the loneliness of home than anything else. The column of ragged people with their scotch carts and disorientated offspring had moved on. The ice-cream man was mopping the pavement.

'So, what happened?' Thomas asked. 'Where did the snake man go?'

The man continued mopping, not looking up.

Thomas tried again. 'I didn't really like his act.'

'Act? What act?' The man seemed incensed, 'That man took his own life.'

Thomas was stunned. He had witnessed it all, not realising it was for real.

'Why would he do that?'

'Didn't you hear him? He said he had lost everything. That the police had come with bulldozers and destroyed the shack where he lived with his family. His son died when the shack collapsed on top of him. They had nowhere to go. They have been living in the bush for weeks, without shelter or food. His wife got sick and she died too. He said he had nothing left to live for.'

'But why would the police do this?'

'The president told them to. They call it Operation Murambatsvina – drive out the filth, it means.' The man continued sweeping. 'And anybody who does not stand for ZANU-PF is filth. They are punishing us for voting against them in the election. Punishing the poor. Driving them out of the towns into the country where they will have no voice.'

Thomas shook his head and returned to the car; ice cream no longer seemed appropriate. Half a kilometre down the road he came upon them again, the refugees, stooping under the weight of their carts and barrows, these 'enemies of the state'. He tried to avoid their gaze as he drove past – he, in his new smart clothes, with his aspirations of owning a yacht and an island.

Driving into his yard, Thomas veered off the driveway and skidded to a halt next to the pool. Snatching up the blue book of liberated leviathans and laureates, he hurled it into the murky waters.

It quickly sank in a noisy tilapian swirl, bashed from side to side by the gaping mouths of a hundred bream before settling in the sludge on the bottom. Like Mister Chikorobho's goblins in the nearby village, it too had become too hot for Thomas to handle.

Once inside, Thomas threw himself down on Marie's bed to collect his thoughts. From their positions above, the Great Ones seemed to focus their attention on him. Staring down from the opposite wall was Robert Mugabe, his picture taken twenty-five years before, looking elegant, sophisticated and full of promise.

Thomas leapt up and fetched the scissors from the kitchen. Snipping quickly and decisively, he cut the picture of Joseph Chiswa from *The Herald*. Placing it over Robert Mugabe's image, he hung the frame on the wall. Joseph Chiswa, a genuine leader who loved and cared for those under his guardianship, had earned the right to be among the Great Ones.

49

Teddington Seeks
a New 'Arrangement'

Teddington was sick of the place. The entire farm was deserted; besides himself, there was not a soul on the property, apart from the times he brought women back to the now decrepit farmhouse, and even then it was only his money they were interested in. Initially, Comrade Shuranyama and the guys had come out quite frequently for barbecues and drinks, but since the liberation of the Comrade Sizemore Chinovhiringa Country Club, they preferred to meet up there. Frankly, the facilities were better, and as a couple of Taffy Jones's staff had been permitted to resume living on the property – as long as they cleaned up after the parties – the place was kept in some order.

Estranged from his family and community in Hatcliffe, it had been months since Teddington had been back there, and none of them ever came out to see him, despite numerous calls to old friends, inviting them for parties. Perhaps they were afraid. After all, he was very senior these days. He had risen rapidly to his station, which was certainly pleasing, but as he had recently confided to Comrade Shuranyama, it could be lonely at the top.

Comrade Shuranyama found this admission hilarious. 'Don't confuse lonely with broke, Teddy-Boy!' he chortled.

The more Teddington thought about it, the clearer these words became. What was the point of hanging around a deserted, run-down old farm, with no companionship? He needed another place, one that could generate an income stream, with people around to respect him and his position. Like it was before Tony left.

There were problems, though; these days, there were few commercial farmers left. There was only a handful in each district, particularly in areas close to Harare, as no new landowner liked having to drive too far out. All the best farms had been taken by the ZANU bigwigs and military top brass, and the few remaining farmers were already yoked into a profit-sharing arrangement – usually with a Party member or war veteran far more important than Teddington – which was supposed to protect the farm from further interference and guard its income.

Teddington knew the score well, as he was often the one tasked with enforcing the terms of such arrangements, just as Comrade Shuranyama had done for him in his early days at Cotswold Downs. To make ends meet, he had scoured the farm for anything worth selling and had made a bit here and there from selling a tractor and some piping, but a lot of the stuff had been looted while he was away in town, and the police had been useless in recovering it. He hardly even had money for sadza these days, let alone booze.

It was rumoured that the government planned to 'indigenise' all businesses, meaning they would be taken from whites and foreigners, and then be redistributed. Teddington was hopeful that he would be getting something out of the process, but who could say for sure when it would happen, and who would be in line to benefit. Certainly, the senior Party loyalists would be first, followed by the military, and presumably only then the war veterans with whom he was associated.

Maybe he should focus on getting higher up in ZANU-PF? Throughout the day, Teddington pondered his dilemma. Something had to be done. Surely there was a solution out there somewhere? He did not want to bother Comrade Shuranyama with his problems again, but maybe, just maybe, he knew of a place that Teddington had not heard of, which was worth liberating.

With his new Isuzu twin cab clean out of petrol, and no airtime on his cellphone, he had no option but to walk up to the manager's cottage where Tony and Patsy had lived before their sudden departure. For some reason the phone there still worked; obviously Tel-One had not noticed, for no bills had been paid in a long time. It was a baking hot afternoon, and sweat poured from every pore of Teddington's body, soaking his shirt so that it stuck to his flabby stomach. He was panting so hard he had to stop every so often to catch his breath. He really should go on diet, he told himself.

It seemed like the manager's house had been ransacked again. This time they had made off with all the remaining curtains. Some of the steel window frames had been chiselled out, and the parquet flooring pulled up for firewood. No doubt soon they would pull down the ceiling boards and make off with the roofing tiles. Thank goodness the phone was still where he had hidden it under a broken beer crate in one of the bedrooms.

He dialled the number. 'Comrade Shuranyama! *Makadiyi!*' he started off cheerfully, setting the tone of the conversation.

'Teddy-Boy, long time no see. What's been going on?'

'Ah, you know, Comrade, with this farming there's always something that needs to be done.'

Comrade Shuranyama guffawed. 'How can I help you, Teddy-Boy?'

'Well, Comrade, I was hoping you might be able to point me in the right direction. I'm looking for a new arrangement.'

'What kind of arrangement?'

'You know, like we had with Tony.'

A wheezy snigger ensued.

'Well, there's a place out in Kwekwe I heard of … you interested?'

Teddington frowned. He had gained a reputation in this area, not to mention seniority and respect. To move districts would be to throw all that away. 'Well, actually, I'm hoping to stay in the district, anything from Harare to Marondera, really. Maybe up to Macheke if something nice comes up.'

'Okay, I'll keep an eye out for you. It's going to take a while, though. I'll come out there sometime and we can take a drive around. See who's planting and who's still got cattle, all that kind of stuff.'

'That would be great, Comrade. *Tatenda*. You know where I am.'

'Of course I know, Teddy-Boy. I took you there, remember!'

50

Surviving
Operation Murambatsvina

Thomas recognised them at once. With their creaking scotch carts and bewildered children, they had made their way from Eastlea to the William Westward. The wheel of fortune had finally turned: the brief months of prosperity in which the William Westward had recently basked, came to an abrupt end as dozens of families sought refuge on the grounds. One among them, an elderly man by the name of Limon, was Robson's uncle. Evicted from their homes on Cotswold Downs Estate in Goromonzi over a year ago, and then again from a squatter camp outside Harare just a month before, they had nowhere else to go, Limon explained.

Baba Chiswa and Robson led the families to the bush behind the mealie field. They must be hidden from the authorities, and kept well out of sight of the Green Bombers, ZANU-PF's youth militia. With axes and pangas, a clearing was prepared for the shacks to be assembled, but in the meantime the prep rooms provided shelter to nearly two hundred refugees, all of whom had to be fed, and some of whom needed blankets and clothes. Initially, Brother Moth was stretched beyond its limits in covering the costs, but gradually, the bedlam caused by Operation Murambatsvina began to abate. Soon, the tin sheets and warped planks, hammered together with salvaged nails, became homes. To secure the community's future, several meetings were held under the msasa trees behind the new camp. There were many mouths to feed, and no one had any kind of employment. Each person was asked to record his or her particular skills in a school exercise book. There was a handful of carpenters, mechanics and teachers, but in the main, the settlers were farm workers who had been born on commercial tobacco farms, and had worked on them from a young age – planting, tending, reaping and then curing. Though this was all they knew as a means of liveli-hood, they knew it well.

So it was decided that the home's two largest fields would be set aside for planting tobacco. One fifth of the profits were to be paid to the William Westward as rental for the land, while the remainder would be shared among those who contributed labour, in fair and equal portions.

At four o'clock in the morning, one day late in September, the men and women assembled in groups alongside the fields which, over the preceding weeks, had been tilled by the tractor, and pre-pared in long straight rows of rich red earth in anticipation of the planting. They all stamped their bare feet and rubbed their arms to keep warm until each had been given a hoe, or a bucket, or a tray of seedlings, and then the back-breaking labour of planting tobacco by hand began. Two weeks later, the exhausted teams stood back to survey their work with a quiet sense of pride. After so many years of working Tony Willoughby's soil, they had for the first time planted their own crop.

Blessed with early and abundant rains, the settlers at the William

Westward watched their crop grow with interest and attention. By mid-December, aided by fertiliser procured through the proceeds of Brother Moth, theirs was some of the finest tobacco in the land. To the passing motorist, it was an oasis of cultivation.

51

In Flagrante Delicto

Distant memories filled Thomas's head as he sat back in Father's wingback chair. He wondered about Leviticus, about his return to his *kumusha*, and his final resting place. If only they had done more for him. If only they had taken him to the doctor. Thomas was filled with regret. At the very least, he decided, he should visit Leviticus's home to see where he had been buried, and to pay his respects to the family. In Marie's black address book he found a number for his brother, Clement. A woman answered, and Clement was called to the phone. They exchanged pleasantries before Thomas proceeded.

'Clement, I'm calling about Leviticus, to find out what happened in the end.'

'Leviticus,' replied Clement, 'has been in a very bad way.'

Thomas's heart leapt, he could hardly contain himself. 'You mean he's still alive? That's excellent!'

'He's still alive, yes, but barely.'

'Can you tell me how to find him? I would like to visit him.'

Though he had some difficulty hearing Clement, Thomas took down the directions to Numwa Secondary School in Hwedza. There, another brother, Michael, a teacher, would guide him on. Thomas thanked Clement before replacing the receiver. His mind was made up – he would set off at dawn the next day. There was no time to spare.

It was mid-morning when Thomas arrived at Numwa Secondary School. Michael's resemblance to his older brother, Leviticus, was striking. The teacher agreed to accompany Thomas as the trail to Leviticus's *kumusha* was unmarked, and the last part was unsuitable for vehicles. Thomas drove the Datsun as far as he was able, after which they walked for half an hour through the granite koppies, passing small patches of maize, and dusty pastures cropped to the ground by goats and cattle, before reaching Leviticus's home.

In the darkness of the hut, Thomas could barely recognise Leviticus. His emaciated figure lay motionless on a blanket on the far side of the room. At first he seemed confused as they woke him, but the familiarity of Thomas's voice stirred him. He tried to get up to greet him, but was too weak. Tears came to his eyes when he heard the news of Marie's passing. There was a pause before Thomas stated the purpose of his visit – to take Leviticus back to town, to the doctor, to get him the pills that would help him. Leviticus protested, nothing could help him at this stage.

Thomas's reply was uncharacteristically firm. 'No, Leviticus, you said that once before and we let you down, my mother and I. Not again, so let's go.'

Defeated, Leviticus fell silent while Michael arranged a scotch cart and a donkey to pull it. Back at the car, Michael and Thomas lifted Leviticus onto the back seat where he could lie down and rest. They drove back to the school, where they shook hands before Thomas set off back to Harare, proceeding directly to the clinic where Marie had previously taken Leviticus. The clinic brought out his test results and prescribed a course of antiretrovirals, to be taken immediately. After stopping off at the pharmacy, Thomas drove Leviticus back to the house, leaving him in the car as he walked to Leviticus's old room and opened the door.

With the exception of a pile of old *Herald* newspapers and an empty tin of Cobra polish, the room was empty. Thomas gasped in horror as it all came back to him. During his time in the rabbit hutch he had burnt all the furniture – Leviticus's bed, his cupboard, it was all gone. Thomas closed the door quickly; Leviticus would have to sleep with him in Marie's bed, at least until a new bed could be purchased for him. Thomas hurried back to the Datsun and lifted Leviticus into his arms. Carrying him slowly through the kitchen he placed him on Father's side of the bed, propping him up on a couple of pillows. Leviticus struggled to eat a few mouthfuls of mashed potato before taking his tablets and immediately falling asleep. That night Thomas lay on Marie's side of the bed, listening to Leviticus's shallow breathing until he, too, fell asleep.

Around midnight, the sound of groaning woke him. Gripped by fever, Leviticus tossed and turned, crying out, covering his face with the backs of his hands as if to protect himself. Again and again, Thomas shook him to bring some sense to his confusion, and wiped his brow with a damp facecloth. Shortly before dawn the fever seemed to subside, and Thomas, himself completely drained, lapsed into a deep sleep.

At a quarter to seven, the sound of a man clearing his throat with a stately 'Ahem' drifted across the yard outside, but Thomas remained oblivious – the brown arcs of Jimmy Moverley-Smith's archaic hearing apparatus were resting sedately on the bedside table next to him. A frosty circle, the size of a modest milk tart, appeared on a window pane, with a pink dot in the middle where Reverend Harold Hardcastle pressed his pitted parson's snoot unparsimoniously against the glass, squinting inquisitively to see inside. Ignorant of any notion of respect for personal privacy, the reverend remained ever true to his seminary nickname, 'The bull in the Bible shop'.

As his eyes adjusted to the dim light within, the reverend rapped his knuckles impatiently against the window. Startled, Leviticus poked Thomas in the back. Thomas shot up with a start, just as the reverend's vision adjusted. He – Thomas, that is – was raising his hand in greeting when Leviticus also sat up, unclothed from the waist up on account of the fever, and glistening with sweat, as if from some extraordinary exertion. The reverend's expression instantly mimicked Thomas's well-known look of surprise. He uttered a peculiar croon, as if he had just slipped off a bicycle seat and landed awkwardly on the crossbar – a sound which slowly transformed to that of a man choking on a kipper. Thomas jumped up in his threadbare Spiderman pyjamas and waved cheerfully at the reverend. He seldom, if ever, had visitors these days.

'Reverend! Morning, come in for some tea. Please.'

The reverend curled his lip in contempt and sprang back from the window. His ankle caught the side of a flower bed and he toppled over in a near-somersault, which all but lost its symmetry in the final stages of execution. He landed on his hip with a thud, his tweed jacket covered in leaves and dried grass.

'Are you all right, Reverend?' Thomas cried out in alarm. 'Please come in!'

The reverend struggled to his feet.

'Not bloody likely!' he called out as he turned briskly toward his red parish Anglia, followed by inaudible mutterings of disgust which included the phrases, 'Filthy sodomists!' and 'If old Reginald had only known!' peppered with an outraged 'God help us, whatever next!'

Thomas ran through to the lounge, but only managed to catch a glimpse of flaring nostrils and piously puckered lips which extended into a full pout oscillating from side to side of the reverend's puce face as the Anglia completed a full turn before disappearing out the driveway.

Perplexed at the reverend's sudden appearance and dramatic departure, Thomas prepared porridge and tea for their breakfast, then quickly dressed so as not to be late for the Eucharist at St Luke's at eight. Settling into his regular seat in the back left corner of the church, where he had always felt close enough to be included but not so close as to feel threatened, he lost himself in the ritual, chanting the responses that he knew so well. The subtleties of Reverend Hardcastle's stirring rhetoric on the shameful descent into immorality among today's youth were lost on him as he yawned occasionally, his eyelids heavy from lack of sleep. By the end of the service, the peculiar incident with the reverend earlier that morning had become a vague memory.

The remains of St Luke's ever-dwindling congregation collected in a line at the rear of the church to shake hands with the reverend. Thomas joined the end of the queue and was the last to greet him. The reverend's face turned crimson. He blinked furiously, his brow deeply furrowed. With a vice-like grip on Thomas's hand, which threated to crush his fingers, he pulled Thomas towards him, whispering forcefully. 'Young man, whilst there may be those in our church – in America, even some in England, God forbid – who condone such heinous acts, here at St Luke's we stand firm in our opposition!'

Thomas looked blank. He had no idea what the reverend was referring to. 'What do you mean, Reverend?'

Reverend Hardcastle snarled, and showers of spittle rained over Thomas's face. 'Do you take me for an ass, young Threscothic?'

'No, Reverend, I –'

'I caught you, dammit – red-handed – *in flagrante delicto*, as they say. With that garden boy of your mother's, by Jove! In your mother's bedroom, of all places. I should've hauled you out and given you a jolly good hiding, there and then!'

'But Reverend, you're quite wrong. That man is very ill, he needed a bed, he –' Thomas stopped himself in mid-sentence. The reverend's misunderstanding suddenly hit him. Even if he were a homosexual, a concept that had always vaguely unsettled him, the church had no right to turn him away. Why should he have to explain himself? Had not wars been fought in this country, and across this continent, to end discrimination? What was the difference now?

'You are wrong Reverend, in more ways than one,' Thomas said calmly.

Trying to keep his cool, he wrenched his hand free and moved to the tea table. With a cup and saucer in his hand, he turned to greet some of his mother's friends. The congregation had dispersed into several circles, engaged in lively discussion, all glancing in his direction, shaking their heads and smirking. He stood there defiantly, sipping his tea, staring back at each of them. When he had finished his tea, he poured himself another cup and again turned to face them. To pass the time, he pulled apart a Romany Cream biscuit and licked the icing off, slowly, with the tip of his tongue. Everyone was watching, but he would not be driven away. He would go when he felt like going – after his tea, after his biscuit. And he would never return. Not to this church, nor to any other that practised discrimination of any sort.

Leviticus seemed slightly better when Thomas arrived home and brought a glass of Mazoe through to the bedroom. Late that afternoon, Thomas was fishing for his dinner in the swimming pool, when a vehicle appeared at the gate. Two young men got out and walked towards him. They were fashionably dressed, wearing tight jeans and silver cowboy-style belt buckles.

Thomas reeled in his line and put down his pole to greet them.

'Hi,' said the one, stretching out his hand with a warm smile. 'I'm Richard, and this is my partner, Tony.'

'Hi. I'm Thomas.'

'Yes, we know. Listen, my mum is a member of the congregation at St Luke's. We used to be too, but that's another story,' Tony said, rolling his eyes. 'My mum told me what happened at church today, and we just wanted to come and say to you that we thought you were very brave taking a stand like that. After all, choosing your sexual orientation should be your right.'

Thomas blushed. 'But it's not like that, really.'

'Oh, come on, that's what they all say.'

'No, really, my gardener is very sick. He's just come back and doesn't have a bed, so he's sleeping inside with me, just until we get him a bed of his own.'

Tony raised his eyebrows. 'Hmm … interesting.'

'Well, anyway,' said Richard, 'if you're ever looking for an Anglican Church that doesn't ask questions, there's one we can recommend. It's not really a church, I suppose, as we get together at the minister's house on a Sunday afternoon. Reverend Edgar Muyambo is his name. He's a good guy. Anyway, here's his number. He's one of us, in orientation, if you know what I mean.'

Richard passed Thomas a piece of paper with a number on it.

'Why don't you come in for some tea,' Thomas said, his face lighting up at the prospect of company.

As Tony sat back in Father's chair in the lounge, Louis the crow descended on him with a terrifying caw, transfixed by the glinting belt buckle. Drawn to all things metallic and shiny, much of his time was spent rearranging piles of motley treasure on the pelmets. Alarmed at Tony's cries of surprise, Thomas leapt to his feet and snatched Louis up in his hands.

Thomas waved goodbye as they drove off. Although he was unlikely to take up their invitation, he was grateful for their kindness and concern.

52

The Invasion of the William Westward

It was an unusually cold morning, with low banks of clouds obscuring the sun, overcast yet refusing to rain. The children shivered in the dining hall, clasping their hands between their legs for warmth as they waited for their porridge. Following the headmaster's lead, they all stood up. Silence fell as each head was bowed in anticipation of grace that would, however, not be said that morning, as the sudden screech of tyres and the vulgar blast of hooters from the car park interrupted their routine. All eyes turned to Joseph Chiswa.

'Sit down, children,' he said. 'No one is to leave the hall until Miss Mukadota says so.'

Frowning, he nodded to Betty to take over supervision, an uneasy feeling knotting his stomach as he walked outside. As he rounded the giant msasa tree in its dense coat of delicious monster leaves, several pickups and one enormous orange vehicle came into sight.

The car park was swarming with men, each with an axe or a panga, some with knobkerries. They descended on Joseph, forming a circle around him. Many were dressed in the distinctive green overalls of the Green Bombers; they were young – some as young as the home's older children – with bloodshot eyes and wild, excitable expressions. Fearing for his life, but unable to flee, the headmaster's heart was pounding. A large gentleman dressed in an elegant navy sports jacket stepped through the ring of youths, followed by his corpulent sidekick whose shirt buttons were undone to his bulging navel, a panga in his hand.

The tall gentleman raised his hand. Instantly, the mob fell silent.

'Mister Chiswa?' said the gentleman in a deep voice, followed by a chortle from the depths of his belly. He clearly found the situation amusing.

'Yes,' Joseph ventured cautiously.

'Let me introduce myself. Comrade David Shuranyama. And this is my colleague, Comrade Teddy-Boy Chiwafambira.'

Joseph nodded.

'You have a nice place here, Mister Chiswa, very nice. Nice tobacco crop, too. Not to mention the vegetable gardens and chickens. Very nice. And an illegal settlement at the back, which has not gone unnoticed by the authorities. As this farmland has been designated for redistribution, we are fully within our rights to evict everyone here, and without your co-operation, we shall certainly do so –'

'But this is an orphanage,' Joseph interjected. 'Where have we to go?'

Comrade Shuranyama chortled again, a little louder this time. 'Heh, a consideration that, fortunately for you, we have not overlooked. A compromise has been proposed, which I believe should work well for all parties.'

Joseph Chiswa could not believe what he was hearing. This was beyond his worst nightmare. He recognised this man from the papers – Hitler Jesus, they called him.

'By seven o'clock this evening, that entire wing shall be vacated,' Comrade Shuranyama said calmly, pointing at Paget block. 'I'm sure, with some ingenuity, you will find the other block adequate for your purposes.'

'But, Comrade, the dormitories are already overcrowded,' the headmaster protested.

Comrade Shuranyama smirked at this. 'Oh, so you don't think the arrangement will work? What a pity. We'll be back at seven, and by then all the buildings will be vacated for the new owner – Comrade Chiwafambira here.'

Joseph Chiswa panicked, realising that perhaps he had said the wrong thing. Maybe the compromise offered was better than outright eviction. 'Please, Comrade, at least leave us with somewhere to live,' he pleaded.

'Ah, so the compromise retains some appeal, does it? Well, there's more to it. Once Comrade Chiwafambira has moved in, he'll be expecting half the revenues of this farm, including … what was it again that we heard about, Comrade Chiwafambira?'

'This moth business,' he replied, grinning at the prospect of replenishing his coffers.

'This is extortion!' the headmaster protested. 'I will not allow this!'

Comrade Chiwafambira saw his chance to assert his dominance, to convince not only the assembled militia, but also himself, that he was a man deserving of his position. He swung his panga and struck Joseph on the side of the head with the flat side of the blade. Joseph Chiswa dropped like a stone. He was momentarily stunned, as blood trickled from a gash above his ear. A child who had been watching from the Paget dormitory windows above gave a cry before returning to the dining hall to spread news of what he had witnessed. As neither Robson Shambari nor Gilbert Mashoko was at hand, all hope for rescuing Baba Chiswa lay with Mister Thomas.

Making his way through the crowd of terrified children who had gathered outside the dining hall, Thomas had no idea what to do in this crisis. Cornered by a band of Green Bombers waving pangas and knobkerries, all clearly itching for some action, Thomas ran in front of the children to protect them, stretching his arms out on both sides of his body indicating that they should stand behind him. He saw Joseph below the giant leaves of the delicious monster, sitting on the ground, holding his head.

As the children cried out for Thomas to do something, the commotion caught Comrade Shuranyama's attention. 'And who is this?' he bellowed.

Aware of the gravity of the situation, Thomas knew he must rise to the occasion. He stood his ground.

'I am Thomas Threscothic. And I stand for these children!'

At least that is what he intended to say, had it not been for a sudden malfunction of one of Jimmy Moverley-Smith's hearing aids, causing an excruciatingly high-pitched squeal to erupt in his ear. He fell to his knees, shutting his eyes tightly and clasping his ears, crying out in agony as if possessed by a hoard of demons. Comrade Shuranyama shifted uncomfortably. Whatever conclusion he reached, the nuances of Thomas's heroic intentions had been utterly lost, though the incident had distracted him.

Comrade Shuranyama turned to Joseph, who had managed to get to his feet. 'Seven o'clock this evening, I said. If that building is not vacated, these men will not show such leniency.'

He turned promptly and marched back to his orange Hummer, followed by Comrade Chiwafambira, whose newly acquired shiny Zhing-Zhong dog tags – a must-have, he thought, for military types like him – jingled as he walked briskly to keep up with his idol. The Green Bombers and assorted throng also withdrew to their vehicles, wary of displeasing their boss. In a minute the car park was once again silent, a cold, biting wind sweeping across it.

Betty Mukadota stepped forward. 'Come on, children,' she said, 'back to breakfast.'

Thomas helped the headmaster back to his office before fetching the medical kit and a plastic tub filled with warm water. Using balls of cotton wool, Thomas cleaned the gash. It was a nasty cut, which certainly needed stitches. Since Joseph seemed disorientated, Thomas offered to take him to the doctor; he refused, though, insisting he could drive himself, adding that he did not want Betty and the children left alone.

As Joseph left, the full weight of the challenge ahead struck Thomas. How could they possibly manage with only one dormitory? In the past, Thomas might have called Reverend Hardcastle for advice, but that was no longer an option. He raced home to fetch Marie's little black book, in which he had written the number for Reverend Muyambo, given to him by Richard and Tony. Without delay, he called him from Mai Rutivi's phone. A cheerful, well-spoken man, the reverend agreed to come over immediately to see if he could help.

Joseph returned with a large bump on his head, where the doctor had shaved the hair to stitch the gash. He looked anxious and flustered, and seemed relieved to meet the Reverend Muyambo, who arrived shortly afterwards, hoping perhaps he might have a solution. In truth, there was none; nobody could stand up to Hitler Jesus, whose political connections, it was said, went right to the very top.

To bolster flagging spirits, Reverend Muyambo undertook to discuss the situation with the war veterans when they arrived that night. Surely he could reason with them about the welfare of the children? Surely they would respect a priest? Betty seemed dubious; these were not the type of men to respond to reason. Ever practical, she suggested that they should instead spend the day vacating Paget Block, and try at least to find alternative accommodation for the displaced children.

Just after eleven o'clock, the labour began. The tables and benches from the dining hall were carried down to the barn, and the seventy

267

beds from Paget would be squeezed into the dining hall. Wishful thinking, this was – the hall could accommodate only twenty-five, at most. Things seemed hopeless. A good number of children would have to sleep in the barn.

Thoroughly dejected, Thomas retreated to his office. Oblivious to the drama, Louis the crow leapt onto Thomas's head and tugged at his curls. Thomas hardly noticed as he stared out the window across the playing fields. In the far distance he caught sight of Mister Chikorobho's dwelling with its thatched roof, a thin wisp of smoke drifting from the chimney. Next to the house lay the cabbage patch where the flaming *tsikamutanda*, goblins in hand, had dived head-first. Thomas recalled the fear on the villagers' faces. Few things, it seemed, could arouse as much terror as a trio of goblins on the loose. Suddenly it dawned on him. That's what they needed: those goblins, and the only man with the skill to manage them – Cuthbert Kambazuma.

Thomas pushed open the door of the headmaster's office without knocking, something he had never done before. Joseph was sitting on the floor on the far side of his office, a screwdriver in his hand. A tired old Hoover lay in pieces on a copy of *The Herald* spread open in front of him. He looked up as Thomas burst in.

'I've got a plan, Joseph, I've got a plan!'

The older man's face looked anxious, dejected. 'So, what is your plan?' he asked.

'We need goblins. Those goblins from the village. You saw how frightened the people were that day we went down there. We can use them to protect ourselves.'

Joseph smiled, but shook his head. 'Thomas, these are things you know little, if anything, about. You can't save the home in that way. Please, let's be realistic.'

Thomas would not be dissuaded. 'No, I disagree. If there's a better plan, I'll hear it. Until then, I'm going to try and find that man, that *tsikamutanda*. I'll even pay him with my own money.'

The two men stared at each other for a moment, then Thomas turned and left. He sprinted across the field and through the gate. Mister Chikorobho opened the door with an expression that seemed to say, 'It wasn't me.'

'Take me to the *tsikamutanda*. Please. Take me to Cuthbert Kambazuma. I'll pay you,' he wheezed, completely out of breath, waving a twenty-thousand dollar bill in front of Mister Chikorobho's face.

Mister Chikorobho snatched it from his hand. 'Right! Let's go!'

The two walked briskly across the playing field, to where the Datsun was parked. Under Mister Chikorobho's instructions, Thomas navigated the vehicle along a patchwork of gravel roads and dirt tracks. Suddenly, his passenger called out, 'Stop! Stop! That's it, over there.'

Thomas glanced across to where he was pointing. A rusty barbed-wire fence enclosed an area around a small house. Built with concrete air-bricks, it had a roof of corrugated iron. Appended to the fence was a large hand-painted sign. In bold red letters on a white background, it promised the following:

DR KAMBAZUMA CAN TREAT & SOLVE MANY PROBLEMS SUCH AS:

Bewitched pple
Swollen Body
Lost Lover
Insanity
Diarhea
Madness
To make mens pennis strong
Women with pregnancy problems

Vomiting all the time
Misfortunes
Demand Debts
Remove misunderstanding with anybody
Court Cases
Casino specialist
Bad luck
Customer attraction
etc ...

Leaning from his window, Thomas squinted closely at the sign. Impressive, he thought – but no mention of goblins. Perhaps they fell under the broad category of 'Bewitched pple'. He pulled the Datsun over, and despite calling out several times, there was no answer. It was one o'clock already, time was of the essence. The two men walked around the dwelling, and there he was. With a half-smoked marijuana cigarette rolled in a strip of newspaper clasped between his fingers, and a red-and-black blanket pulled neatly up to his waist, he was fast asleep in a homemade hammock strung up between two msasa trees. Swaying gently from side to side in the breeze, lulled by a soothing snore, he was the picture of contentment.

Thomas leant towards him. 'Cuthbert,' he called out softly, not wishing to give the man a fright.

The mysterious *tsikamutanda* did not stir.

'Cuthbert!' Thomas called out, this time in a louder voice. Still there was no reaction.

'CUTHBERT! WAKE UP!'

Cuthbert opened an eye, uttering a barely perceptible groan of complaint. 'What time is it?' he asked in a hoarse whisper.

'It's ten past one,' Thomas replied.

'Hey, guys. We're closed between one and two. Come back later,' muttered Cuthbert, closing his eye again.

Thomas and Mister Chikorobho looked at one another in disbelief. In the world's fastest-shrinking economy, one seldom encountered people who turned away business in such a brazen fashion.

'Cuthbert, come on! Wake up. We need your help.'

'Guys … please. What does a man have to do to get some peace and quiet around here?' protested the *tsikamutanda*, his eyes still closed.

'Cuthbert, we need those goblins of yours – for protection. The war veterans came by this morning. They want to take over the William Westward.'

At the mention of goblins, Cuthbert's eyes sprang open and he lifted his head ever so slightly.

'Goblins,' he said, 'Ooooooooooh, that'll cost you … And war veterans, you say? Tricky combination.'

'Of course. But I'm willing to pay.'

Cuthbert scratched his chin. 'Goblins … dangerous work that. Hmm … how many do you need?'

'Three,' replied Thomas. 'Those three from this man's house.'

'So … its *zvikwambo* you're after. Very nasty. That'll be fifteen large. Each.'

'What?'

'You heard me, fifteen million each, forty-five for the lot. Take it or leave it … that's my final price.'

Cuthbert closed his eyes again. Thomas grimaced; for him, forty-five million was an absolute fortune. He would have to scrape together every last cent he had in the world.

'That's too much. Can't we negotiate?'

'Take it or leave it. But there's nowhere else around here to get *zvikwambo* at short notice.'

With a sigh, Thomas capitulated, 'Okay, Okay. But you better come right now, to the William Westward.'

'No, no, not now,' Cuthbert said, 'I told you, it's my lunch hour. I'll be there at two-thirty.'

Thomas glared at him, 'Don't be late, Cuthbert. I'm warning you.'

With his eyes still closed, Cuthbert dismissed them with a carefree flick of his fingers.

53

The Unlikely Genius of Doctor Cuthbert Kambazuma

Back at the William Westward, Robson and Gilbert, assisted by Reverend Muyambo, had already begun the arduous task of carrying the remaining forty-five beds down to the barn. Wishing to talk with Robson, Thomas joined in, grabbing one end of a bed, and Robson the other. As they lugged it across the playing field, Thomas slipped in a mention of his visit to the *tsikamutanda*. Robson instantly dropped his end of the bed and turned to Thomas. Contemplating the proposal for a second, he shrugged his shoulders and said, 'No harm in trying, I guess. Let's see if that fellow turns up.'

Sure enough, at exactly half past two, the dreadlocked *tsikamutanda* appeared at the administration block, asking for Thomas. An assistant accompanied him – a boy of about fourteen years old, introduced by Cuthbert simply as his 'monkey-man'.

Slung across Cuthbert's back was a cage with rusty iron bars

272

and a door that slid up and down. Inside was the *tsikamutanda*'s ubiquitous plastic packet filled with bark and roots, as well as several balls of twine, a canister of silver spray paint, and a dirty hessian sack with the heads of a couple of filthy old mops poking out. An unusual assortment of items, Thomas thought, when all he really needed was the leather pouch filled with sex-goblins, which, disturbingly, was nowhere to be seen. Thomas eyed the *tsikamutanda* suspiciously. He was about to lay out an awful lot of money – this man had better deliver the goods.

Cuthbert asked to be taken to meet the headmaster. He needed a full account of the morning's events, he said. Joseph Chiswa seemed distracted, however, and it was difficult to draw his attention away from his son's disassembled radio-controlled beach buggy that lay next to the shell of the Hoover in a corner of his office.

Thomas helped Joseph back to his chair and introduced him to Cuthbert. With some difficulty, the headmaster recounted the visit that morning by Hitler Jesus, Comrade Chiwafambira, and their crew. There were tears in his eyes as he explained their predicament: at seven that evening, Comrade Chiwafambira would be taking up residence in Paget Block to begin what the refugees of Cotswold Downs Estate anticipated would be a reign of terror. Cuthbert listened intently. He waited patiently until the headmaster had finished, then asked to be shown the car park where the events had taken place. Leaving Joseph to his buggy and Hoover, Thomas led the way down the courtyard path.

Cuthbert halted at the spot where the path from the administrative block joined the car park, just in front of the giant msasa with its jungle-like cloak of leathery leaves. Deep in concentration, he surveyed the scene for several minutes, in absolute silence.

'Bring me an exercise book and a sharp HB pencil,' he instructed, without turning his head.

One of the children from a curious group that had gathered was dispatched to the prep room and promptly returned with a sky-blue mathematics exercise book and a yellow pencil, sharpened as requested. What then followed, baffled all present. With large but even paces, Cuthbert measured the length and breadth of the car park, stopping from time to time to record his results in the exercise book. That in itself did not seem particularly unusual, but when he began pacing across the open asphalt in seemingly incongruous zigzags, Thomas's suspicions were again aroused.

Returning to his spot at the head of the path, Cuthbert turned and gazed intently at the buildings, examining every window and door in great detail, all the time taking notes.

'What's up there?' he asked Thomas, pointing at the second floor of Fairbridge block.

'That,' replied Thomas, somewhat irritated, 'is one of the dormitories.'

'Excellent,' was Cuthbert's response. 'And that thing there with the cable?' he asked, pointing at the contraption suspended from the Fairbridge balcony. 'Does it work?'

'That's the slide. And yes, it does work.'

'Excellent,' Cuthbert muttered, scribbling furiously in the book. 'And them,' he said, gesturing towards the children, 'what kinds of noises can they make?'

'Well,' Thomas replied, clearly unsettled by the question, 'the usual ones, I suppose.'

'Hmm,' was all Cuthbert said, as he pushed his way through the circle of children. He crawled under the spreading leaves of the delicious monster – rather like a Mau-Mau warrior preparing for an ambush – and remained there for several minutes. 'Can you see me?' he eventually called out.

Thomas was at the end of his tether.

'Sort of, yes. I can see your leg.'

'And now?'

'I can see your head.'

'And now?'

'I can see your leg again.'

'I can tell, this … this bush here, is going to be our main challenge,' Cuthbert muttered from the undergrowth. Emerging with a frown, he asked, 'And how many staff will be available tonight?'

'Five,' Thomas answered, counting on his fingers. 'Myself, Betty, Gilbert, Robson and Joseph Chiswa … if he's feeling all right.'

'And me,' Reverend Muyambo called out. 'I'll be there to meet the war veterans when they arrive, to try to reason with them, that is.'

Cuthbert chuckled. 'Very good, very good. So you intend to have a speaking role, do you?'

'Eh … yes,' replied Reverend Muyambo, 'I had thought so. Will that be a problem?'

'Not at all, not at all.'

Turning to Thomas, Cuthbert asked for a room – somewhere to distil his thoughts, he said. Thomas led him back to the administration block and opened the door of his office, startling Louis the crow, who was busy rearranging a pile of tinfoil strips, teaspoons and silver Parker pens on the desk.

'Does it always do that?' asked Cuthbert, pointing at the pile.

'Yes, he collects shiny things wherever he can find them.'

'Are you sure? Can it be relied upon to do that?' Cuthbert asked, narrowing his bloodshot eyes. 'It's very important that you're absolutely certain on this point.'

'Well, generally, yes.'

Cuthbert sat on the desk and opened the exercise book to study his notes. Thomas was about to close the door behind him, when Cuthbert called out, 'That buggy of Mister Chiswa's. The one he's fixing. Will it be working by seven?'

'I really don't know. I'll have to ask him,' Thomas replied. By this time, he had had just about enough of this farce. 'But why do you want to know? What do you want to use it for? To ferry the goblins in?'

'Precisely' the *tsikamutanda* responded with a wink. 'Not all of them, though, just one.'

Shaking his head and closing the door behind him, Thomas proceeded to check on Joseph's progress with the buggy.

Cuthbert closed his eyes and sighed. After five minutes of what may have seemed like a quick forty winks – but which in reality was the ruminations of uncommon genius – Cuthbert opened his eyes, picked up the exercise book, and opened it to a fresh new page.

Raising his HB Pencil, he began to write:

Act 1, Scene 1

Stage left: Enter Hitler Jesus, Cde Chiwafambira and mob.

Centre Stage: Enter Rev Muyambo.

Rev Muyambo: 'Bla-bla-bla-bla, etc … Christian mumbo-jumbo … etc etc.' (30 seconds)

Centre Stage: Exit Rev Muyambo (in a hurry).

Half an hour passed – almost four o'clock, but still no sign of the *tsikamutanda*. Thomas was gravely concerned. What on earth could he be doing in there? He knocked on the door. There was no answer. He knocked again.

'All right, all right, I'm coming. Two more minutes.'

Thomas felt a wave of anger rising within him, when the door burst open and Cuthbert emerged, beaming. 'So, will the buggy be ready?'

'It should be,' said Thomas.

'And where is my monkey-man?'

Thomas rolled his eyes in annoyance. 'He's waiting outside for you … where he's been for the last half hour.'

Cuthbert strolled into the courtyard to find his monkey-man. Thomas followed, determined not to let the *tsikamutanda* out of his sight again.

'There you are,' Cuthbert said. 'Right. *Ndinoda kuti uyende kunovhima ubate tsoko nhatu*. Catch me three of them. Nasty ones. Big as you can find. Take the cage with you. Do you understand?'

The monkey-man set off at once with the rusty cage slung over his shoulder, across the playing fields to the bush beyond.

It was the number of monkeys that set alarm bells ringing in Thomas's mind. Three of them, the *tsikamutanda* had said.

'Cuthbert,' Thomas asked, 'where are the three goblins you promised?'

The *tsikamutanda* looked away, frowning.

'Cuthbert, where are the goblins?' he repeated, his voice trembling.

The *tsikamutanda* opened his mouth as if to speak; a peculiar gurgling noise emerged, but there were no discernible words.

'Cuthbert! Did you bring those goblins with you?'

The gurgling noise resumed. Thomas detected a smile on the *tsikamutanda*'s lips.

'God damn you, Cuthbert Kambazuma. You think this is funny, don't you? You want forty-five million dollars, for three blasted monkeys. What are you going to do, dress them up in suits and send them out to negotiate?'

The *tsikamutanda* spluttered, 'But there will be goblins ...'

'What kind of goblins? Speak up now. This is not a joke.'

'Goblins of the mind,' he suggested whimsically. 'Far easier to manage than the real ones, I find, and equally effective. Perfect for an occasion such as this. Honestly, the real ones are a nightmare to handle.'

Thomas scowled. It was clear this man was all hat and no cattle.

'And I bet you're not a real *tsikamutanda* either.'

'What one tends to find nowadays is an evolution of sorts,' Cuthbert responded adopting a quasi-academic tone, 'in certain of the traditional practices. Some of us are now ... how does one put it? ... self-trained.'

With just three hours until the war veterans returned, Thomas knew he had no other option but to go along with the machinations of this phony *tsikamutanda* – he could only hope that Cuthbert had something up his crooked sleeve. 'Dammit, Cuthbert, ten million, then. That's all you're getting. Take it or leave it. Leave right now if that's not enough for you.'

'Well, you know,' countered Cuthbert with a sheepish grin, 'it's for a love of the arts I do it, not for the money. Okay, ten million it is.'

'This better be good,' warned Thomas. 'Now get to work. I'm going to my house to get your money. When I come back, I want to see some progress in this scheme of yours.' With that, he turned and strode decisively towards the Datsun.

'Don't be too long now,' Cuthbert teased. 'Cast meeting at four-thirty.'

Cast meeting? Thomas shook his head and walked on.

Once home, Thomas made his way directly to the pantry. Using a step ladder, he pulled down a large cake tin. Charles and Diana smiled at him from its lid – the Royal Wedding. The tin was stuffed with bricks, all his savings. He counted out ten and squeezed them into his pockets. Before getting back into the Datsun, Thomas had a thought. From the side table next to Marie's bed, he fetched Mister Mkhize's little jar of Vaseline, the holy embrocation from Lawley – that, and Father's most beloved book, the Winston Churchill one, complete with a flotilla of bookmarks at all the important speeches. Tonight they would need all the encouragement they could get.

Back at the William Westward, it was Cuthbert's turn to restrain his impatience. 'Where've you been?' he shouted, using a plastic orange cone as a megaphone. 'It's quarter past five. We've been waiting for you, for the dress rehearsal.' Before Thomas could reply, Cuthbert thrust the blue exercise book into his hands. 'Here's the script. I'll be directing from up there,' he said, pointing up at the near corner of Fairbridge block.

Thomas noticed a commotion under the leaves of the delicious monster. Shovel-loads of soil flew through the air, landing on a fresh heap of earth nearby. Robson's head popped up from a small, deep hole to greet Thomas, sweat pouring from his temples.

'What's going on down there?' Thomas asked, perplexed.

'That,' replied Cuthbert, 'is the ground control centre – to be operated by Miss Betty Mukadota.' Then he added by way of whispered theatrical aside, 'If we can get her in there, that is.'

'Why can't I go in there rather?'

Cuthbert stared at him impatiently. 'If you'd had the decency to to attend the cast meeting at four-thirty, as I'd asked, you'd know that your role is up there with me – technical support: management of the slide and the spotlights, and that crow of yours. A central role. Vital, in fact.'

Thomas peered under the leaves of the enormous plant. A peculiar howl rang out, and a small furry hand grabbed at his nose. He recoiled in horror. Barely visible in the darkness was the wire cage. In it were three of the largest, angriest vervet monkeys that Thomas had ever seen, with bulbous blue scrotums and livid black faces. The monkey-man had certainly been hard at work. A labyrinth of thick twine zigzagged all across the front of the car park, wrapped around spikes that had been driven into the asphalt. The ends of each length of twine ran into the hole that Robson had been digging. Using gravel and loose earth, which he poured carefully from a bucket, Gilbert covered the lines of twine around the hole, obscuring them from view in the dim evening light.

'Okay, bring me the rope. It's time to get her in,' shouted Cuthbert through the cone, pointing up at the rope used in the annual tug o'war competition, which was now hanging over a large msasa branch. One of the senior boys stepped forward and handed it to Cuthbert.

'Betty Mukadota. Stand forward,' called Cuthbert. 'Quickly, now.'

Betty came forward. Cuthbert skilfully transformed the end of the rope into a hangman's noose and dropped it over Betty's head.

Thomas gasped. 'Hold it right there, Cuthbert. This … this … show of yours has gone too far. Take that off Betty now, right now. They'll be no hangings here tonight.'

Ignoring his protests, Cuthbert widened the noose so that it slipped down to Betty's hips. He pulled it up under her arms and tightened the noose behind her shoulders. 'Right, team, hoist her up!' he shouted.

A group of senior boys took their positions in standard tug o' war formation, holding the other end of the rope.

'Ready! Steady! Heave-ho!' shouted the boys.

Betty's enormous frame was yanked instantly off the ground. She began spinning uncontrollably in the air. Cuthbert grabbed her feet to steady her, and positioned her above the hole.

'Heave-ho!' cried the boys, and up Betty went again, even higher into the air, gasping as the noose tightened around her frame.

'That's enough, that's enough!' roared Cuthbert.

'Okay, pull back those leaves. Steady, now, steady! Let's lower her into the ground-control centre. Gently, now. Gently. That's it.'

Within seconds, not a part of her was visible, save for the top of her head and her face. It was an extremely tight fit, but Betty somehow managed to wriggle her hands and arms free, and reached out for the pieces of twine that ran into the hole – trip wires, she'd been told.

A cheer went up from the tug o' war team – Betty Mukadota was in position. The boys who had been holding back the leaves of the delicious monster gently released them. From where Thomas was standing, the ground-control centre and its operator were now completely invisible.

'There's no need to cover her with soil for the dress rehearsal,' Cuthbert called out. 'Now, will someone get that pile of earth out of sight.'

There was a flurry of activity as the remaining lengths of twine were concealed and the wheelbarrow loaded with soil and hidden behind the far side of Paget.

'Right! Opening positions!' Cuthbert's voice rang out.

Thomas watched in amazement as a hundred and twenty children broke up into small, well-ordered groups, which then dispersed to various locations across the property. The tug o' war team, under the captaincy of Gilbert, took up their positions, crouching behind the desks in the prep room closest to the car park. Other children were seen clambering into the branches of the msasas and jacarandas around the playing field. Still others concealed themselves at regular intervals in the hibiscus hedge surrounding the car park, but the vast majority filed up the stairs to the dormitories where the beds had been pushed aside, allowing them to form themselves into neat choir-like units.

Joseph Chiswa, his composure well-nigh restored, walked to the far side of the playing field and squatted inconspicuously under the grandstand. Reverend Muyambo disappeared into the shadows at the base of the Paget stairs.

'Remember, Reverend, no matter what happens, do not move until my command,' Cuthbert instructed. Then he turned to Thomas. 'Follow me, Thomas, to the Director's Suite! But first, fetch the crow.'

Cuthbert marched up the Paget stairs and across to the front windows, where Joseph Chiswa's stately armchair had been placed on top of the laundry table, providing a commanding view of the car park. In front of the chair, fastened to the windowsills, was an array of spotlights with multi-coloured gels – relics from the early days of the William Westward, when the Rotarians and Round Tablers had staged an annual Christmas pantomime to raise funds. In the corner, still enclosed in its dirty hessian sack, was the mop, which now had a large picture hook screwed in between the shaggy fibres of its head.

Cuthbert took his position in the director's chair and turned to his runner, young Tanaka, who had risen to the occasion and forced his way into the coveted position.

'Coffee! Make it strong, and make it snappy!'

Tanaka dashed down to the kitchen and returned in record time with a steaming mug of instant coffee.

'Ahh,' said Cuthbert, taking a sip, 'now that'll put the hair back on any *tsikamutanda*'s chest.' Standing on the table, he raised his makeshift megaphone to his lips and pushed his head out the window. 'Checking all positions. Sound Effects Group 1?' he boomed.

His voice echoed across the silence of the car park and playing fields. From the recesses of the hedge by the gate, a chorus replied, 'Check!'

'Sound Effects Group 2?'

'Check!' was the response from the branches of the jacarandas and msasas.

'Sound Effects Group 3?'

'Check!' resonated from the bike shed behind Fairbridge.

'Sound Effects Group 4?'

'Check!' roared Gilbert's tug o' war platoon from behind the desks of the prep room across the courtyard.

'Scene 5, General Sound Effects?'

'Check!' chorused the dormitory choir groups from Paget as well as Fairbridge.

'Lighting and Airborne Props?'

There was a brief silence. Cuthbert lowered the megaphone and whispered across to Thomas, 'That's you!'

'Check!' called back Thomas, echoing the enthusiasm of the various sound effects groups.

'Ground-control Centre?'

'Check!' came Betty's high-pitched call from the cavernous underbelly of the delicious monster in the courtyard below.

Cuthbert climbed down from the table and walked across the

dormitory to the window overlooking the playing fields. Raising the megaphone, he cried out, 'Mechanised Props?'

'Check!' Joseph Chiswa responded from the grandstand, some distance away.

'Mechanised Props Control?'

'Check!' Robson called out from the windowsill, next to Cuthbert.

'Communications?'

'Check!' answered a line of children, seated one behind the other in a long chain that extended from Cuthbert's director's chair, right across the dormitory and down the stairs to the reverend.

And finally, 'Divine Intervention?'

'Check!' hollered Reverend Edgar Muyambo, from the base of the stairwell.

'Right!' Cuthbert concluded. 'Full house, then. Lights off!'

Gilbert snapped down the switches of the main electricity box, leaving only one for the all-important socket feeding the spotlights and the buggy's radio controls. The William Westward was plunged into darkness.

'Okay, Reverend, let's rock and roll!' was Cuthbert's final instruction before he resumed his position in the director's chair in Paget.

The first dress rehearsal was, somewhat predictably, an unmitigated disaster. Beads of sweat formed on the director's brow. By now it was a quarter past six. With so little time remaining, there was, quite simply, no margin for error. Some measure of relief came with the second dress rehearsal. Bar certain mechanical hitches from Lighting and Airborne Props, and the failure of Sound Effects Group 3 to come in on cue, the show seemed to hold some promise. Cuthbert quaffed the tepid remainder of his coffee and grabbed his smoking paraphernalia; his mood had regained its former buoyancy.

'Back in five,' he said to Thomas as he leapt down the stairs. Presently, the pungent smell of marijuana came wafting up from the courtyard, together with the cheerful whistling of 'There's No

Business Like Show Business'. The maestro's final preparations were in place.

Along with the break came a renewed sense of dread. The children had reassembled, and were milling about at the entrance to the administration block, waiting for final orders to resume their positions. Sensing their anxiety, Thomas checked his watch. It was already half past six – time to fortify the children's resolve.

From his window in Paget overlooking the courtyard, Thomas called down to everyone – to the children, the staff, Reverend Muyambo and to Cuthbert – asking them to come up and assemble in the dormitory. Even with the beds pushed back against the walls, it was a tight squeeze. While the children were settling down, Thomas spoke briefly with the reverend. Prayers must be said, and the holy embrocation administered. Reverend Muyambo stood up on the laundry table next to the director's chair, with Thomas and Joseph Chiswa beside him. He gestured, and all bowed their heads. The reverend prayed fervently for their safety and deliverance before asking them to join him in the Lord's Prayer. As the last amens died down, he asked the children to form a line and to come forward, one by one.

The first child stepped up. Thomas opened the jar of holy Shembe Vaseline, and with his index finger scooped a smear of the soft petroleum jelly. The reverend placed his hands on the child's head and delivered a silent blessing as Thomas gently marked the sign of the cross on the child's forehead, for protection. One by one, the children came forward, until precious little remained in the jar. Thomas ran his finger around the inside surfaces, eking out the remainder, until each child and every member of staff had been blessed and crossed. Even Cuthbert came forward, smirking slightly. Thomas then turned to the reverend, and finding a small sliver on the inside of the lid, made a cross on his forehead and then on his own.

Silence descended on the congregation and, expecting to take up their positions, they all turned around.

'Wait!' said Thomas. 'Wait for the speech.'

The staff looked at each other in surprise as Thomas climbed back onto the laundry table. Holding Father's book – the contents of which he knew like the back of his hand after years of paging through it – Thomas opened it at one of the bookmarks. To his mind, no words could possibly be more fitting than those of Sir Winston Spencer Churchill on the eve of the Battle of Britain.

Thomas closed his eyes for a second to collect his thoughts; without any preparation he would need to improvise. He knitted his brow and commenced in a loud, clear voice:

> *'I have, myself, full confidence that if all do their duty, if nothing is neglected, and if the best arrangements are made, as they are being made, we shall prove ourselves able to defend our home, to ride out the storm, and to outlive the menace of tyranny, if necessary for years, if necessary alone.'*

The children shifted uncomfortably. Taking no notice, Thomas continued:

> *'We shall go on to the end, we shall fight from the dormitories and from the prep rooms, we shall fight with growing confidence and growing strength from the trees and hedges, we shall defend our home, whatever the cost may be, we shall fight in the car park, we shall fight upon the playing fields and in the streets, we shall fight from inside the delicious monster. We shall never surrender.'*

An uncertain silence followed. Thomas quickly flipped forward to the next bookmark.

> *'Let us therefore brace ourselves to our duties, and so bear ourselves that if the William Westward and its lands last for a thousand years, the children will still say, "This was their finest hour."'*

Thomas looked up at his audience to confirm that the rhetoric had done the job. Perplexed, the children starred at him with gaping mouths. From the back, Cuthbert chuckled and called out, 'You tell them, brother!' followed by a loud 'Yahoooo!' The children looked around, still unsure. The sound of a solitary person clapping echoed about the room. It was Reverend Muyambo, eager to keep spirits afloat. The headmaster joined in, followed by Robson, Betty and Gilbert. Taking this as their cue, the children responded with tumultuous applause – clapping, cheering and whistling. Thomas beamed. A sense of camaraderie embraced the William Westward. It was some time before the hullabaloo died down.

Cuthbert pushed through the crowd and grabbed his orange megaphone as he leapt onto the laundry table. 'Right. Code Red. Opening positions!'

The mood of jubilation instantly transformed into one of resolute purpose. The children ran down the stairs to take up their positions across the property, and the tug o' war team busied itself lowering Betty back inside the ground-control centre, this time covering her with soil, right up to the eyeballs. A couple of minutes later, Cuthbert again called out the checklist. Each position responded instantly. The William Westward was ready.

'Right!' shouted Cuthbert. 'Lights off! Remember, keep still in your positions until you get your cues!'

A cloak of darkness descended on the William Westward. Not a single ray of moonlight penetrated the low-hanging clouds. All across the property, a hundred and twenty-seven hearts pounded, anxiously anticipating the final showdown. Predictably, Hitler Jesus and his mob were late; they were still deeply immersed in an all-day drinking session on the verandah of Comrade Teddy-Boy's residence at Cotswold Downs Estate. Quarter past seven, at least, estimated Cuthbert, as he whispered to Thomas to cover the lamp with a hessian sack and switch it on, so that he could check his watch. Thomas leant forward and flipped the switch. There was no response. He tried again, but to no avail.

'Try one of the spotlights,' hissed Cuthbert.

Thomas draped the sack over a spotlight and switched it on. Again, nothing. Both Cuthbert and Thomas began to panic – without electricity, the show would be doomed. Telling him to sprint over to the prep room, Cuthbert whispered a message to his runner: Had Gilbert remembered to leave the switch on in Fairbridge block? Tankara tripped over the children forming the communications line on the stairs, and then scampered across the courtyard and into the prep room. Seconds later, low whispers and the sound of a switch being snapped up and down could be heard from the Director's Suite. Thomas tried the desk lamp again, but with no joy. Then, glancing across the car park, he noticed that the street lamps outside the home were also off. This was the worst-case scenario – once again, the Zimbabwe Electricity Supply Authority had failed them.

Just then, the roar of vehicle engines disrupted the darkness. The outline of Hitler Jesus's orange Hummer was briefly illuminated in the headlights of the ten-ton truck behind it, laden with a highly inebriated mob of Green Bombers and assorted hangers-on, all singing and slurring, itching for some violence. Fortunately, in the confusion of the day's drinking and the subsequent scramble onto the trucks, none had remembered to bring a torch.

The children stiffened with fright as they held their positions. The vehicles came to a halt at the far side of the car park, and the rowdy gang leapt out. Several lost their footing in the darkness and landed heavily on the gravel, grazing their elbows and knees without even noticing, numbed by the alcohol. They congregated around the wooden guard house next to the gate, and some even went inside to sit down for yet another drink before the fun began.

Thomas crouched down, frozen with fear. Suddenly a vision popped into his head – Hennie van Aswegen's antiquated Kawasaki generator, collecting dust down in the barn where Robson was raising the day-old chicks. Since the chicks needed lights to warm them, Joseph had run an extension cord from the socket in the dining room right out to the barn.

'Cuthbert, I've got a plan,' Thomas whispered. 'Think of something to distract them, I need five minutes.' He fumbled his way across the dormitory, climbed out the window and slid down the drainpipe, momentarily overcoming his aversion to heights and poor coordination. Within seconds, he was down the drainpipe and sprinting across the playing fields.

The menacing sounds of the mob became louder. 'Come out, Chiswa,' a voice called, 'it's time to face the music!'

Distorted renditions of what may once have been ZANU-PF liberation songs spontaneously broke out.

'Come out, Chiswa! I'm not asking again!'

Cuthbert knew something had to be done, and quickly. He turned to the first child in the Communications line and whispered, 'Send the reverend out.'

The message went from one child to the next, right across the dormitory and down the stairs: 'Send the reverend out'; 'Send the reverend out ...' – although somewhere along the line, things got slightly garbled, so that when the message finally reached the reverend, ever so subtly it had changed. 'Send your rear end out, Reverend,' was the message he eventually heard. The reverend was not at all amused. What an inopportune moment for an oblique swipe at his sexuality. 'What?' he whispered back to the child, in gravely offended tones.

Up the line the message went. Seconds later, it reached Cuthbert, who was every bit as confused as the reverend. Very clearly, very precisely, Cuthbert tried again, whispering to the child next to him, 'Go. Out. Reverend!'

This time the message went through without a hitch. From his position at the bottom of the stairwell, the reverend got to his feet. Following the path as best he could, he rounded the delicious

288

monster. The movement caught Hitler Jesus's eye.

'Is that you, Chiswa? About time you showed yourself!'

Gathering his wits, the reverend cleared his throat and called out, 'It is I, Reverend Edgar Muyambo.'

'Ah, Christ, what's this now?' Hitler Jesus responded, his patience wearing thin. 'Where's Chiswa, dammit!'

'I understand you have come here to take over the one wing of this orphanage. Gentlemen, in the name of God, I appeal to you, rethink this decision,' the reverend pleaded.

'Listen here, preacher man. Bugger off with your white man's witchcraft. You bloody Christians! Last I heard, God fell behind with his ZANU-PF membership fees. Now get the hell out of here and send Chiswa down before this gets nasty!'

In the pale evening light, the reverend saw Comrade Teddy-Boy raise his panga to swing it at him, and so he stepped back in horror. Betty was right, it was hopeless trying to reason with these men. He had no option but to leave the situation in the hands of the *tsikamutanda*.

'All right, all right,' the reverend capitulated. 'Wait here while I find him. There's been a power failure, so it might take a few moments to locate him.'

Upstairs, Cuthbert was in a flat spin. What was he to do? Thomas had disappeared, ostensibly to find a solution – who knew when he'd be coming back? The drunken singing at the gates became rowdier. All around, clusters of anxious children wondered why there were no signals from the director.

'Come out, Chiswa, dammit. Or we're coming in. Do you hear?'

Cuthbert knew he had to do something. Mimicking the high-pitched voice of a young girl, he called out, 'He's on his way! Just finishing up in the bathroom.'

Feeling his way about in the barn, Thomas finally located the old generator under a wooden workbench. He had no idea when it had last been used, or even if there was any petrol in the tank. Taking the rubber handle of the pull-start cable in his right hand, he wedged his foot against the petrol tank and gave an almighty yank. There was not even a cough in response. Thomas gritted his teeth and tried again. They had come this far; they could not be defeated. There are occasions when one's determination is so strong as to overcome even the most recalcitrant of machines. Whether it was that, or divine intervention, no one will ever know. The important thing was that the second time round, with a reluctant splutter and the violent expulsion of a mass of dried leaves, the aged Kawasaki KG 1500C burst into life with a roar – an extraordinary tribute to the quality of Japanese engineering.

Thomas unplugged the extension cord from the lamps that hung over the chicken pens and forced it into the socket on the side of the generator. He flipped a white switch down, hoping against hope that this was the right thing to do. The roar of the engine seemed to subside slightly – a good sign, Thomas thought. From his position under the grandstand, Joseph Chiswa caught a glimpse of a lone figure flying across the playing field.

Hitler Jesus's patience had by now expired. It was time to set the mob loose on the buildings. Barely metres away, buried below the spreading leaves of the delicious monster, with one hand fastened to the end of the cords that crisscrossed the car park, and the other on the wire lever of the monkey cage, Betty was unable to dislodge a wandering worker ant that had scuttled up her nostril. She had tried all manner of abrupt head movements, and nose twitches, but nothing would work – the tickle persisted. Just as Hilter Jesus raised his hand and the mob fell silent, Betty could contain it no more. A loud sneeze burst mysteriously from within the plant.

Hitler Jesus looked across at Comrade Teddy-Boy. 'Did you hear that?'

'What?'

'Like a sneeze or something. From that bush over there.'

'Let's take a look.'

Betty froze. The two men advanced and peered under the leaves. Comrade Teddy-Boy pulled a box of matches from his pocket and lit one. A pair of huge eyeballs and a cross of holy Vaseline glistened in the flickering light. The men recognised her immediately – it was the large woman who had shouted at them earlier that day. Both were instantly unsettled.

'What on earth are you doing down there?' Hitler Jesus demanded to know.

This was the moment upon which the success of the entire operation would stand or fall. Momentarily dumbstruck, Betty whispered the first word that came to mind, which – though she had no way of appreciating it at the time – was in fact the only word in the world that could have saved the day. '*Zvikwambo!*'

Comrade Teddy-Boy and Hitler Jesus recoiled in horror. Though neither would admit to it, deep down, nothing was more frightening than the suggestion of traditional black magic, with its array of goblins, surreptitious curses and evil spells. There was something strange in this neighbourhood. Why else would this enormous woman bury herself to the eyeballs in a hole under a delicious monster? From above, the sinister croak of a solitary crow, hoarse and unnerving, sent shivers down their spines.

On the other side of Paget block, panting loudly after his dash across the fields, Thomas reached inside the dining-hall window and yanked from its socket the plug for the cable that ran to the barn. Clenching the cable between his teeth, he scrambled onto the window ledge and hauled himself back up the drainpipe to the dormitory above. Robson leant out the window and grabbed Thomas's arm. Without uttering a sound, he effortlessly lifted Thomas through the window. Dragging the generator cable behind him, Thomas scampered past rows of crouching children to the Director's Suite. There, Cuthbert snatched the plug from him and rammed it into the power socket, which was linked to the spotlights and the buggy's radio controls. At last, the moment of truth had arrived. Covering the desk lamp with the hessian sack, Thomas snapped the switch. By God, it worked – there was light. The show would go on.

Cuthbert turned to his little batman, Tanaka, with a whisper. 'Send out the signal: Sound Effects Group 4, to commence!'

Tanaka scampered to the side windows overlooking the courtyard. Knowing that Gilbert and his tug o' war platoon would be waiting for their signal, he wasted no time in striking a match under a bed and raising the lid of a large cake tin. With great precision, he angled the inside edge of the lid so that it reflected the light across the courtyard, invisible to the invaders. Gilbert counted two quick flashes, the designated commencement signal. He raised his right hand in the darkness of the Fairbridge prep room. Crouched below the desks, each and every boy drew in a deep breath and counted the strokes of Gilbert's hand as he whispered, 'Three, two, one!'

Like clockwork, with perfect synchronicity, Sound Effect Group 4 set the mood with a chorus of heartbeat sounds, which came from their closed mouths and pulsating gullets, frog-like and in unison. The ominous throbbing floated from the windows of the prep room, reaching the ears of the mob outside. Befuddled with booze, and disquieted by Betty Mukadota's utterances, Comrade Teddy-Boy gulped. Had his spurious war veteran's honour not been at stake, he would have bolted right away. Pulling a half-jack of Mainstay Cane from his pocket, he took a few healthy swigs to steady himself. Hitler Jesus, a seasoned veteran of literally dozens of such raids, stood firm, though. Behind him, the silent band shifted uncomfortably on their feet as the eerie sounds enveloped them like vapour in the surrounding darkness.

Cuthbert again turned to his batman. 'Send out the signal for Mechanised Props to commence!'

Tanaka scampered across to the far side of the dormitory where Robson, the sole member of Mechanised Props Control, stood at the ready with the buggy's radio controls in his hands. Two cake tin flashes appeared at another window, and Joseph stepped out from under the grandstand to start the buggy's engine and switch on the torch taped across the bonnet to illuminate its hideous cargo. Without a sound, the buggy shot forward, now under the control of Robson, who eyed the torchlight with an owl's intensity, walking from window to window of Paget dormitory to maintain his view of the rapidly advancing buggy. Within twenty seconds, it passed by the lonely outpost of Sound Effects Group 1, huddled as they were in the hibiscus hedge by the gate. Right on cue, beginning softly, and working up to a terrible crescendo, Sound Effects 1 emitted a series of blood-curdling screams – the sound of piglets in an abattoir, just as Cuthbert had instructed.

The eyes of every drunken Green Bomber, thrill-seeker and hired thug instantly shifted to the origin of the sound. Even Hitler Jesus's pulse shifted up a gear as he spotted the fast-approaching apparition making its way under the jacarandas and msasas, whence further chilling screams emanated as Sound Effects 2 went into action. Covered with black-painted hessian, the buggy was entirely invisible. Only the ghastly voodoo doll could be seen gliding towards the veterans, illuminated in the torchlight – Cuthbert's unearthly creation of a doll-shaped cardboard cut-out, spray-painted silver, and attached to a mop head, emerged from the dark. The mob's taste for war was rapidly evaporating.

As the buggy neared the outer perimeter of the assembled mob of invaders, Cuthbert raised his makeshift megaphone to Thomas's ear. 'Lighting and Airborne Props – go!' he hissed.

Thomas lept forward and snatched up the second mop-doll, the wicked voodoo stepsister of the one below, and attached it by the hook in its head to the wire-and-pulley slide. Controlling the speed of its descent with a length of fishing line, he flipped on the spotlights that were aimed down the slide, illuminating the doll's sinister descent from the dark sky above. The mob below, almost blinded by the intensity of a line of purple, green and orange spotlights, could no longer contain their fear of the voodoo dolls apparently besieging them on all sides. Thomas's timing was flawless – to prevent the spotlights from revealing the hessian-covered buggy, he switched them off just as the wicked stepsister hit the ground, a split second before the buggy passed by Hitler Jesus. Comrade Teddy-Boy could not remember fear like this since being hauled before the Spin Doctor on charges of mishandling ZUPCO property.

Sound Effects Group 3 from the bike shed began a bone-chilling caterwauling the moment the voodoo buggy rounded the corner of Fairbridge and disappeared out of sight. And then, suddenly, everything fell silent, except for the pulsing echo of a heartbeat, steadily increasing in tempo. Cuthbert stood up from his director's seat and drew a deep breath. Then, in the voice of a demonic overseer, he roared into the darkness, 'GIVE THEM THE WORKS!'

Thomas flipped on every single spotlight. Every child present, including the auxiliaries in both dormitories, began screaming with apocalyptic venom, so shrilly it seemed the window panes might crack. The mob below instantly covered their ears. From his Paget window, Thomas released Louis Cyphre, who had eyes for one thing, and one thing only: the Zhing-Zhong dog tags around Comrade Teddy-Boy's neck. His worst nightmare came true as the bird clawed relentlessly at his chest and battered his face in a frantic flapping of wings, cawing excitedly. Louis Cyphre had done his bit for the team.

All that remained was for Betty Mukadota to deliver the coup de grâce. With her left hand, she yanked the cable attached to the monkey cage, sliding the door open. The enraged monkeys sprang out of the cage, howling for revenge. Two of them leapt onto Hitler Jesus, setting to work with a torturous combination of teeth and nails. Hitler Jesus bellowed as he fought to fling them away. However, it was the third monkey that rose fully to the occasion. The largest and most incensed, a silverback among vervets, it lunged towards Comrade Teddy-Boy. Using his sadza belly as a springboard, it gashed his face with razor-like claws and bit off the top of his ear, which it then spat out in disgust before bounding victoriously back to the bushes.

The mayhem had by now gripped the mob. They turned and ran for the truck, bawling and screeching. With Amazonian strength, Betty yanked at the hidden trip wires that crisscrossed the car park, raising them from the ground. Not a man among them escaped without a nasty fall onto the asphalt. Some became tangled in the twine and cried out for mercy, but not a single man turned round to assist his fallen comrades. With a frantic spinning of tyres, the Hummer and the truck roared into the night.

Cuthbert Kambazuma had pulled it off. Indeed, this show had been his magnum opus – the crowning achievement of a glorious career in special effects, dishonesty and fabrication. Up in Paget dormitory, in the dim candlelight, Thomas took the *tsikamutanda*'s money from his pocket and slapped it onto Cuthbert's outstretched palm. 'Well earned, well deserved, and well done, Cuthbert!'

Down below, the children were cheering and whistling as they gathered in the courtyard. 'Cuthbert! Cuthbert! Cuthbert!' they began to chant.

Thomas switched on a spotlight and turned it to illuminate the triumphant artist as he stood on the laundry table in full view of the jubilant crowd below. As the applause reached a crescendo, Cuthbert flicked a loose dreadlock from his face and delivered the most elegant of bows – befitting a maestro from one of Vienna's grandest opera houses.

When the excitement abated, Thomas and Cuthbert went down to the courtyard. Together with Reverend Muyambo, they walked across to the guard house by the gate. Cuthbert lit a candle on a table in the middle of the small room. It was only when the three had seated themselves on some plastic beer crates that a profound sense of relief began to sink in. Thomas noticed an open scud of Chibuku and three tin mugs on the table, left there by the Green Bombers. Although he had resolved never to drink again after his time in the rabbit hutch, this was a truly special occasion.

He stood up and filled the three tin mugs right to the brim, handing one to the reverend, and one to Cuthbert. Thomas raised his mug. The others stood up and followed suit. All three mugs were raised high, casting huge, flickering shadows on the wooden roof.

'All for one, and one for all!' declared Thomas jubilantly.

The three men looked at each other – an unholy trinity if there ever was one – an Anglican priest with a personal secret, the bogus *tsikamutanda*, and the young man who'd fallen from the sky on Independence Day as a peace offering from the British.

'All for one, and one for all!' the three repeated loudly in unison, clinking their mugs of Chibuku.

The skirmish may have been won, but deep down, each man knew: this was only a temporary reprieve in a battle of attrition, from which ultimately no one would emerge a winner.

Acknowledgements

Every effort has been made to credit all known copyright holders. In the event of any inadvertent error or omission, please contact the author or publisher so that it can be corrected in the event of a reprint.

I would like to thank the following people most sincerely for their contributions towards this book: Jonathan Ball, Jeremy Boraine and Francine Blum of Jonathan Ball Publishers; Willemien de Villiers and Helen Moffett for guidance and advice as regards earlier versions of the manuscript; Lynda Gilfillan for her meticulous editing of the final manuscript; my wife, Katherine, and son, William, for their constant support and encouragement; and certain friends in Zimbabwe whose personal stories lent much to the book's content.

While the characters and their specific locations in this book are entirely fictional, many of the events described resemble events that did in fact take place in Zimbabwe's recent history. Research therefore relied heavily on Zimbabwean newspaper and online news articles published between 1999 and 2007, mainly by *The Herald*, *The Daily News* and *ZWNews*. These sources are gratefully acknowledged below, together with the books, articles and films that I consulted:

Books

Churchill, Winston S, *Winston Churchill's Speeches: Never Give In*, Pimlico, 2004

Conrad, Joseph, *Heart of Darkness*, Dover, 1990

Cooper, Richard, *Butterflies of Zimbabwe*, Longman Zimbabwe, 1991

Kipling, Rudyard, 'The Elephant's Child', in *Just So Stories*, Chartwell, 1902

Pinhey, Elliot, *Emperor Moths of South and South-Central Africa*, Struik, 1972

Roberts, Austin, *Roberts Birds of South Africa*, revised by Gordon L Maclean, John Voelcker Bird Book Fund, 1985

Steinberg, Jonny, *Three Letter Plague*, Jonathan Ball Publishers, 2008

Woodhall, Steve, *Field Guide to Butterflies of South Africa*, Struik, 2005

Underhill, Evelyn, *The Spiritual Life*, Hodder & Stoughton, 1937

Articles

'Headmaster Flees as Hysteria Grips School', *The Daily News*, 30 July 2002

'Magic Medicine of Dr Juma', *Growabrain*, 10 June 2007

'Man Loses Property after being Accused of Using Mubobobo', *Daily News*, 30 January 2003

'Man Surrenders Goblins to Chief', *The Herald*, 24 January 2005

'Mugabe Says "Gay Gangsters" After Him', *Independent Online*, 7 November 1999

'Mushroom Drug Creates Mystical Experience: Study', CBCNews, 10 July 2006

'The Needless Suffering and Terrible Death of Emmanuel', Jan Raath, *The Zimbabwe Situation*, 20 April 2005

'Nicotine does it for Drugless Mental Patients', Independent Online, 7 July 2002

'Quantifying a Mystical Experience: Hallucinogenic Research Gets to Grips with Spirituality', *Science a Gogo*, 11 July 2006

'Shembe is the Way for Millions in Southern Africa', *World Wide Religious News*, 13 November 2006

'Shock Treatment for Widows as Pandemic Ravages Zimbabwe Women', *Africanews*, March 2002

'South Africa Flooded by Two Million Refugees from Robert Mugabe's Zimbabwe', Zakeus Chibaya, Institute for War and Peace, AR No 65, 31 May 2006

Acknowledgements

'Ten Trillion Zim Dollars Lost when Currency was Revalued', Gideon Gono,
   Association of Zimbabwe Journalists, 25 August 2006
'Virgins, Potions, and AIDS in Zimbabwe', Eugene Soros, *Worldpress.org*,
   22 October 2002
'War Veterans besiege Marondera Country Club following alleged anti-Kabila
   Sentiments', CFU Farm Invasions and Security Report, *The Zimbabwe Situation*,
   29 January 2001
'Zimbabwe: Makwavarara Donates $1m to Children's Home', *The Herald*,
   19 January 2007
'Zimbabwe: Ruling Party Supporters Declare War on "The Daily News"', *All Africa*,
29 January 2001
'Zimbabwe: South Africa Tries to Close the Back Door', *IRIN Africa*, 3 March 2007
'Zimbabwe Traditional Healer Burnt by Goblins', *Newzimbabwe.com*, 12 November
   2009
'Zimbabwe's Inflation Tops 1 000%', BBC, 12 May 2006
'Zimbabwe's Fuel Prices More Than Double Amid World Oil Hike', *Xinhua*,
   8 September 2005
'Zimbabweans have "Shortest Lives"', BBC, 8 April 2006
'ZISCO: The Cost of Zimbabwe's Kleptocracy', *Sokwanele*, 14 December 2006

Report
*Report of the Fact-Finding Mission to Zimbabwe to Assess the Impact of Operation
   Murambatsvina by the Human Special Envoy on Human Settlements Issues in
   Zimbabwe*, Mrs Anna Kajumulo Tibaijuka, United Nations, 18 July 2006

Films
No Direction Home, Martin Scorsese, 2005
The Cave of the Yellow Dog, Byambasuren Davaa, 2005

Cover photography

Our cover, designed by Cape Town's Michiel Botha, is made up of several images. We thank the relevant photographers for their contributions:

Hans Hillewaert – Shona witchdoctor
Billy Alexander – leaf
Santiago Arce – moths
Kevin Forbes – vervet monkey
Manu Mahon – single crow
K Rayker – silhouette of birds
Michal Zacharzewski – bus